My Grumpy Single Daddy

AN OFF-LIMITS AGE GAP ROMANCE

ANNA PIERSON

CHAPTER 1
Dara

I barely flinch as the Escalade flies at breakneck speed towards me.

Getting hit by a car seems like a fitting end to the day. I close my eyes, internally bracing for the impact.

It's too late for me to move out of the way, and it's going to hurt.

Strangely enough, I'm almost fine with that.

It wouldn't be the worst thing that's happening to me today. In fact, it's probably at the bottom of my list—I just lost my job, and I'm getting evicted from my apartment.

A kind neighbor also just informed me that my landlady is currently tossing out all my belongings on the street.

I should have expected it. I received an eviction notice on my door a few days ago, but I pleaded with the landlady for more time. *I just need to take a few extra shifts at the restaurant,* I begged, *and then I'll be able to make it up.*

Except now I can't because I have no job.

"Downsizing," my supervisor muttered vaguely before he went on to attend to his customers. Right after, he told me that I was fired. My horror meant nothing to him. Neither did my panic. I asked him again if there was anything else I could do—mop floors, clean toilets—but he shook his head and shooed me away like I was a bother. Once again, I should have expected this too. Pepe's is a seasonal restaurant. It's packed during the spring and sometimes the summer, but it's usually empty during the fall when all the college kids have gone back to school.

And this fall is emptier than most.

Mentally, I say goodbye to Lisa and the handful of people who care about me in this life. I hope that I can meet them again in the next.

Then, I wait for the impact.

But it never comes.

There's no whack, no pain, no screeching tires.

Just a smooth hum of a decelerating engine that is more than capable of handling a sudden stop.

I pry one eyelid open to see the sleek black vehicle perch an inch away. My t-shirt billows in the wind, and its hem touches the angry-looking car lights. The glass is tinted, and I can't see who's driving, but I can sense their irritation from here.

Get off the road, you crazy bitch, they probably want to yell. *Are you trying to die?*

No, I would answer. But on second thought, I'm not sure I want to live either.

Today is just the peak of months and months of suffering. I can't catch a break. I keep trying to look on the bright side and keep trying to stay moving, but all the roads are closing in on me.

And I'm just so, *so* tired of trying.

But you don't need to make it this person's problem either.

I wave a little in apology, and I'm about to leave when the back door of the car opens.

2

One large foot comes out first encased in sleek leather loafers that scream wealth.

I think I saw those shoes in Vogue once. I muse distantly. *It probably costs ten times my rent.*

Another foot quickly follows, and the man stands out of the car.

My heart jolts and then stops for a good two seconds.

Because hot damn. What a man he is!

I didn't think men like him existed in real life. Men who tower over you at around six foot five, with a leanly muscular frame attired in an all-black ensemble. He's wearing a shirt that looks tailored to accommodate his wide shoulders and narrow waist and trousers that hug his muscular thighs in all the right places. His hair is pitch black with silver streaks running through it, and his face...

His face is something from Greek mythology.

Dark sunglasses sitting on an aristocratic nose. Perfect symmetry. Lips that look punishing but soft at the same time.

In the past, women would have called him a demigod, and poets would have written sonnets about him. They would have followed him and declared him their leader based on his looks alone.

And as he takes off his sunglasses, revealing piercing blue eyes, my heart stops again.

His eyes tell it all.

He is a beautiful but extremely dangerous-looking man.

And I have no defense against such potent desirability, so much so that I'm frozen, staring at him for possibly up to a minute before he finally speaks,

"Are you okay?"

"Huh?" I answer dumbly.

He gestures to his car, eyes flicking to the front of the car and then back to me. "You didn't get hurt, did you?"

His accent is a bit strange, not entirely American, but not un-American either. I can almost detect a hint of a Slavic accent but also a French tilt. Sort of like he's an American who lived in a handful of European countries and adapted accents from each.

He raises an eyebrow, and I realize that I've been staring at him for even more seconds without saying anything.

"Uh yeah, I'm fine," I manage to sputter out, touching my hair self-consciously. Heck, I didn't even bother brushing it before I left and it probably looks insane right now after I sprinted for up to a mile. Not to mention the sweat likely staining the back of my t-shirt. "Sorry about that. I'm not suicidal, I swear. I just wasn't watching where I was going."

Shit. I flush. Why did I have to phrase it like that and mention the suicidal part?

He doesn't comment on it, but I can tell that he wants to.

"Are you in a hurry?" he asks instead.

"Um…kinda," I say. "Sorry, but I need to—"

"Let me give you a ride."

I blink. I wasn't expecting that at all, but then again, nothing about this interaction has been expected so far.

How does one expect to chat casually with a Greek god?

"Oh, don't worry about it," I respond because he probably feels guilty for almost hitting me, which is why he's offering. But I don't want to spend more time in his presence. I'll continue stuttering like an idiot. "It's just around the corner."

"Even more reason for me to take you. It won't be out of my way." He taps the car bonnet twice, and the driver's door opens. A shorter brunette man in an expensive suit and sunglasses steps out of the car. He shoots me a smile before he heads over to the other side opening the car door.

It takes me a few seconds to realize that he's opening it for me.

4

A sense of apprehension immediately trickles through me.

Why does he want me to come with him? Is he just a kind stranger, or is there something else? Maybe a kidnapping?

Well, it's not like you have anyone left to pay a ransom, I think morosely.

Besides, the more time I spend here arguing with him, the more things my landlady is probably throwing out.

I still have a few miles left to run to get back to my apartment, but it might already be too late by then. If I get there in time, maybe I'll be able to salvage my most valuable items, including my treasure box.

"Alright, um…thank you," I say and head to the door, taking a second to pause at the luxurious interiors. It's spotless black leather, smooth and cool. The perfect temperature. The car smells of luxury, too, and some other indescribable herbal scent.

I start to climb in before I realize that I'm still covered in sweat and grease from working at the restaurant. I don't want to get it over the seat.

But turning around shows that the handsome man is right behind me.

I jump a little, stunned at his appearance, his subtly spicy scent surrounding me.

"Um, sorry, I'm sweaty. Do you have a towel or napkin or something?"

"Don't worry about it."

"I thought you were in a hurry," he says, a touch of amusement on his lips. "Oh shit, sorry." I didn't even realize I was staring at him again. *Get a hold of yourself, Dara.*

Mortified, I turn back and enter the car.

The doors shut behind me, and the driver gets into his

seat. The other passenger door opens, and the gentleman gets in beside me.

It's like the entire air is sucked out of the space instantly.

He doesn't look at me, but he doesn't need to. His entire aura spreads across to fill the car, and he doesn't seem to realize he's doing it. Or perhaps he realizes it, but he doesn't care.

He's staring out the window thoughtfully, and then suddenly, like a serpent, he turns, and his eyes catch mine.

It's electrifying.

Something dangerous but so invitingly mysterious lurks in his gaze. A flush spreads through my body, and the longer he stares, the worse the heat burns.

And it's then that I realize I made a huge mistake.

I may not have any money to give this man. But I do have my body.

This could be human trafficking.

My fascination with him immediately turns to horror.

Is this how it works? They send in incredibly handsome men to pick up unassuming girls from the street and then take them somewhere to do whatever it is they want to do with them.

Shit.

And I made it so easy for them, too. I just got into the car with them without any argument or even much conversation.

I'm such an idiot.

I want to say something, but the words get stuck in my throat.

I can't quite accuse him of human trafficking to his face, can I?

"Where do you live?" he asks.

A sense of relief cuts through my panic. He wouldn't be

asking me where I live if he was planning on selling me, right?

Unless he wants to make sure I live alone and that no one would miss me.

"In Lansing Heights," I tell him. "Um...I live with a ton of roommates. They're expecting me right now."

He gives me a bemused look. "I'm sure they are."

As the car pulls off, I try to figure out any escape routes. The window looks sturdy, but I could probably smash it in a bind.

With what, your imaginary muscles?

Hey, not so imaginary anymore. Scrubbing pans at Pepe's has given me some lean musculature. Plus, a little bit of adrenaline would lend me some strength. And if I grab that glass of whiskey in his cupholder, I could probably smash it and have a good, sharp piece to jam into the corner of the window. I've heard that's the best place to break a car window.

Then, I will jump out of the window and escape.

Yeah. And if he and his henchman are distracted for two minutes, it will likely take you to manage that. You can be home free.

A muffled sound has me glancing back at him.

He's staring at me again, and he still has that whisper of a smile on his lip, as if he can see everything I'm thinking.

Why does he keep watching me?

I give him an awkward smile back, trying to hide what his gaze is doing to me internally. I'm stuck between wanting to hide and wanting to twiddle my hair like a teenage girl with a crush.

But Jesus, he is handsome. I thought maybe if I looked back at him, I would find that I had exaggerated, but no.

He really is as magnificent as I remember. Probably even more so.

And the car keeps on the path to my home, so I start to relax a little during the ride.

I want to say something, but I don't know anything to say. And he doesn't make conversation either.

It's a good thing we arrive a few minutes before we're supposed to. I didn't even notice that we were speeding. The interior is so quiet that everything just hums.

And then once we turn into the broken road leading to Lansing Heights, I immediately see my landlady, Rena.

She's still in her bathrobe with rollers in her hair.

My clothes are a heap at her feet, my box in the middle.

And she's furiously trying to light a match to set the clothes on fire.

"No!" I immediately shoot out of my seat, reaching for the handle of the car.

I jiggle a little, and it comes unlocked. My legs bolt out before my mind can process the horror.

I'm running to her to save my treasures. "Stop!"

The landlady, Rena, has a facemask, but I still see her cock her eyebrow as I approach.

"Well, well, well," she says. "If it isn't the whore of Babylon herself. I'm glad you came to get your stuff because I was about to burn it all to hell. And if you come near my husband again, I swear I'll do the same to you."

A horrible pressure builds up in my chest.

My loathing wants to burn out of me and slam into her. I want to say something obscene and nasty to her, but I'm still focused on everything I own in shambles on the floor, clothes piled on the dirt.

My box, holding my most prized possessions.

My parent's ashes.

The box is opened and overturned.

I can only cry.

All my emotions, fury, sadness, and profound hopelessness slam into me all at once, and I'm weeping my eyes out with not a single sound leaving my mouth.

The strength leaves me, and I drop onto the floor as I see her walk away. I hate this. I hate my life.

I'm so tired of this.

Time must have passed but I don't know how many minutes it is until I feel a body next to me and a hand on my shoulder.

"Come," the man from the car says. "I'll help you."

I shake my head. "No, it's fine. Just leave me here to cry. And maybe if I'm lucky, a bolt of lightning will hit me, and I'll just die."

"Dara," he says. "Let's go."

Surprise presses pause on my tears.

"How do you know my name?" I frown.

"Because I know you," he says. "My name is Kane Leon. I'm a friend of your brother."

I gape. "You mean Carter?"

"Yes," he says, then puts two hands on my elbow, slowly drawing me to my feet. "Come with me. I'll tell you all about it."

CHAPTER 2

Kane

This isn't how I expected my day to go.

I watch from the car as she rushes to confront the stout woman who has her hands on her waist. I can't hear what they're saying from far away, but I resent the smug smile on the woman's face.

Then my gaze switches to the abject devastation on Dara's face, and my annoyance turns into full-blown hatred of the other woman.

"Is that her?" Pope, the driver asks in the silence.

"Yes," I respond. She certainly matches the description and the picture that Givings sent to me. Of course, I didn't expect to meet Dara like this, and I didn't imagine I would be watching her being evicted.

It was hard enough finding the woman in the first place. I knew Carter had a sister, but when Dad's PI searched for her years ago, it seemed she and her father had vanished off the face of the earth. They moved around quite a bit, and each address on file led to either an old PO Box or a dead end. No social media presence, no other family, nothing. Just two people gone with the wind.

Finally, my PI landed on an obituary for a David Dalton.

Eventually, that led me to his daughter.

Pope doesn't know much about her or why I need to find her. But he was there for my meeting with Givings and knows I'm looking for a woman who fits her description.

"There's not a lot to her," Pope comments. He sounds disapproving as he watches the scene in front of us, clearly also troubled by the display. The older woman is a bully through and through. She seems to enjoy the havoc she caused and walks away with an extra bounce on her step. Dara, on the other hand, looks devastated.

"She looks awful young too," Pope adds.

Yes.

Young and innocent.

That was the impression I got the first time I stared into her eyes. There was no guile in her face, with every expression clear as day.

It's dangerous to exist like that, especially for a pretty young woman like her.

The world we live in is full of beasts and terrible creatures. They'll eat her up in a second.

The thought disturbs me, burrowing into a part of me that I've long since locked shut.

I don't want to care about the girl, but she clearly needs someone to.

Her brother should have been here to fulfill that role. But the coward is too busy running from his crimes.

It frustrates me that she's not even fighting back. The way she dashed out of here, I half expected her to grab the other woman's hair and throw her on the ground, maybe pound her into the grass.

That was how I always handled bullies back at the British boarding my father sent me to. Somehow, the gothic castle with its perfectly manicured lawns housed the most terroristic individuals I've ever met.

Hormonal teen boys packed together under the thin veil of civility turned out to be pack animals, each trying to show they're the biggest man on campus.

Once you make them bleed though...they simmer down real quick.

In the distance, Dara falls to her knees, crying, and that uneasy feeling spreads around my chest. Fuck I hate watching this.

"You should go help your honey before she combusts," Pope suggests.

"She's not my honey." Even without the eighteen-year age gap, a woman like Dara could never be with a man like me.

I'm a ruthless businessman surrounded by other ruthless people like me.

She would be eaten up and spit out in my world.

Still, I can't exactly sit here watching her cry, so I get out of the car and approach her.

I'm not entirely sure what I'm going to do once I reach her. Soothing crying women isn't my strong suit.

I can manipulate as easily as I breathe, burrow into my competitor's brain, and figure out how to get what I want from them.

I can hold a boardroom hostage and make grown men beg after I take everything from them.

Most of the time, my heart is a cold, hollow box where logic dominates.

So now, I'm out of the depths, approaching my best friend's little sister. And the inadequacy turns to annoyance at being in this situation in the first place.

When I get close enough, the annoyance turns to rage.

But not at her.

At the fucking animal who threw all her fucking shit on the floor.

I observe the things on the ground, a few items of clothing, and a wooden box, and wonder distantly if that's all she has.

That would be shocking. Her brother stole enough from us to buy his sister a small island. Why on earth is she crying over a few measly clothes?

Her sobbing draws my attention back to her, and I sigh.

I touch her shoulder, feeling just how slight it is. It shakes with the weight of her wailing.

I pat her awkwardly, and she turns around to stare at me. Her green eyes are filled with tears. It tugs at something inside me, adding to the discomfort spreading across my chest.

"Come," I say. "I'll help you."

"No, it's fine." She shakes her head. "Just leave me here to cry. And maybe if I'm lucky, a bolt of lightning will hit me, and I'll just die."

"Dara. Let's go."

She glances back at me in shock. "How do you know my name?"

Shit. I slipped up. But I need to introduce myself at some point, and there's no time like now.

"Because I know you," I say. "My name is Kane Leon. I'm a friend of your brother."

Her mouth falls open in shock. "You mean Carter?"

"Yes." I bend and pull her up to her feet. I can't stand looking at her kneeling in the dirt anymore. "Come with me. I'll tell you all about it."

She allows me to pull her up, still staring at me in shock.

Her tears are still rolling down her cheeks, and she blinks five times in under ten seconds.

"Are you okay?" I ask her.

She shakes her head and sniffles. "I can't…" she hiccups. "It's just too much. I just lost my home and my stuff and my parent's ashes…" With a shaking hand, she points at the black dust on top of her clothes.

I nod and immediately squat, carefully lifting the shirt with the dust and pouring her parent's ashes back into the box. Then I close the box.

The broken latch prevents me from locking the box.

Someone intentionally broke it to spill out the contents. And I know exactly who that someone is.

I glance at the ugly yellow apartment complex.

No one saw it fit to stop that woman.

They all let this happen.

Disgusting.

They'll pay for this, too. Because I may not know much about comforting crying women, but revenge was my forte.

Isn't your own revenge what you're here for?

That douses my indignation slightly.

That's right. I'm not a knight in shining armor and I'm not here to rescue this damsel from distress. If anything, I'm here to distress her even more.

But all that can wait.

"Who was that woman?" I ask.

She doesn't ask who I'm talking about.

"My landlady." Her voice cracks on the last word as she visibly tries to stop crying, swiping at her face. "Rena."

I nod, digesting the information. Rena. She'll pay the highest price for every tear Dara has shed today.

Dara rubs her face clean and suddenly takes the box from me. "It's okay. I'll take it from here."

Then, she bends and sets the box aside. She starts packing up the clothes into a single garbage bag tossed to the side. She does it with quick, jagged movements that hold an edge of desperation.

I gesture to Pope, who almost immediately appears at my side.

"Yes, sir?"

"Help her pack her things into the car."

Dara turns those tearful eyes to me, and once again, it breeds a host of uncomfortable emotions inside me.

"No, it's fine. I don't…" She bites her lip. "I haven't even figured out where I'm going yet."

"Do you have anywhere to go?" I ask.

Her face falls, which tells me that she doesn't.

I cock my head, and to my surprise, she doesn't fall apart again. Instead, she brushes her hair back and nods as if coming to a decision.

"No, but it's okay. I'll figure it out. I always do."

And something in the determined set of her lips tells me that she will, too.

Admiration sets in. Perhaps she isn't as helpless as I thought she was.

You're not supposed to be admiring her, I remind myself. *You're supposed to be figuring out how to use her.*

"At least let me help you then," I say. "It's the least I could do for your brother."

She squints a little when she stares up at me, probably against the blare of the sun. "You said you were his friend?"

I must be a better actor than I thought because I don't cringe at the word.

A friend wouldn't be how I described my relationship with Carter today. Mortal enemies would be more like it, but

16

for a long time, we were the best of friends. More like brothers.

Of course, that was before he stole from me.

"So why are you here?" Dara asks.

I nod. "He sent me here to look after you. I was actually on my way to your place anyway to find you. It's a good thing I came early enough, or you would have been gone by the time I got here." The lie slips off my tongue as easily as the truth, but my face always masks my true feelings. It seems I've been lying my entire life.

But I am relieved that I found her. It has been notoriously hard to track her down, surprisingly.

"Come, we'll discuss it over lunch," I tell her.

"I'm not hungry," she says in typical female fashion, but almost immediately, her stomach starts grumbling.

I smirk, and she blushes.

Pope takes the hints and gently takes the full garbage bag from her hands, then walks to the car. She's still holding onto the box, and I have a feeling that she's not going to let it go anytime soon. It's still shocking and annoying to me that this is all she has in this world. Where the fuck is Carter, and why is he letting his sister live like a pauper?

I gesture to the car, and she looks at me tentatively, but she doesn't move.

"It's not like I don't believe you," she starts hesitantly, and I'm immediately reminded of her little lie in the car. *I live with a ton of roommates. They're expecting me right now.*

I knew it was a lie the minute she said it. Her eyes shifted a little to the side, and she grimaced a little when she spoke as if she didn't believe what she was saying.

She was not as skilled at lying as I was. Not even close.

But the lie tells me what's on her mind now. She doesn't trust me, a strange man telling her to get into a car.

Smart girl.

Some others her age would have been blinded by the luxury. The second I picked them up, they would have started imagining dollar signs and would have thrown themselves in without caring for their safety.

But in the beginning, after a cursory glance at the car, she didn't give it much thought. She was more so worried that she would stain it or something.

Adorable.

I stop the thought dead, ripping it out of my head. I'm not supposed to find her adorable.

I'm a cold-hearted bastard. I'm only here to analyze and utilize. That's it.

"But you don't believe me," I complete her thought for her, and smile to take the bite out of it.

"It's fine. You don't have to." I pull out my phone and search for a picture I had of her brother and me. It's an old picture pulled up from the cloud. We were in our mid-twenties at my father's estate in Martha's Vineyard. We'd gone to the lake house and taken my father's boat for a joyride despite my father's many warnings for us not to do it.

Back when I was a rebellious teenager, I thought I could trust Carter with my secrets.

I thought I could trust him with a lot of things.

I show her the picture. Her eyes caress the image of her brother, and she reaches out to touch it. "Carter."

"He traveled soon after this and has been doing some business abroad," I say. "We kept in touch for a few more years, and he returned to visit a few more times. But then, for the past few years, I lost touch with him. He only reached out recently to tell me to find you."

"Really?" There is a naked hunger in her eyes, a hunger to be seen and heard and loved.

I take advantage of it.

"Yes," I say, disgusted that Carter hadn't even asked anyone to look after his sister while he was off doing God knows what. "I didn't think much of it at first. Now I see he has a reason to be worried."

"How did you know where to find me?"

"He sent me a picture." I showed her pictures of her when she was younger, noting her expression. She was about twelve in one of the pictures with a toothy grin. "He used to talk about you all the time, Dara. Eventually, I got a PI and —" Her stomach growls, interrupting the rest of my words, and I smirk. "I'll finish the story after we get some food in you."

She nods, finally relenting. "Okay, but can we not go anywhere too public? I don't feel like being around people right now."

"Fine." I gesture to the car, and she eyes it uncertainly, but eventually, she follows.

The start of the ride is silent. Dara stares out the window as we drive away, looking back at her old apartment morosely.

"Do you like Japanese food?" I ask her, and she glances at me and then shrugs.

"I guess," she responds.

"Pope, have Nobu deliver a spread to the condo at Lincoln Park."

"Is that where we're headed, boss?" Pope asks.

"Yes," I respond.

"We're going to your house?" Dara asks apprehensively.

"One of them," I say smoothly. "It's more of a guesthouse where I have visitors stay sometimes. You can stay there until you figure out where you want to go next. The food should be there by the time we get there." I can already hear Pope placing the order on the phone.

"Oh, okay. Um, thank you," Dara says. "But I'm not sure I can stay at your house."

"You said you have nowhere else to stay. And Carter would kick my ass if he knew I just left his sister out on the street."

She is thoughtful for a few seconds, and then she says, "You said he's out of the country? On business?"

I nod. "He didn't explain much about it. Initially, he worked with our company, but then he received an offer he couldn't refuse abroad. And so, he left."

"He didn't even tell you where he was going?"

"No. We communicate mostly by email."

"I see." She glances out the window as we merge onto the highway to take us to the city.

"Every time we email, he mentions you," I say. "He tells me you want to be a chef."

"Oh." Her eyes widen in surprise. "I can't believe he remembered that."

Her voice feels even lighter now, and I can tell that the emotions from before have drained her. We don't talk much again until we arrive at the condo.

Pope instantly gets out of the car heading to her door. I'm about to step out, too, when my phone rings.

I pull it out of my pocket and frown at the caller ID.

It's my father.

"Kane?"

I glance up to find Dara out of the car, staring at me with concern.

"Pope will show you the apartment," I tell her. "I'll be right up. I need to take this phone call first."

She eyes me uncertainly, then nods and follows Pope while still holding onto her box like a lifeline.

I answer the phone. "Yes?"

"Did you find her?" Samson Leon's light voice comes through clearly on the phone speakers.

I don't ask my father how he knows I was looking for Dara. I've long suspected that he placed spies on me.

"Yes," I answer.

My father lets out a relieved breath. "Good. That's good. It's great, actually."

My suspicions grow, and an uneasy feeling sets through me. My father has always had a strange way of doing things, but he's gotten stranger with age.

"What do you want with her?" I ask.

The phone is silent for a few seconds, and then he says, "You know her father, and I started this company together. He put a lot more into it than I did, and I…after everything he's been through…it's only fair that his daughter gets what was supposed to be his."

Horror fills me at the implication of my father's words. "You mean you plan on giving your shares to her?"

"I don't plan on *giving* anything," he says calmly, then shatters my ease with the next words. "Nothing that isn't already rightfully hers, that is."

CHAPTER 3
Dara

M y eyes open, and I blink a few times at the roof.
I don't recognize it.

Neither do I recognize the mid-century industrial light fixture hanging from the middle of the room, like an abstract flower with petals that seem to be formed from legitimate crystals.

They look like raindrops, and I stare at them for a few seconds, wondering if I'm dreaming again.

And then it hits me—everything that happened yesterday, that is. The memories return one after another like an unending storm.

I'm not dreaming, and this isn't my apartment.

Technically, I don't have an apartment anymore.

A muted despair sneaks through my senses, and I blink back tears even as the searing pain spreads through my chest. I don't want to cry anymore. I already cried enough last night. Better I distract myself by marveling over just how gorgeous this place is.

It's about three times the size of my apartment, with a classic design and a modern touch. Minimalistic and sterile, with white walls and beige furniture, the only sign of character in the apartment is in the lights, which look hand sculpted metal.

I roll out of bed, stretching and wondering that the back pain I physically have every morning isn't there anymore. Then again, my last mattress was hard as a rock, so that may have been a contributing factor. This king-size bed was so soft it snatched me to sleep before I realized what was happening.

As I roll out of bed, one foot meets the cool tile floor while another sinks into a soft, plushy, decadent cream rug. I get up and walk towards the bathroom, admiring the pristine ceramic bowl and sand-colored his and hers sinks. The mirror lights up automatically when I get close, and I bink in surprise to see my reflection so starkly highlighted.

I look exhausted.

My eyes are red with pronounced bags underneath. My cheeks are splotchy, and my hair is a brown rat's nest. I slept in the same clothes I was wearing yesterday, which are now crumpled beyond belief. I look like I went to hell and back.

Which I guess I did.

I turn on the faucet and resist the urge to dunk my face under the rushing water. Instead, I cup my hands under it and splash the water on my face once and then twice. Each splash brings an extra level of clarity.

Last night, after I walked in, I didn't even have the energy to admire the place. There was a spread of food waiting for me on the table, and as exotic and elaborate as it all looked, I simply ate without tasting much and then fell asleep. Pope and Kane left soon after we arrived, with Kane promising he'd be back tomorrow.

Now, as I step out and look around, I see the remnants of the food still on the counter. I note lobster, sushi, and soup. I head over and begin placing the plates in the fridge, although it might be a little too late for some of it.

Now I have the mind to look around. I can see how gorgeous this apartment is.

But I can't stay here.

At least not for long. In my experience, nice things never happen to me for no reason. Everything has a price. It was something my father hammered into me since I was young. He was not a rich man, but he had a lot of pride and never accepted charity from anyone. The lesson remained, and it doesn't matter how desperate I have been after his death, I don't accept expensive gifts like this.

Especially those from men like Kane.

Kane Leon. I don't know if I'm terrified of him or attracted to him. Probably a little bit of both.

Even though he knows my brother, I still don't entirely trust Kane. It all seems to be too much of a lucky coincidence that he was looking for me right when I was getting kicked out of my apartment.

And where is Carter anyway? Why didn't he tell us before he left the country?

Why didn't he say goodbye to me or Dad?

And why didn't he answer my letters?

Carter and I had been writing letters to each other since I was young. During one of his sporadic visits, when I was about ten, he gave me a PO box number to always send letters to if I needed to reach him. We rarely sent texts because he insisted letters were more fun.

And when I was ten, I thought so, too.

But now, not so much.

My last two letters to him were over a year ago, first telling him Dad was sick. And then I sent another one when Dad died.

He'd never responded to either, nor had he written anything else.

Sometimes, I feared he was gone too.

Because if he were alive, wouldn't he respond? He and Dad didn't get along much, but still. I thought he cared about me despite the fact that he rarely visited.

Carter was an adult when I was born, so I figured he was simply busy.

But if he's alive and didn't bother to check in on me after Dad's death, then what does that mean?

And why is he checking in on me now through his friend?

It's all so confusing, but even if everything wasn't confusing, I just knew that this little respite couldn't last. It's the story of my life.

Whenever I have any bit of luck, disaster quickly follows.

I need to immediately have a game plan. I need to start looking for a job ASAP, and I need to move out of this place.

The thought of getting another waitressing gig depresses me even more.

In my dream world, I would be going to culinary school. It was what I was doing before Dad's death, studying to open my own restaurant. Dad had been so proud of me when I got into culinary school. I knew Carter would be proud of me, too. That is, if he had ever read my letter telling him about it,

But, of course, culinary school is expensive, and even with the partial scholarship I had, there was no way to sustain it.

So, I dropped out and have been surviving as a waitress ever since.

The phone ringing echoes through the quiet house, shattering the silence. I turn and frown, trying to remember where my phone is. I follow the sound of the ringing, locating it in my bag that I left on the couch.

"Hello?"

"Oh my God, thank God, I was about to call the police." My best friend Lisa's words are a rush of breath, shaky with panic. "Where *the fuck* have been? I've been calling you since last night, and I went over to your place, and it was in chaos, and I've been freaking out. You're not at work either—"

"Lisa, calm down. It's fine," I interrupt, feeling guilty for not updating my friend in time. I can only imagine how scared she must have been. "I'm sorry I didn't call. I'm not at work because I got fired, and as for the apartment...I got evicted."

"Wait, you got fired? Why?"

I shrug before realizing she can't see me. "Downsizing."

"That's bullshit. They can't just fire you like that. And evicted?"

"Yeah. I'm pretty sure Rena thinks her husband was hitting on me that one time we were talking about reducing my rent because she's had it for me ever since. And this was the perfect excuse for her to make good on her threats, I think."

I still remember her look when I saw my parent's ashes. The way she smiled gleefully.

Never have I felt such hate in my heart for another human being before. I've always known Rena was mean, but there's cruelty, and then there's that.

"Bitch." Lisa's heated tone gives voice to my anger. "Well, believe it or not, it's probably a good thing that happened. I went over to your apartment this morning, and it was not a pretty sight."

"What do you mean?"

"The building was surrounded by police. Apparently, there have been several building code violations, and they

27

were talking about demolishing the whole thing. And fast, too. It might be gone within the next few weeks."

Surprise lashes through me. "What?"

Not that I'm surprised that the building has violations. But several other buildings in that neighborhood are not exactly up to par. They can't charge low rent and afford to be up-to-date on everything.

"Someone called the police for that?"

"No, I think the police were there for a different reason," she says. "Someone mentioned that Rena and her husband were being taken for tax evasion or something like that."

I blink.

That was sudden.

Again, I'm not surprised Rena would be involved in something like that. No matter how many times she portrayed herself as an upstanding citizen, she always seemed a little shady to me.

But once again, it feels too...sudden. The apartment is getting shut down, and at the same time, the police find out that Rena has been evading taxes. The day after I was evicted.

It's all too convenient.

For some reason, an image of Kane pops into my mind. I remember his eyes as he looked down at my stuff, the brief flash of rage when I told him what happened before he hid it under a cool, placid tone.

The look on his face when I told him Rena's name.

Could it be... I mean, did he have something to do with this?

"But dude, I'm so sorry for everything that happened to you," Lisa continues, her voice quiet now. "I can't believe you're going through all this."

"I can," I say wryly. My life has just been a series of bad news lately. "But it's fine. I'm okay with it."

"You shouldn't be. That's awful."

Not knowing what to say I shrug again. "Yeah."

"Well, where are you right now?"

I bite my lip, wondering how to tell Lisa what happened.

She is going to have a conniption if I just blurt out that I went home with a stranger and was currently still at his house. Maybe I should tell her a different story.

Then again, I've never been very good at lying, and she's going to find out the truth anyway.

I sigh. "Okay. I'm going to tell you, but you have to promise me not to freak out until I finish saying what I have to say."

She pauses for a second. "*Okay.*" The word drags out. "I promise."

That doesn't exactly ring with confidence, but I venture on anyway. "Remember I have this brother, right?"

"The older one who disappeared when you were sixteen and hasn't said a word to you since?"

A pang hit me. Leave it to Lisa, to be brutally honest. "Yeah, that one."

"What about him? Did you hear from him?"

"Not exactly. But...um...he asked his best friend to look out for me. The best friend found me yesterday when I was trying to get my stuff from the apartment. He told me I could stay at his place, and that's where I am."

I don't add that Kane nearly ran me over with his car. That would freak her out even more.

I don't have to wait too long for her reaction, and it does not disappoint. "Excuse me? Was that a roundabout of telling me that you went home with a stranger?"

"No," I say. "I'm not home *with* him. I'm in one of his condos."

"Did you say one of his condos? Who has multiple condos in Chicago these days? Who is this guy, the mafia?"

Of course, her mind goes there. But Lisa thinks every rich guy is shady. She has multiple brothers in law enforcement and one who's a prosecutor, so she essentially looks at the world through a lens of crime.

"No, Lisa, he's not mafia. He's a..." I pause, realizing I actually don't know what Kane does.

I try to think of something to cover the silence but it's too late. Lisa already catches on.

"You don't know what work he does, do you?" she asks. "And you're in his house?"

I sigh. "Yeah," I admit.

"This is a colossally stupid idea, Dara. This is how people get trafficked and stuff."

"If he wanted to traffick me, he would have already," I say. "Plus, he had a picture of me in his wallet. An old picture of when I was younger. He says my brother gave it to him. He has pictures with Carter, too."

"A picture can be faked."

"Yes, but he knew things about me, things that I only told Carter," she says and sighs. "Look, I know it's crazy, but I don't have a choice, do I? It's either this or be homeless."

"No. You could come to stay with me."

"You know I can't do that." Lisa lives in a three-bedroom apartment with her Dad and three of her brothers. It's already a tight enough squeeze as is, and even though I know they'll welcome me, I don't want to burden them with my problems.

"Why not?" she asks.

You know why," I respond. "Look, it's fine. I'm going to

look for a job today, and then when I get one, I will move out. Easy peasy."

"Dara—"

"Hold that thought. I need to shower and get started with my day. I'm going to visit a few of the restaurants in the city to see if anyone needs a waitress. You can lecture me when I get back." Hopefully, I'll have a job by then.

"Fine," Lisa says reluctantly. "But keep your phone on you. I'll call you every hour, and if you don't answer, I'll call the police."

"Alright. I love you."

I hang up and release a deep breath. Then I get up and head to the bathroom. There's already a fresh towel hanging on the hanger, so I simply strip and step into the large shower.

It takes me a second to figure out all the fancy dials, but by the time the hot water touches my skin, I sigh in pleasure. I haven't had a hot water shower in what felt like ages. The hot water at my last apartment was broken, which made for a very miserable winter.

I enjoy the shower for ten minutes and then step out, grab the towel, and tuck it around myself.

And then I walk out of the bathroom and scream.

Kane is there.

He's sitting on the living room couch, ankle on the opposite knee, and eyeing me in amusement.

"What are you doing here?" I ask.

He raises an eyebrow, and I realize how silly the question is. It is his condo, after all.

"Sorry. It's just that I didn't hear you come in."

"I noticed," he remarks and then gestures to the seat. "Come on. We need to talk. I got you some breakfast as well."

Only then do I notice that there's a cup of coffee, another

cup of orange juice, and some pastries resting close to him. They smell divine.

"Um...okay. Let me get changed first."

"No need. I won't be here long."

I tuck the towel even firmer and then move to him. I notice his eyes dip to my legs for a split second and wonder if I imagine the way they darken. The intensity in his gaze has awareness skittering over my skin, my pulse ready for flight.

Or maybe I'll just lay there and let him do whatever he wants with me.

Don't be ridiculous. I tell myself. It's probably inappropriate for me to be thinking about Kane like that for so many reasons.

If he's around my brother's age, then he's much older than me, even though he doesn't look it. Besides his silver-streaked hair, his smooth skin and striking facial features place him anywhere from late twenties to mid-thirties.

But then there's a cold shrewdness in his eyes that tells me he's seen and done far more than I can imagine in two lifetimes.

His gaze does something to me. A part of me feels terrified of it, but it also makes a different part of me come voraciously alive. My body can't decide which sensation to settle on, so it makes me jumpy instead.

He doesn't say anything as I sit and draw the coffee closer to me, bringing it up for a sip.

And when he does speak, his voice is deep and serious.

However, what he says is just about the most ridiculous thing someone can say to another person they just met.

"Marry me."

CHAPTER 4
Kane

It's all my father's fault.

Samson Leon has been obsessed with the Dalton family since I was young.

First, it was Carter Dalton, whom my father invited to live with us as a teenager. Even after he grew up, my father treated Carter like a son, inviting him to meetings with us and holidays everywhere. He gave Carter a job as his aide, while I had to work hard and prove myself in my role.

I didn't mind their relationship since Carter was my best friend, too, but I did wonder about it sometimes.

Of course, all that ended with Carter's betrayal.

And now, with her, Carter's sister Dara, the old man is talking about giving away vital shares of Leon Inc., the company I've given my entire life to.

Over my dead body.

Leon Inc. almost fell once. It was right after Carter disappeared. I assume as a final 'fuck you' to us, he leaked information about the company to our competitors, who beat us out on making the next model of smart TVs. They copied our entire design and innovation, but it didn't matter because they did it first.

Our stocks crashed at that time.

We didn't have anything new to offer to the market and were to rely on old stock.

Our profits dwindled, and Leon Electronics, our leading moneymaker, looked like it was becoming a relic of the past.

It would have if it hadn't been for me.

While my father succumbed to the seemingly inevitable defeat, I burned the midnight candle and figured out how to save us. After months of sleepless nights, daily meetings with scientists, and spending endless amounts of my own money, we finally managed to make a product that would not only stop our stocks from freefalling but also catapult us back to the top.

We've stayed at the top for ten more years due to continuous innovations driven by my flank of the company. I drew blood for that company.

I've given my life energy to keep us where we are.

And the old man wants to take that all away and give it to a girl who can't even stand up for herself, much less for two thousand people working for her.

Not fucking likely.

I don't know if my father was joking or not about his comment, but he's proven enough times that he's not entirely rational when it comes to the Daltons. And so, I must cover all my bases.

I could only see one solution.

A marriage proposal.

A bout of coughing overtakes Dara, and the coffee sloshes as she slams the cup back to the table. I would try and rise to help her, but I'm not sure touching her is such a good idea.

Not when she's wearing only a towel held tentatively by a single knot on her chest.

The towel covers pretty much everything that needs to be covered, but I can't stop myself from admiring the smooth, delicate lines of her shoulders and the nicely curved tone in her legs.

And fucking pervert that I am, I can't help imagining what lies underneath.

Don't think about that. She's too young for you. And that's not what you're here for.

"Drink," I order, my voice harsh to cover the desire tainting my tone. It's a completely inappropriate desire for a woman who is far too young for me, amongst other things.

Dara obeys and takes the cup, sipping tentatively and swallowing in between coughs.

As she eventually manages to regain herself, she gapes at me, and a horrified shock settles itself onto her expression. "I'm sorry. Did you just ask me to marry you?"

"I did," I respond, smirking a little as her eyes grow even wider. I probably should have explained everything first, but I'm enjoying her shock so much. *She does make the most arresting expressions.* "Preferably today if we can manage it, but I suppose we can do it sometime this week, too."

"Wait, excuse me." She holds her hands up and shuts her eyes, visibly thinking. Then her eyes open again, and...they're not entirely green, I note. They're mostly green, but with intense emotion, and with the sunlight falling in through the huge kitchen windows, there are flickers of gold in her eyes.

Beautiful.

"I just met you," she announces.

"Yes."

"I just met you, and you asked me to marry you."

"Again, you're correct. And?"

She gives me a look that suggests that it should be obvious. "And I can't marry a man I just met. A man I don't know or love."

Love? How adorable. "Arranged marriages are a fixture in many cultures and are typically successful across the board," I inform her. "So, if that's your only reservation, I assure you—"

"It's not my only reservation." She frowns.

"My main *reservation* is that I don't know anything about you, and you probably know very little about me."

Oh, but I do know a lot about you, Dara Dalton. In fact, while trying to locate you, my PI sent me quite the list.

She went to college for only two months before dropping out to go to culinary school. And then she stopped that too to start working at a restaurant.

Her father died recently, and she never held a funeral for him. Simply had him cremated and put in that box of hers.

She doesn't have nearly enough money to sustain herself but somehow spends a lot of time volunteering at the animal shelter.

She's a very odd woman all around.

"Why would we get married?" she asks.

"Why not?"

"I think we've already been over that."

It's not like I expected her to say yes immediately, though there were certainly a few girls who would have. Down on her luck and with a billionaire offering marriage…, there were worse things that could have happened to her.

Suddenly, my mood dims.

I don't want to think about those worse things.

For some reason, my stomach tightens when I consider what could have happened if she was homeless and I hadn't shown up when I did.

I rise and stride towards the bookshelf above the flat-screen TV, searching through the decorative magazines there. I pull out one with my face on it. I don't usually have magazines of myself, but an old college friend brought over my Forbes magazine issue and left it here during their stay.

I return to the couch and slide the magazine across to her.

"That's who I am," I tell her.

Her eyes fall on the cover, and then she gapes. "Wait, your last name is Leon? As in Leon Electronics, the people who make the TVs?"

"Yes." And the phones and the cameras and just about every other major device.

Her eyes are like saucers now. She appears a little taken aback, more so than impressed. And then she purses her lips.

"I meant that's great and everything," she says. "But I still don't know why I should marry you."

Now, she has truly surprised me.

Me being a billionaire isn't enough?

I don't mean to sound arrogant, but usually it is. Even though it's not something I advertise, most people in my circles already know who I am, and it attracts a lot of—often unwanted—attention from women.

So, what makes Dara Dalton seem less than impressed with it?

And why does that intrigue me so much?

"My father is dying," I say, the lie rolling smoothly off my tongue. "He has about a year left to live, and his last wish is to see me married. I would like to fulfill that. The marriage only needs to last till his death. And in return for helping me with my Dad, you receive two million dollars."

She blinks quietly as she digests the information

"Wait, for real?" she sputters.

"For real." I nearly smile at the various comical expressions that pass over her features. She hasn't learned to guard her expressions yet. I wonder how it feels to be so open and vulnerable, to show every emotion without fear.

I've never had that luxury, not even when I was her age.

"I'm very serious about this. My lawyer is drafting up a contract as we speak and I'll have you read over it before we go through with it."

"Why me, though?" she asks. "I mean, you don't know me?"

"I know enough," I assume with an unaffected shrug. "You're my best friend's sister, and you seem like a good person who's going through a hard time and could probably use the money."

She blushes at my assessment but still doesn't deny it. "Yes, but you don't know that though? That I'm a good person. I could be a money-hungry gold-digger who's pretending so she can steal all your money. Or a murderer."

I bark, and a surprised laughter escapes me. She frowns.

"What, you don't think I could murder someone?"

"I wouldn't know. I haven't been around a lot of murderers to tell if you fit the MO."

"I am fully capable of being a violent criminal," she says and assumes what I suppose is supposed to be her scary face.

"I'm sure you can," I say, trying to hold back my laughter.

After a few seconds, she cracks a smile, too.

She sighs. "Okay, fine, I'm not a murderer. But the point still stands that you know nothing about me, and this could all end up very badly for you."

Another bolt of surprise.

She's worried about what could happen to me? Worried that she could be getting one over on me?

How cute.

A trickle of something resembling guilt drops into my conscience, but I crush it immediately.

I can't feel guilty. It's my father's fault that I have to do this in the first place. I need to protect my company no matter what, and it's not like she's getting nothing out of this deal. She's getting a handsome reward, by most metrics.

Sure, it's probably less than she would be getting with controlling company shares, but even if she had that, she wouldn't know what to do with it. She's far too soft and kind and inexperienced to run Leon Inc. It would go belly up in a month.

Wait.

Soft? Kind?

Why on earth did I just assign those traits to her when I just met her?

That was how Carter seemed at first, too.

You forget she's a Dalton. They're very good at hiding their true colors at first.

"Believe me, you won't cheat me," I tell her, hardening myself against any delicate emotion. "I have very powerful and very vicious lawyers on my end who won't let you."

Her eyes widen. "Okay, now I'm a little scared for myself."

"You don't have to be. It's a very simple deal. We sign a contract in which you'll marry me for a year. You will receive a hundred thousand dollars every month we stay married and the bulk payment at the end of the year. And then after that, you're free to do whatever you want, millions of dollars richer. It doesn't get any simpler than that."

Her eyes narrow, her teeth nibbling her lips. Lines furrow into her forehead, and I have the mad urge to smooth it over.

Or maybe I just want to touch her.

She thinks for so long, which is odd because I imagine that kind of money must be life-changing for her.

But still, she hesitates. I don't know why.

I decided to give her the final push.

"I understand you might need time to think about it, but I need an answer today," I continued. "I already told my father I was married, and he insisted on meeting my new wife by the end of the week."

"That soon?"

"Yes." I want to rush this now. The more she thinks about it, the more likely it is she'll talk herself out of this. Her caution will only grow with time, or perhaps someone will finally clue her into what a ruthless bastard I am.

She shifts in her chair again, and the towel falls open, exposing a little more of her thigh.

Suddenly, a hunger rumbles inside me and robs half my attention.

She seems to notice at the same time that her towel has moved, and her eyes are meeting mine. But behind the faint embarrassment, there are also threads of desire in her eyes.

It's the same look she'd given me on the car ride, a cautious hunger.

I knew then she wanted me, but I brushed it off as a young woman's crush. I never planned on acting on it.

But instantly, I know what to do to get her to not think so hard about my proposal.

I rise from my seat and stride to sit right next to her. Her breath quickens when I do, her gaze tracking my path intensely.

She doesn't move away.

The desire in her eyes only builds, feeding into the hunger she seems surprised to feel.

I'm surprised myself by the corresponding desire growing at the base of my stomach.

This is just a game, I tell myself. It's a game I have to play to win.

I lift my hand and skim at the side of her face, silently watching her reaction. Her eyes darken, and she moistens her lips, but she doesn't back out of my arms. Neither does she protest.

Her submission curls through me like a drug, teasing at the dark corners of my psyche.

Just a game.

My thumb passes over her lips, and I observe the way they part slightly to accommodate me. My finger tingles at the touch of her breath fluttering out. Her lips are soft, the lower one a little plumper. She's nervous but she's approachable to the desire.

"I want you," I admit to her, surprised by how true the statement is.

I might tell myself it's a game all I want, but my cock is hardening, and my heart is picking up pace, urgency driving me closer.

I want to kiss her right now and I only let my forehead lean forward to touch hers. "I want someone to be my wife, and it needs to be you."

"Why?" she whispers back

"Because I want you." I let my lips touch hers, and a shock of desire bolts through me.

I know instantly that this was a mistake.

CHAPTER 5

Dara

I don't know what I was thinking.

I mean, I probably wasn't thinking at all. Thinking likely escaped me the second Kane got up and stalked over to me like a panther stalking prey. All I could see was that dark intent in his eyes and the little curl of his lip as though he was amused by something secret he wasn't telling me.

He was dressed in all black today, too, with the silk shirt falling open at the top, showing the hint of hard, sculpted muscle underneath.

And I wanted to touch it.

I wanted to kiss it and lick his bronze skin.

The crazed thought took hold of me as he sat next to me.

I've never had such dirty thoughts about anyone before, but everything about Kane exuded virility and stoked a desire I'd never felt before.

In fact, all the sensations pounding through me felt foreign, this mix of trepidation and fascination, this desire that alarmed and thrilled me.

It was like he was a creature sent from hell to seduce all good girls.

And then, when he got closer, all thinking stopped entirely. His spicy scent surrounded me. I could feel a pulse starting in my belly, something inside me aching for more.

Kiss me.

His face came closer, and my eyes slid shut. I could already imagine the sensation of his mouth, and although I knew it was probably a bad idea, that voice of reason was lost to the abyss, drowned out by the pure lust thrumming through me like a drum.

Kiss me. Kiss me. Kiss me.

His lips touch mine, barely a breath, but the sensation chugs through my whole body like syrup. He brushes his mouth against mine, almost experimentally, then to the corner, where he presses down a little in a soft kiss.

It's gentle and sweet. The kind of kiss that could be construed as innocent under a certain light.

But I don't want innocent. The feelings thrumming through me are purely carnal, and I want to indulge in them.

Without any thought to what I'm doing, I push closer to him, my tongue licking the seam of his lips.

He freezes.

Then he releases an explosive groan.

That seems to be the straw that breaks the camel's back.

Suddenly, his hands are in my hair, grasping, pulling me close for a kiss that sears my brain. His tongue licks at my lips, and I open up for him. He plunders my mouth and then coaxes my tongue into a dance with his. His other hand goes around my waist, pulling me closer, and I throw my arms around his neck, kissing him back just as ferociously. Our lips meld together in a senseless rhythm and a dance that we're both learning together. He seems much better at it, though, so I follow his lead as the kiss gets more heated and more violent. His hands tighten around my waist, abruptly pulling me flush against his body.

Yes. The lust is an inferno now in my pussy. The low pulse turns into a pounding beat. It's a drug overtaking my senses, demanding more.

Suddenly, he's gone.

I blink to reorient myself as a dizzying splash of reality hits me right in the face.

Kane is not sitting with me anymore. He's somewhere by the window, hands braced against the wall as his back faces me.

For seconds, nothing but our harsh breaths can be heard. His body is rigid, and his fists are clenched against the wall, but I think I see an almost imperceptible tremble go through him, "I'm sorry," he says in a voice like gravel. "I shouldn't have done that. I...lost myself."

"No, it's..." I clear my throat to get rid of the huskiness. "It's my fault. I shouldn't have..." Licked your lips? Kissed you back?

Somehow, none of that feels appropriate to say right now.

Kane is silent for a few more seconds and then grits out, "Your towel. Fix it."

I glance down to note that the towel has shifted down a few inches, and my breasts are dangerously close to being exposed.

I blush and grab the knot, shifting it higher. Still, Kane remains by the window for a few more seconds, pulling in breaths and pushing them out again.

By the time he turns back around, his face is placid once more. He's schooled it into that unflappable, vacant expression.

But as he gets closer, I note there's still a simmering in his eyes that he didn't quite get rid of.

He goes back to sit across from me and then asks, "Well? What's your answer?"

It takes me a second to recall what we were talking about before the kiss scrambled my brain.

Oh yes. He just asked me to marry him.

Somehow, the idea doesn't sound as crazy as it did before the kiss.

And he does have a point that it would probably benefit me the most. I get to marry a hot billionaire for a year and get two million dollars out of it at the end.

At the same time, I'm apprehensive. I know that when things seem too good to be true, they typically aren't, especially for me.

But what if this is different? What if your luck is finally looking up?

Kane shifts, crossing his arms over his chest. To most, that would be an intimidating stance. But there's a little something defensive about it, too.

I recall his eyes when he spoke about his father. His intonation remained the same, but there was a little something there, some emotion I couldn't put my finger on. It was like sadness flickered across his face before he leashed it once more.

Or maybe it was nothing at all, and I was just imagining it.

But I'd lost a parent before. Two, in fact. My mother died giving birth to me. I didn't remember it, obviously, and couldn't miss what I never had.

But my Dad…watching him get sick and slowly deteriorate until he was gone was brutal. It's something I wouldn't wish on my worst enemy.

And if there's anything I can do to make it even a little better for Kane, then I will do it.

So, despite my reservations, I find myself nodding and saying, "Yes. Let's do it."

∼

It's only on the drive to the courthouse that I think maybe I made a mistake.

Maybe I rushed into this too quickly without thinking it through.

This time, it's just the two of us riding in a sleek black Corvette with the top down. The wind whips my hair, and the car purrs, but I still hear when Kane says, "The lawyer will meet us at the courthouse with the papers detailing our contract. You can read through it and have it sent to your lawyer if you want."

"Uh…sure." My mind is a whirlwind, and I can't believe this is happening. *Am I really doing this?*

Lisa is going to blow a gasket when she finds out.

But, a voice of reason permeates the panic. *This is like a once-in-a-lifetime opportunity. Like with people who win the lottery. Two million dollars will literally solve all your problems.*

You can pay off the rest of Dad's medical bills with ease. You can go back to culinary school. And you can have a little extra to treat Lisa and pay her back for all those times she helped you out.

I feel my heart racing in excitement as I imagine it. I can start planning for the future instead of just living day to day, hand to mouth.

I can donate to the animal shelter!

Kane makes a sound, and I glance at him from the corner of my eyes.

Can I really trust him? Is that why he's doing this to help me?

His eyes are covered by shades now, and I can't read his expression when he turns to me.

"It will be alright," he tells me in his deep accented voice. "You'll see."

I nod. I don't know why, but I trust him.

It's a blur to get to the Cook County Marriage court. Lisa called at some point during the drive, but I texted her, telling her I was in a job interview and I'd call her in a few hours.

Once at the court, we head up the marble stairs, and Kane strides directly to a redheaded, elderly man standing in front of the doors who shoots us a friendly smile.

"This is Warner, my lawyer," Kane says to me, then asks the lawyer. "Do you have the documents?"

"Yes, sir." Warner pulls out some papers from his folder and hands them to me. "This is your copy, dear."

"Thank you," I take it from him, reading through the first few lines. A part of me is tempted to send the contract to Lisa's brother, who's a lawyer, but then I'd have to explain to him what it's for, and the news will certainly reach Lisa, who will shut this entire thing down.

And as trepidatious as I am, I don't want this to be shot down.

Besides, it's only a few pages long, and the language is pretty simple. I read over twice as we stand there and then nod.

"Sounds good," I say. "Where do I sign?"

Kane smiles, satisfied, and Warner pulls out a pen from his pocket.

The rest of it is done shockingly fast.

In the several blinks, we're standing in front of a court official, with Warren as our witness, signing marriage documents. I hesitate for only a second before I sign mine, thinking once more of any catch-22s.

But there is none. I don't have anything for him to scam me off. I have nothing to lose here and everything to gain.

Then, a thought occurs to me.

"Wait, what about…" Pen poised over paper, I turn to Kane instantly, and he raises an eyebrow. "You know…we're only going to be married on paper, right? No… consummation?"

He smiles, and I blush. Curiosity bid me to ask the question, although I don't think I would mind so much if the answer was no.

"Of course," he says. "Would you like me to add that to the contract?"

"Um, I don't think it's necessary." I turn away the heat on my face.

And then, I finally signed my name on the dotted line.

Afterward, we're back in his car driving on the highway, and I'm still sitting in shock about the whole thing.

I genuinely can't believe I did that, shaking internally. I feel like a hummingbird is stuck inside me, and I'm not entirely sure if that feeling though is terror or excitement.

"Where are we going?" I ask when he merges off the highway onto a winding backroad surrounded by woods.

"To my home," he responds. "I had Pope pack up your things while we were at the courthouse and move them there. It'll probably be a lot more comfortable than the condo. Besides, I don't know how I feel about you living alone in the city."

"Oh," is all I respond. So many changes in so little time. "My box…"

"I told him to be extra careful with it," he says. "And you might want to consider getting an urn."

I'm about to say something in reply, but whatever it is dies in my mouth as the car swerves in front of a tall, spiked iron gate.

I gape. "This is your home?"

"Yes," he responds.

I don't even know why I'm shocked. Except this isn't a home.

It's an estate.

Beyond the gate railings, I see a large sprawling grass with a mansion sitting in the middle. It's surrounded by the woods, and a fountain sits in the center of the yard, with statues dotted all over.

It's like something out of a storybook.

Kane presses a button in his car, and the gate opens automatically. He drives around the cobbled path to the front door, and when we arrive, there are men and women in uniforms standing at the entrance.

"Welcome back, Master Kane," one woman says.

Kane exits the car and comes around to my side to open the door for me.

"This is Anna," he says to me, gesturing to the woman who spoke. "She'll show you where you'll stay in the second wing."

"Where are you going?" I ask, a little scared of being left on my own in this huge place.

"I need to check on something," he responds shortly. "Anna will tell you everything you need to know, and I'll stop by for dinner. But the most important rule is this." He takes off his sunglasses, meeting my eyes with his icy blue ones. "The entire estate is yours to explore as you wish. But never, ever go into the first wing. Do you understand?"

Something harder than steel enters his voice when he says it, and I can do nothing but nod.

"Good," he says.

But as he walks away abruptly toward the large imposing building, I feel like I just might be in over my head.

CHAPTER 6
Kane

I stride through my apartment, compartmentalizing the thoughts currently rushing through me.

I should feel gratified that I got exactly what I wanted. By marrying Dara, I've ensured that no matter what, I get to keep my company.

But I still feel faintly unsettled. And the worst part is that I'm not sure why.

No doubt my father will find out about the marriage soon enough, and he'll want to meet Dara. He'll probably integrate her into the family the same way he did her brother, receiving her as a surrogate daughter of sorts.

A jaded part of me wonders if he planned this from the get-go. He mentioned giving her the shares so I could find a way to bring her and attach her to me.

After all, my father has been looking for Dara since before I did. Dara and her father moved around quite a lot and left only little traces of their next destination each time. I have no doubt Dad attempted to find them several times.

His PI is just not quite as good as mine.

This is one way to get what he wants. He can finally have

a Dalton in the family again, and I will get to keep running the company I was raised to.

I've trapped myself in this marriage to a woman nearly half my age for him. And he likely knew I would.

Is this his end game? Or is there something else at play here?

Something I'm not seeing.

Because the old man has never been particularly predictable when it comes to things like this.

And lately, he's grown more unpredictable with age.

My shoes don't make a sound against the sleek floors as I walk down the broad parlor leading to the first wing. A maid dusting the Moeller Vintage French dining table stops and stares at me as I cross, apprehensively as If I'm going to take this time to analyze every surface for dust or something.

I pause.

"Where's Kenny?" I ask her, but before she can respond, I hear a loud crash.

That, I suppose, answers my question as well as anything else.

I immediately continue my walk up the spiral staircase toward the location of the crash. As I get closer, another crash sounds followed by the sound of running and a singular woman who swears, "Kenny, if you don't come down from there, I swear you're going to regret it."

"You'll have to catch me first," Kenny's ten-year-old voice challenges and I nearly smile at the audacity in his tone. He's a Leon true and true, audacious even when he's clearly in the wrong.

And a complete terror to his nannies.

I watch the commotion from the doorway. Kenny's wing is a sixteen hundred square foot space equipped with his living room hosting the latest technology, games, toys, and everything a ten-year-old could want.

So, it surprises me that he would neglect all that to instead climb on top of his dresser and dangle a necklace over his head.

"This isn't real, is it?" he frowns, eyeing the gem of the pendant. "It has so many scratches on it. Dad says if it has scratches, then it's not very good."

"Give that back, Kenny," Nanny number three, May I think her name is, cries out, looking red-faced and out of breath. No doubt, she chased him all over the room. And the clatter I heard earlier was from the breakfast table that was now overturned, likely in Kenny's haste to get away. That and a coat hanger.

Kenny's other two nannies, Sophia and Lacey, don't look any better for the wear. One of them holds her hands out in fear of Kenny falling and the other looks nearly apoplectic with panic.

Only May looks stern-faced and holds out her hand. "I'm going to count to ten, Kenny, and if you're not back down here by the time I'm done, then…"

"Then what?" Kenny mocks. "You're going to ground me?"

May's lips tighten. Even she knows that grounding doesn't mean much to a kid like Kenny who has everything in his room at his disposal.

"I can take your new X-Box away," she threatens and Kenny smirks even more.

"You can't do that," he says. "You don't have the authority."

"No." I finally step forward from my spot at the doorway, drawing eyes from everyone in the room. "But I can."

Sophia and Lacey gasp.

"Mr. Leon," May stammers. "I was just trying to—"

I hold up a hand to stave off any explanation she has. She probably thinks she's in trouble and wants to explain why she was scolding my son, but she was right to do it.

I'm not one of those parents who believe that their children must be coddled from all forms of discipline, and neither do I think my child is an angel who can do no wrong.

Truthfully, my son is a real demon when he wants to be.

"Get down from there," I order, crossing my hands over my chest.

Kenny's expression morphs from dissatisfaction at his game being interrupted to mulishness. He sticks his nose in the air. "I don't want to."

"What you want is irrelevant," I tell him. "You're being a pill. Now get down before you break something."

I walk closer and reach out my hand. If I want to, I could probably reach the top of the dresser and snatch him down myself but I wait for him to realize that he's lost this little game.

It doesn't take long.

With an exaggerated huff, he starts scaling the side of the Arabic-style dresser, using the decorative ridges on the side. I seize him when he's about halfway down and drop him on the floor, then hold out my hand.

"The necklace," I order. "Give it to me."

Familiar blue eyes glare at me as he shakes his head. "I don't want to."

"Remember what I said about wants?" I raise an eyebrow, but he still doesn't relent.

I squat so that we're at eye level. His lips curl churlishly, and he further clutches the necklace like a lifeline, hiding it behind his back. From the glimpse I got, it's not an extremely beautiful necklace. Not too hard to find in any flea market. I could have it custom-made as well. "I'll get you one exactly like it if you want. But taking someone's item without their permission is stealing. And Leons aren't *thieves*."

The emphasis I place on the last word has Kenny reacting.

He jerks a little, and a blush spreads across his face. My son likes to commit a crime, but apparently, he hates being called out on it.

"Fine," Kenny says, practically tossing the necklace in my hand before running into his bedroom and slamming the door. The lock turns.

I remind myself to get rid of that lock if he continues this behavior.

I sigh, straightening, and hand the necklace to May, who's standing to the side and receiving it hesitantly.

"I apologize," I tell her. "I'll have a talk with him about this."

Yet another of many talks that will probably do nothing to curb his bad behavior.

I wonder if I should just take a page out of my Dad's book and send him to boarding school. Or lock him in a room until he relents.

But every harsh punishment my father ever gave me only reinforced my antics and made me more rebellious.

It's why I'm trying the gentle parenting route with Kenny, but so far, it's not exactly yielding fruit.

"It's alright," May says graciously, blushing a little as her finger grazes mine in the exchange. "He mentioned that it looked like something his mother owned and wanted to take a closer look, so I gave it to him. That's probably why he didn't want to give it back."

Ah. I was wondering what would fascinate him so much with a woman's necklace.

The topic of Kenny's mother, Rosa, is a sore one. She's an actress with whom I had the misfortune of spending a single night in Paris. That night, she conceived Kenny but Rosa didn't tell me this at the time. In fact, she didn't tell me for nearly six years until she was tired of being a mother and decided to show up at my doorstep one day with Kenny.

From the first moment I saw Kenny, I knew he was my son. I didn't even need a DNA test to tell. The resemblance was far too strong.

I never expected to be a father. It's not something I've ever wanted, but I can't say that I'm too upset about having a son.

And Kenny, for all his mischievousness, has been a bonus to my life so far.

Whether or not I'm doing a good job as a father is another question.

But since his mother has decided not to parent anymore, I guess I'm all he has.

"He was looking forward to breakfast with you today," May ventures carefully as though navigating a minefield. "You know, since it's a weekend."

"Something came up," I tell her. "I'll have dinner with him." Although perhaps not even that. Because I have a meeting right now that I'm currently late for.

I hold out my hand, and May hands me the spare key to Kenny's bedroom. I let myself in to find him underneath his blanket, probably sulking.

"We have a guest staying with us at the second wing," I tell him. "She'll be here for a while."

"She?" Curiosity penetrates the distaste in his voice.

"Don't bother her," I tell him because the last thing I need is for him to initiate his pranks on Dara. "And don't go to the second wing."

"Okay, Dad. I guess I'll stay in this prison then."

I try not to roll my eyes because this bedroom just might be the most comfortable prison known to man.

But he's a kid, so I suppose the melodrama is to be expected.

I exit the bedroom and tell May, "Watch him. He's going to start plotting something in the next few hours."

"Yes, sir," The nannies respond in a chorus as I walk back to the second wing.

I should give Dara time to settle in and unpack herself. Anna is likely giving her a tour, and I should probably leave them to it and head to my meeting.

But I want to see her again.

I tell myself it's because of the item in my pocket and not because of that kiss.

That kiss continues to replay in my mind, at the base of my consciousness. Perhaps that's what has been unsettling me this whole time.

I didn't expect to enjoy the kiss as much. The word 'enjoy' even seems like too mild a description of what happened.

I loved it.

I didn't expect to lose my fucking mind by kissing her. Her lips were soft, and I could taste her inexperience but also her eagerness as she gave in to it.

I've never been that hard that quick in my entire life.

I nearly lost myself and fucked her right there. Only the strongest willpower enabled me to pull back in time.

I hear voices as I approach and a tinkling laughter that does something to me. I see Dara laughing with Anna as they walk down the hallway. Anna sees me first, and she draws back as I approach.

"Hey," Dara says, coming forward to meet me.

"I have to go to a meeting tonight," I tell her. "But I wanted to give you this before I leave."

I pull my black card out of my pocket. She frowns at it. "What is it?"

"An Amex," I tell her. "There's unlimited funds on it. I want you to spend something each day."

"How much?"

"At least fifty thousand," I say. "It's apart from the payment for our deal."

She gapes.

"I can't take that from you," she whispers, looking alarmed.

"If you don't spend at least that, I'm just going to spend more than that each day buying you things. And trust me, my imagination is more expensive than yours." I lean in. "Don't forget. You have to play the role of my wife and make it believable. And my wife gets showered in gifts and luxury and everything she wants."

Her eyes darken, and she gazes at me.

Fuck I want to kiss her again.

But I can't. I remind myself of the series of reasons why I can't.

She's Carter's very young, very naive sister. I may be using her to keep my company, but I'm not a big enough bastard to use her to slake my lust, too.

It takes herculean effort for me to draw back and walk away.

CHAPTER 7
Dara

I stare at Kane's retreating form and swallow the words in my throat.

I wasn't even sure what I was about to say. My mind is still stuck somewhere between shock and disbelief.

My life has done a complete three-sixty in the last few hours.

And part of me wants to cry and tell him how grateful I am for everything. But I don't want to get in his way.

He seems to be in a hurry somewhere. And he's probably got a lot of work today.

I turned to find that the woman who was showing me around, Anna, was no longer behind me. But it's fine. I can find my way back to the bedroom through hallways wide and grand like those of a castle.

Which I guess is what this house is. A castle.

And it's suddenly unsettling standing alone in the vast expanse of its magnificence.

Maybe I'll feel better if I unpack, I tell myself as I head back in the direction of the room Anna showed me. As we go,

I admire the gothic decor of the house and note the hints of classic elegance.

Everything here looks old and new at the same time. There are paintings on the velvet walls, golden burnished knobs on doors, and every corner seems to feature some antique sculpture or vase.

At the same time, the designer knows just when to pull it back. The colors are subdued and simple, and there's a subtle sophistication in the simplicity of the decor. Plus, it's pretty technology-friendly—there's a coded lock on every door, too, and cameras are placed in corners.

When I reach my room, I take another moment to take it all in.

It's not just a room.

It's a space that's about three times the size of my last apartment, and it's the perfect mixture of vintage and modern decor that runs throughout the whole house. There's a flat-screen TV in the middle of the lounge area, but also a legitimate chandelier on the ceiling. The platform bed has sashes that remind me of the Victorian era, but it also has buttons on the side for a massage. A patio overlooks an elaborate, colorful garden.

The place is beautiful.

But also, kinda lonely.

I guess I'm just not used to being in such a large, quiet space on my own, and it's a little disconcerting. And rather than get better, it gets worse as I start to unpack, so I stop halfway through.

I place the parent's treasure box into a safe dresser and then head back to the bed.

Maybe I should rest.

But I can't.

The entire day runs through my mind again, in a loop that restarts every time I think about Kane's 'threat.' *If you don't spend at least that, I'm just going to spend more than that each day buying you things. And trust me, my imagination is more expensive than yours.*

It all feels so surreal. What has my life become?

And was he serious? I don't think he would joke about something like that.

But fifty thousand dollars a day? I wouldn't even know how to spend that much if I tried.

I immediately sit up and get on my phone.

Either way, I could at least try to spend it on something I want rather than have him buy me a fifty-thousand-dollar bag or something equally ridiculous. I take out the card with one hand as I head to the website of the school I was attending until about a year ago. They placed my attendance on hold until I fulfilled the balance on the account.

Experimentally, I begin typing the card details onto the website, excitement fluttering in my heart. I hold back and try not to hope too much. Every time, I hope I end up disappointed.

This could be another one of those times.

But it's not. Because the website loads for a second, the balance is clear within the blink of an eye.

Congratulations. You may now resume attendance.

I throw my hand over my mouth and nearly sob. It's real. It's nearly the beginning of a new semester and I made it just in time.

Gratitude overflows in my heart. Happiness pulses inside me so potent that it bursts out of me in a single laugh.

I don't know what to do with myself, but I do know who to thank for this.

Kane.

However, this turns out, I will always be grateful that he gave me my dreams back.

And I want to show him my gratitude.

It takes me a second to decide how to do it.

With a renewed sense of purpose, I immediately head to the door and throw it open just as a young woman in a maid's uniform is about to knock.

"Oh!" she exclaims, startled.

"Sorry," I say, holding my hand out. "I didn't mean to scare you. Are you okay?"

"Yes," she shoots me a kind smile as she presses her hand over her chest. "Sorry, I just wanted to find out if you wanted to eat here or in the dining hall."

"Oh...um...I'm not hungry actually. But I did want to know where your kitchen is. If you can show me?"

"Of course!" she beams and says. "It's on the first floor. You can follow me."

"Thanks," I say and do just that. "Is Kane around?"

"No," she responds, her footsteps quick and efficient. "He actually just left."

"Oh," I say in disappointment. *Which means that I'm at home alone.*

Nevertheless, at least I can take this time to get accustomed to the place. My phone rings instantly, reminding me of something I haven't done yet.

"Give me one second," I tell the girl, and she pauses. I step away from her for a little privacy, turning around to call Lisa.

Nervousness sinks in my stomach as the phone rings. I think of how to tell my best friend that I just married a guy I don't know.

"Hello?" Lisa answered a lot faster than I would have liked.

"Hey, it's me."

"Of course, it's you," she answers sarcastically. "Who else is saved under this number on my phone." I can hear loud voices in the background telling me that she's at work. She works double shifts at the Farmer's Market on weekends to pay her tuition, and during the weekdays, she interns at a graphic design studio.

"Are you safe?" she asks.

"Yes, I'm good. Just…" I glance behind me a little, hoping the girl can't hear me. She's looking away pointedly. "Just hanging in there."

I laugh a little nervously, but Lisa doesn't return the laughter.

"I'm so sorry this happened to you." Lisa's quiet voice only worsens my guilt.

"Not it's fine. Worse things have happened to better people."

"Did you manage to find a job?"

"Um…something like that." Should I still get a job? I want to, but somehow, I don't think that will go over well with my new husband. We haven't exactly discussed the rules of engagement yet, but I have a feeling that part of playing the 'wife' role is not working at some restaurant for less than minimum wage.

Also, speaking of which, if I'm going to be meeting his Dad soon, shouldn't we get straight the story of how we met? And shouldn't we discuss things about each other that married couples would know?

We'll unpack that later.

"It's still up in the air right now, but I think something should come through soon."

"It will," Lisa says. "And I have a few ideas, too, of other things you could do in the meantime. How about we meet for dinner tonight and discuss it?"

"Dinner? Um…I don't know. We can do breakfast tomorrow."

"Tomorrow?"

"Yeah. I'm still sending out job applications, and I'll probably be doing that all through dinner."

"Oh," she says and then asks. "Okay then. Listen, I gotta get back to work because Mo is giving me the stink-eye, but you tell me if you need anything, right? And I do mean anything."

"Sounds good, I will."

"And tell me if this brother's friend asks you to do anything weird."

Does marrying him count? I think a hysterical laughter bubbles up, but somehow, I hold it back.

"Sure," I croak and then hang up before I can give myself away. Then I release a breath.

Breaking it to Lisa is going to be hard.

But still, all things considered, this marriage is off to a good start.

As we wander through the hallways, I venture to ask. "So, um…I'm sorry I don't have your name."

"Faith," she responds.

"Faith. I'm Dara."

"I know. The boss announced you would be coming today."

"He did?" I say. *How did he know I would say yes?*

And then in the next thought, I wonder if his staff knows about the true nature of the relationship. I don't imagine he would explain it all to them, but strangely, none of them seem surprised that I just showed up married to Kane today. Even

Anna didn't bring it up, spending most of her time telling me the history of the mansion.

I want to ask all these questions, but I don't want to potentially blow our cover.

"How long have you worked here?" I ask instead.

"About two years," she answers. "But I used to hang around long before that because my Mom used to work here, too."

"So, you knew him when he was younger?"

"Not really. But my Mom did. She always said he was a mischievous boy, always getting into one thing or the other. It was worse when his friend was around. Carter."

I stumble a little over the rug.

"Wait, you met Carter too?" I blink at her in surprise, and she nods.

"Yes," she responds. "Not personally, of course, but he was close to Beverly, Kane's mother, who was also close to my Mom."

Something shifts in her expression, but it's gone before I can pinpoint it. But before I can ask more questions, we arrive at a wide, open area, which is the kitchen.

About a half dozen people freeze when they see me.

I wave self-consciously. "Hello."

One man extracts himself from the group, wiping his hands on a clean rag. "Did you need something, ma'am?"

"No. Well, yes. I wanted to make something and was wondering if I could use the kitchen for that."

Confusion ripples across his expression, and he says, "If you need something, we can make it for you."

"Oh no." I hold out my hand. "I'm sure you can. I don't doubt your abilities, it's just that I like cooking too. I'm in culinary school, and if I don't train, I fear my skills will get rusty."

"Oh. Alright, then, the space is yours to do with as you wish." He gestures to the kitchen. "Let us know if we can help you."

I much prefer cooking on my own, but I can't find a non-rude way to say it.

"Sure," I say instead.

It doesn't end up being as awkward as I thought it would. Everyone is a bit uncomfortable at first, but the man who spoke to me—who ends up being the head chef, Harold—is a huge gastronome, and we get into a lengthy discussion about French desserts as I make Kane a crème brûlée.

"When I stayed in France with the boss, I used to *love* eating crème brûlées," he says. "There was a restaurant across from the condo that made the best ones, and their chef taught me a thing or two. But I gave up trying to make it myself after I got home. I kept messing up the texture."

"Like most things, it takes time and a little practice," I tell him. "It took me about a hundred tries to start making the perfect crème brûlée."

Of course, when I take it out of the oven to torch it, Harold's eyes widen. He gestures to the other cooks.

"Guys, come see this," he says. "I think that really is the perfect crème brûlée."

They gather around and murmur their appreciation. I blush at the compliments. "Thank you."

At that point, Faith comes in to announce that Kane is back and will eat in his study. Sophie directed me to study in the second wing, and I arranged the food on a plate and took it to him myself, already reciting the words in my head.

Thank you for everything. This is just a small token of my appreciation.

Kane is not in the study when I get there. I place the food

on the table and leave, resolving to come back in the next few minutes.

As the time elapses, I can barely contain my excitement. I head back to the study after about ten minutes.

He's not there.

But also, the food isn't on the table anymore.

It's in the trash.

CHAPTER 8
Kane

Mild sounds of laughter reach me as I approach the conference room at the Marriot where the meeting is taking place. The low orange lights cast a glow on the oak doors, beckoning me.

Perhaps I would be in a better mood, too, if not for what I see once I open the doors.

All the board members are already in attendance, seated around a large circular boardroom table.

All board members, including my father.

He was involved in a conversation with another board member, but he stopped when the doors opened and glanced at me, cocking his head.

I narrow my eyes, annoyance rippling through me.

He pretends he has no idea why I might be glaring at him.

My father no longer attends company meetings. Ever since he stepped down from his directorial role at Leon, he stopped coming to meetings, and I filled his spot.

But he's here now.

And he's sitting in my spot, at the head of the table,

clearly in a bid to provoke me in some way. I don't take the bait, sitting at the other end.

"Gentlemen," I announce in the sudden silence. "Let's make this quick. There are a few things on the agenda, but the most pressing issue is the new prototype we're releasing in the summer of next year."

"You mean the phone?" Elliot, the man seated beside my father, asks. "I know we discussed this already, Kane, but...I don't know how I feel about lowering our prices this long into the game."

"How you feel about it is irrelevant. Our research continues to prove the same thing. While we're by far the most innovative tech company, we're still being outpriced by at least two folds. People aren't getting the chance to buy into our ecosystem because they can't afford to."

"So?" Marvin Hayes calls out. "We've always been for those who *can* afford to indulge in our quality. And if the general masses can't afford it, then they can't afford it. It's not our problem."

He elbow-bumps the man sitting beside him, trying to get him to snicker along, but his partner doesn't dare. Not with my eyes on him.

"Our problem," I say, "Is that the elites don't buy enough phones every year to keep us in business. We need something else for the general masses, as you put it."

"But lowering our prices also lowers our profit margins and leads to less quality products."

"Not necessarily. That's where this new prototype comes into play." I gesture to my secretary who's sitting in the corner of the room. She nods and stands, pressing a button to activate the projector.

"This phone can be the average man's introduction to Leon technologies. A bait, if you will." The second picture appears on the screen, detailing the features. "A phone that is both affordable yet holds the key components of our phones —durability and exceptional camera quality. That's the highlight. It's with this phone that we finally solidify our place in the market and wipe out our competition."

A murmur goes through the room as the men consider the image on the screen. My secretary, Melissa, now gives a detailed explanation of each phone component and how we're able to make it affordable while still maintaining its quality.

A lot of research has already gone into creating this phone, and I'm assured of its impact. But of course, the board needs to be convinced of every fucking thing.

"I thought the entire point of Leon is quality at an expense," Cliff Harley, sitting to my right, says. He's an old friend of my father's, so I know him better than any other board member.

"Yes," I respond. "And we still have that. The rest of our phones will be maintaining their price tag."

"Yes, but people will talk. They'll think we sold out and started creating lower-quality products just to be as cheap and flimsy as our competitors. Then our reputation tanks. And, as you know, if you've been in this business as long as I have, reputation is everything."

"Correct," Marvin says. "People believe our stuff is quality *because* of the price tag. A lower price tag indicates lower grade items."

"Wrong. People think our stuff is quality because it is quality. Every quality assurance test proves it. Our phones, by and large, last about five years longer than the next phone on the list. We don't build for the bin, and we perfect each innovation before we put it out to the public. Our only drawback so far has been our price tag. I'm not saying we need to lower our prices across the board, but I do think market domination is possible with this new phone."

Another murmur reverberates through the room. They begin discussing amongst themselves, dissent warring with approval.

Through it all, I can feel my father's eyes on me.

So far, he hasn't said a word.

And then he speaks up suddenly.

"It's a bad idea," he says, and the room descends into silence at his booming tone. He levels me with his stern gaze and orders, "Scrap it."

I tighten my body to keep from reacting. He's watching me specifically to see whether I'll react or throw a tantrum. It's why he said the words in the most provocative way possible, as though I were just a boy and he was still in charge. No explanations, just directives.

It's a game he's been playing since I was young. And I've learned over the years to get very good at controlling my emotions around him.

"Any particular reason?" I ask.

He glances at Marvin before he speaks. "It's better to stick to what we know. Leon Technologies started with cameras. We should be innovating that."

"Cameras don't make sense for our current direction and research," I say. "Our phones are our money makers."

"Not if you start selling them for cheap."

"They will not be cheap." I feel the frustration rising, but I fight it down to keep from showing it. *How many times do I have to repeat the same fucking thing?*

"Listen, our stocks aren't rising as fast as they should, and we're nearing a downturn. We need to do something, or we're going to sink. We need to build a loyal customer base from the ground up that will not hesitate to abandon our ecosystem. We need to draw them in."

"I still don't think we should change anything."

I pin him a look. "Fine. But a failure to innovate is going to be our downfall. And that will be on all your heads."

The words have discomfort reverberating through the room, but I'm done hearing their excuses.

"Let's put it to a vote," I say. "All those in favor, raise your hand."

Six people do. Three people are against it, and two abstain.

I win by a slim majority. But there's no satisfaction to be had.

Only a soul-deep, unsettling idea that something very vital is happening here, and it's going over my head.

～

WHEN I GET HOME, I HEAD TO MY STUDY, NEEDING TO BE alone to decompress. Thoughts are flitting around my mind, and I need to sort through them.

Chiefly, I'm wondering about my father's actions today. He was deliberately provoking me. Why? What's his endgame in all of this?

When I entered my study, there was a plate of dessert waiting for me. I don't know who put that there, but all my staff knows I'm not a fan of desserts under normal circumstances. Most of them are far too sweet for my taste.

I throw it out without a single thought and then head to the bathroom to wash my hands and take a quick shower.

When I come back out, Dara is there.

She stared with devastation on her face at the trash bin. When I appear, she spins around to look at me in shock.

Irritation and suspicion cloud my mind.

What is she doing here?

The suspicion floats through my mind, and I remember my father's subtle look of satisfaction as he stared at me during the meeting. Was that about the argument?

Or was he simply happy I married Dara Dalton?

Were they plotting something secret together?

Am I the one being fooled here?

I eye her closely, trying to see any trace of guilt or guile in her expression. But her gaze travels back to the trash, hurt stinging her features.

"What are you doing here?" I ask, my voice harsher than I intended.

"Um…" she says quietly. "I was just wondering if you had tried the crème brûlée. Wanted to know if you liked it."

I glance at the food in the trash and frown. Why would she want to know if I liked the food or not? Unless…

"Did you make it?" I ask.

She nods hesitantly.

"Why would you do that?" We have three chefs who are on rotation at the estate. Were none of their cooking to her liking? "You didn't like the chef's cooking?"

"No, I did, I just… I thought…" She shakes her head, and her expression squeezes a little as she swallows. "I mean, it doesn't matter now, but I thought I would make something nice for you. Just to say thank you."

That startles me into blinking twice. "What?"

She frowns at my look. "Don't look at me like that. It's not weird. You're letting me live here for free and everything, and I got to sign up for school today. I *should* be grateful. I thought maybe it would be nice if I…" She shakes her head, and her voice quivers a little at the last part. I frown at her.

Why does she sound like that?

Is she getting that emotional over making food?

Or is she simply exhausted? She has been through a lot today, and the last thing I want is for her to do chores around the house just because she feels indebted to me.

"Don't bother with things like that," I tell her. "You're my wife, not a maid. If you want to make me happy, then you can start by spending the money on the card I gave you. Go shopping. Visit places. Play the part of the spoiled wife."

A flash of pain shoots across her features, but she looks away. "Right."

"And don't come into my office again without asking," I say, unable to get rid of that stray thought. *What if my father sent her as a private spy to infiltrate my life?*

Although, somehow, I doubt it when she covers her clear hurt with a tight smile.

"Noted," she says, and I read the expression on her face.

Anger.

She starts to storm past me, and my hand shoots out to stop her. She stiffens and turns to look at me, her expression schooled into careful indifference.

"Yes?"

"Why are you mad?"

"Why am I mad?" she gaped at me incredulously. "Did you really just ask why I'm mad?"

"I believe I did."

She presses her lips together, but the words seem to swell inside her chest until she has no other choice but to let it out.

"You threw it away!" She points to the trash. "You didn't even take a single bite, I bet."

I glance at the food. "I'm not a fan of sweets," I say defensively. "Perhaps you should have asked me that before you went about making it."

"It was supposed to be a surprise," she says. "I wanted to

surprise you, but you…I…" She sighs and runs her hand through her hair. "Look, if you didn't like it, it's fine. I can't hold that against you. But you didn't have to throw it out. I could have given it to Oscar. Or Harold, he loves crème brûlée."

I raise my eyebrows. Oscar? Harold?

"The chefs," she says, narrowing her eyes at me. "They've been working for you for months now. How do you not know their names?"

"If I know the names of everyone working for me, then I wouldn't have any brain space to know anything else."

"Spoken like a true spoiled little rich boy who's been raised with every single privilege in the world."

Annoyance shoots through me. The assessment isn't wrong, but I resent the implication that I should feel bad for how I was raised. Yes, I was raised with wealth and servants at my disposal. I can't pretend that I wasn't. I can't change how I see these things.

"Real rich coming from someone who is currently enjoying those privileges free of charge," I point out, leading her to flush.

But it doesn't silence her. "You're right. I am a freeloader. I should probably keep my mouth shut and enjoy the money you give me, but I can't stand by treating the people who work for you like shit."

That's a stretch. I pay everyone far above market rate with great benefits. "And you would know this due to your extensive background check on me?" I ask, trying to catch her off guard.

But she doesn't take the bait.

Instead, her eyes spitfire as she says, "I know it because no gentleman would throw out something that was painstakingly made for him without even a single thought."

The words are a shot, but they're overpowered by another overwhelming thought.

Her eyes are pretty when she's mad.

I realize this due to how close we're standing.

And those lips look just as succulent as ever.

Fuck, I want them in mine. Bad.

"I don't want any gifts from you." My voice is darker and grittier with the effort to hold back my desire. "I don't want any favors or any kindness. The only thing I want from you is to do exactly as you're told."

The anger in her eyes darkens into an infernal flame. But it's the same way they get when she's getting turned on.

I mentally trace her lips, wondering if she can sense the potent energy between us. And if she wants more of it.

Fuck. I can't do this. I let her hand go and took a step back, desperately needing some space between us before I did something crazy.

"Noted," she says and crosses her hand over her chest before she walks off.

And I'm left throbbing and more confused than ever.

CHAPTER 9
Dara

I lie in bed fuming, a complicated mess of emotions churning through me.

Chief of them is anger. Of course, I'm furious about the waste of food and how he casually disregarded my kindness. And the way he couldn't even remember his chefs' names.

I understand that he's wealthy, and that's normal for him, but it infuriates me regardless. Particularly the food waste. I've had to go without food a few times. My Dad even more so. I've also seen people worse off than me, people, to whom that food would have meant the difference between life and death.

And he just casually threw it away.

"Asshole," I mutter under my breath.

I tell myself I'm just annoyed because of the principle of it all, but I guess I'm also a little hurt. I tried to do something nice. Instead it feels like someone spat in my face for it. But also, he never asked me to do any of that.

The admission is like hot pokers, stoking my indignation even more.

Of course, I'm hurt, I tell myself. *Anyone would be. I'm human, after all, and he's an ass. A jerk.*

He's also virtually a stranger.

It's like a bucket of water to the face, putting my feelings in perspective.

The worst part is that I don't even know why I'm so hurt. I met the man yesterday. I don't know him, and he doesn't know me.

And yet he's your husband now, which is the most ridiculous part of this. But the more I think about it, the more I realize that I should not be this upset. So, what if he didn't like my food? I probably should not have made it in the first place. Heck, he has Michelin-starred chefs working for him, people who have traveled the world with him and learned his tastes. My crème brûlée is probably nothing compared to that.

And we're nothing to each other. All we have is this little business arrangement.

Reminding myself of it makes me feel like hurling a pillow against the wall, but I resist the urge.

So far, he's keeping up his end of the deal. It's me doing all the unnecessary stuff, trying to show my gratitude.

He doesn't need your gratitude, I remind myself bitterly. *Like he said, just do as you are told and play the part of a rich spouse.*

I have no clue where to start.

Regardless, I'm pretty sure I can learn. How hard can it be to spend money?

In fact, I can start tomorrow right after I get a good night's sleep.

And from now on, I'm going to stop thinking so much about him. No more worrying about whether or not he's in a bad mood or thinking about how to cheer him up. From now on, I'm only going to worry about myself. I'm going to finish culinary school and put aside enough money to maybe start a cute little restaurant for myself. And I'm going to run it.

And then, in about a year or so, we'll divorce, and I'll never have to speak to Kane Leon again.

I'll never have to think about the way his eyebrows furrow in annoyance or the subtle arch of his lips when he finally gives into the urge to smile. I don't have to see the way his eyes darken sometimes when they look at me.

Was he looking at my lips earlier, or was it my imagination?

Because for a few seconds during our argument, I thought perhaps he was.

And I imagined the intense heat of his lips on mine, his body urging mine to his as he kissed me into the abyss.

I slap my hands against my cheek, banishing the thought. I need to stop thinking about us kissing. It was nice, but it probably won't happen again. Snob that he is, he probably doesn't want to taint himself with a commoner like me.

And I don't...*shouldn't* want him to.

$\sim$

KANE IS GONE THE NEXT MORNING WHEN I WAKE UP. SOPHIE tells me this when she brings breakfast to my room. After eating, I head out to start my day, running into another maid I saw yesterday cleaning the tables.

"You cleaned that yesterday," I mention, catching her attention.

She smiles at me in greeting and says, "I know. But they need to be cleaned every day to maintain their luster."

"What's the point of having a table that gets dusty every day? Especially having it so close to the gardens."

She shrugs. "I don't ask questions," she says, still grinning. "Besides, I don't mind. It gives me something to do. And I get to stretch my muscles in the morning."

"Oh." I never looked at it like that. "Well then, good job, I guess."

"Thank you, ma'am."

"Dara," I correct.

She ducks her head. "Thank you, Dara."

"And you are?"

"Gemma."

"Nice to meet you, Gemma."

She returned my wave, and I continued heading outside, meeting Anna, who was on her way in.

"Going out, ma'am?" she asks.

"You can call me Dara. Ma'am confuses me," I say. "And yes, I am going out."

I have strict instructions to paint the town red, so to speak.

She nods. "I'll fetch Pope."

"No need," I call out, continuing on. "I think I'll just get an Uber or something." Or Uber Plus, since I have to spend more money.

Yet when I get outside, Pope is already waiting for me, apparently standing next to the Cadillac.

"Ma'am," he greets.

"Hi, Pope," I say, smiling at him. He smiles back. I feel a little familiar with the man. He has seen me sob over my parent's dead ashes, after all. It doesn't get more intimate than that. "I'm going out, but I don't think I need a driver."

"I think you do," he says smoothly, opening the door for me and directing me into the back seat. "I have strict instructions to take you wherever you need to go today and be at your beck and call."

I have no doubt who those instructions came from. "Oh. Um..."

"Come on," he says. "If you don't let me, then I get to sit around twiddling my thumbs all day. Or worse, sit in the kitchen and listen to their gossip."

"Is it juicy?" I tease as I climb into the car.

"Not even slightly. It's all about this television show Downton Abbey, who's marrying who, and why Mathew still loves Mary despite being engaged to Lavinia..." he shrugs. "Personally, I think Lavinia is far too good for both of them and should run away with a dashing pirate, but that's just me."

I giggle a little. "Alright then. I guess we can go."

On the smooth, comfortable ride, Pope continued telling me all about the show and all the fan theories. I ask questions and try to pay attention, but my stomach is in knots.

I'm going to tell Lisa about everything today.

When we arrive at the Farmer's Market, I direct Pope to drive right up to the entrance where Lisa is standing outside waiting for me.

I roll down the windows as he parks. "Lisa."

She glances around, looking for my voice, and I call out her name again before her eyes zero in on me.

And then she gapes. "What the fuck?"

I blush as I become aware of the attention we're drawing from shoppers exiting the market. "It's a long story. Get in."

She frowns as she approaches the car. Pope gets out to open the door for her, and she hesitates for a few seconds before sliding into the seat next to me. "Why are you in this?"

"This is Pope," I say, gesturing to Pope, who reenters the car with a salute.

Lisa eyes him. "This is the mafia man you married?"

I blush as Pope chuckles in the driver's seat.

"*No*. Pope works for him, and he's not a mafia man."

"Right," she says, unconvinced. "So where are we going?"

"Um, I thought we could try a new spot." A trendy new Italian restaurant in Wicker Park and it's been getting rave reviews from every local food journal ever since. Luckily, it's not too far from here.

I refuse to tell Lisa exactly where we're going, no matter how many times she asks.

But as we approach the glass midrise with a brick base and a sign of Luna projecting from the cream walls, Lisa's eyes bug out.

"Okay," she blows out a breath. "What the fuck is going on?"

Pope drives up right into the dropping spot and parks. Then he gets out of the car to open the door.

"You said you wanted to try it, didn't you?" I ask as I get out of the car.

"Yeah, but I didn't think we would in a million years." Lisa is a lot slower getting out of the car, and she's glancing around as though she's not sure what to do.

"Just trust me," I tell her.

"Alright, but if they kick us out, I'm going to laugh at your face."

We approach the entrance, where a hostess sits behind a table. She gives us a bored glance.

"Um, table for two, please?" I say, trying to inject confidence in my voice.

"Do you have a reservation?"

Shit. I completely forgot to reserve the place. "No-"

"I'll add you to the waiting list," she cuts me off and

sticks her hand out. "It's a two-hundred-dollar deposit for a spot. I need your card."

"Okay, uh...sure." I took Kane's black card from my purse and handed it to her. The hostess takes it, but instead of swiping, she stares down at the card.

Then her eyes widen, and she peers even harder. Then it's like her entire demeanor changes.

She straightens up, and a smile instantly spreads on her face.

"So sorry, ma'am," she says. "I had no idea it was you."

Me? I share a confused look with Lisa. "Have we met before?"

"No, but you're a guest of Mr. Leon, which automatically means you're on our VIP list."

"Oh," I say, not sure how I feel about that.

"Please follow me."

She leads us into the cool restaurant. I try not to gawk at the chic interior with a suspended fireplace and reflective ceiling-to-floor windows.

The hostess leads us to a table on a raised dais next to a softly flowing water fountain with a prime view of an empty stage.

She whips off the VIP reserved placard on the table.

"Please. Sit," she says, smiling tight. "The menus will be with you soon," and then she disappears.

Lisa, who was quiet during this entire thing, finally levels me with a look.

"What's going on?" she says quietly. "Look, I've been patient and everything but now I'm getting worried. We're getting VIP seats at one of the most popular, expensive restaurants in the city. We're riding in luxury cars. What, did you sell this guy your kidney or something?"

"Or something," I say and gesture to the seat. "Come on, sit. Like I said. It's a long story."

She sits, and then I start telling her everything from the beginning. I also include my reservations, why I ultimately decided to go through with the marriage, and what I plan to do after it's over.

She listens quietly, even when some of what I say alarms her.

"Wow," she says when I'm done.

I nod. "Crazy, right?"

"Crazy is one word for it." Her lips purse and she glances around the restaurant without saying anything else.

"Is that all you're going to say?"

"What? You want me to tell you it's a bizarre and possibly dangerous game you're playing?" she shrugs. "You already know all that. And you seem to have measured all the risks already, so there's nothing I can say."

I blink. I was expecting a lecture, not an easy acquiesce.

"Send the contract to Conrad so he can make sure there's nothing fishy in there," she says. "And I want to meet him as soon as possible."

"Uh. Sure." I smile with relief at just how easily she accepted the situation. *That's a huge load off my chest.*

The menu arrives in a few seconds, and the food is served quickly, too. I ended up getting risotto and seafood pasta, and Lisa got the ravioli.

The food is absolutely divine. We devour our dishes within seconds, only stopping to take breaths and nod to each other in approval.

I have a mouthful of spaghetti when I feel a tap on my shoulder.

I turn around to meet the twinkling brown eyes of a handsome man in a chef's uniform.

I nearly choke on my spaghetti.

He grins even more. "I'm glad to see you're enjoying the food."

"Oh." I struggle to swallow the mouthful. "Yes! Everything is delicious. The risotto was the perfect consistency."

"Great. It's always a pleasure when beautiful women enjoy good food."

I nearly choke again, but for a whole different reason. *Is he flirting with me right now?*

I'm about to respond when I sense a prickle at the back of my neck. I'm not the superstitious type, but it feels distinctly like I'm being watched.

I glance around, my gaze freezing on someone. Everything inside me clenches. I see him.

My husband.

He's sitting a few paces away, concealed in the shadows, staring daggers at me.

CHAPTER 10

Kane

Dara's eyes meet mine, and it's like an electrifying current passing through our gazes.

In her face, shock and discomfort battle for dominance.

She pales slightly, but that might have something to do with my countenance.

I'm not sure what expression I'm making, but it can't be good.

Ever since that man walked up to talk to her, a tightness has coiled around my belly, and a simmering heat starts in my chest and travels through my body. I have an insanely possessive urge to go over to her table and snatch her away from him. He's grinning down at her like he has every right to like she's his to be smiling at. Even from here, I can see the clear interest in his eyes. I can't blame him. Dara is beautiful, and any man with eyes can see that she has that rare combination of innocence and untouched sensual magnetism.

And she's smiling back at him.

I think that's what pisses me off more than anything. She's smiling back and enjoying his attention.

And I know I should feel nothing about it. After all, this is simply an arrangement, and we don't owe any loyalty to each other.

But she's my wife, damn it. And I despise the idea of any man looking at my wife with 'fuck-me' eyes.

A crack sounds from the distance, but it's not until my companion says, "Jesus, you're going to break that," that I realize what happened.

I finally glance away from Dara to the saltshaker in my hand. I had picked it up when I saw the chef walk up to her and have been holding it ever since. And yes, the glass has cracked a little under the pressure of my grip.

"Who is that?" Nathan asks.

Nathan's the lead researcher on our team and also someone I would consider a friend if I still believed in such things. He's now regarding me with a puzzled grin as he follows my gaze to where Dara is sitting. "Is she an ex-girlfriend or something?"

"No," I respond smoothly, trying to regain my senses. My tone makes it clear that I don't want to get into it, even though, for some reason, it's difficult to keep my gaze from drifting back in Dara's general direction.

It's ironic that the one time I choose to eat at a restaurant Nathan suggests, she's here. I immediately spotted her and her friend the moment we walked in. They were seated in the VIP area, raised above the rest of the floor.

"Do you want to be seated in the VIP lounge yourself?" the hostess asked us when we arrived, but I shook my head. I didn't want her to see me. She was smiling at her friend and seemed to be having a good time. I didn't want to ruin her day, considering the fight that we'd had yesterday.

The fight that I still worked over in my mind, wondering why the fuck she'd made me that food in the first place.

I also don't know why it bothered me so much that she did.

I asked the hostess to seat Nathan and me at the other corner of the restaurant, which was relatively hidden from view. But I could still see her. Throughout my conversation with Nathan, my gaze would drift there again and again.

I don't know how she captured my attention so effortlessly. Maybe it was the pure joy in her face, for once free of its usual tension. Since I met her, it's like she's always carrying an invisible burden, and today it's just gone.

And it does give me pleasure to see her like this, carefree and unencumbered by the stressors of life. She's eating delicious food with her friend without worry.

She should always smile like that.

This is the life she was meant to live. This is the life she would have had if her brother hadn't fucked everything up.

As my father's assistant, Carter was paid a significant six-figure salary that would have soon climbed to seven figures with more experience. But no.

He just had to fuck it all up by being a damn thief.

I watched Dara as I ordered and wondered why it gave me so much pleasure to see her like that. Most of the women in my circle enjoyed such luxuries as if they were nothing. But Dara's innocent and ecstatic exploration of this new lifestyle made me want to smile.

Of course, that feeling disappeared the minute the damn chef showed his face.

And I shouldn't look her away again, but even as I start to salt my steak, my eyes disobey me. Dara is turned away from me and still talking with the damn chef. He puts his hand on her shoulder, and once again, I grip my fork so hard that I nearly feel the metal bend.

"Okay, now I'm very curious," Nathan says again,

drawing my attention back to him. "I don't think I've seen that expression on your face since the last meeting with your Dad when he suggested we cut the research funding by half."

Mention of my Dad only worsens my mood. But before I can answer, Dara rises and heads off somewhere, leaving her friend and the chef looking on in her wake.

Before I can stop myself, I rise too and follow her.

I naturally draw attention, but I ignore them all, laser-focused on her back. She heads into the single-occupancy bathroom, and before she can bolt the door behind her, I head in, too, locking the door behind me.

She spins around with wide eyes. "What do you think you're doing?"

"I could ask you the same thing," I answer, the tension evident in my voice. "What the fuck were you doing talking to that man?"

"What man?" she asks, but her eyes shift, meaning she knows precisely what I'm talking about.

"Don't play that game with me," I say and walk closer. She blinks, and her breath quickens, but I can't tell if it's desire or anger.

Fuck! At this point, I'm not sure I care.

"This is the women's bathroom," she says, and her whisper tells me that she feels this tension too. I get even closer.

"I don't give a fuck," I tell her, and I can't resist anymore. I lower my head and seize her lips in a violent kiss. She doesn't resist as I ravage her mouth, everything in me demanding to possess her and show her that she's mine.

Dara makes a sound into my mouth but it's not protesting. It can't be because her hands grab my hair, and her body presses closer to mine. I hoist her up on the counter and devour her lips, her sweet taste flooding into me, drowning me in even more desire.

Fuck, she tastes much better than I remember.

I thought I had imagined how good she tasted, but I didn't.

I also forgot how insatiable her taste would make me.

I grab the back of her neck gently, and she moans as I control her movement. Her body shifts against mine, hunger in every tremble. Fuck she gets horny so fast. And I'm not much better because my cock is pounding behind my pants.

I tear my lips away, attacking the pulse, tasting her skin as her head falls back. My hands search underneath her jean skirt, skittering across the edge of her panties. Then I press a finger against her moist center.

"God," she gasps, tearing away from my lips. Her head falls back, eyes rolling shut. I watch her face as I shift her panties aside, slowly trailing the slit of her pussy. Her curls are damp, her scent addictive as it drifts up to me.

It's sweet and musky, and I want to bury my face in it.

But I don't, gently strumming her clit and watching the expressions dance across her face. Tension has her face pulled tight, her eyebrows furrowed. Her eyes open, and there's a plea for more as desire coils inside her, repeatedly pushing her hips further into my touch.

She moves like she can't help herself.

So sexy.

"Don't stop," she whispers, crying out when I exert more pressure on her engorged nub. She moans when I tease her, and I feel compelled to draw out more of her lusty responses.

I've never been so turned on in my entire life.

Everything else falls away, including all the reasons I shouldn't be doing this.

I push my index finger slowly into her center, and it sucks at me.

Then I thrust it in, once, twice, three times.

She mewls.

Her body starts to shake when she hits the precipice. Her mouth falls open, her eyes glassy and unseeing.

She's going to come.

I finger fuck her through her orgasm that rushes through her body, curling her toes and rendering her body in one long arch. It lasts for seconds or minutes, her pussy pulsing around my fingers and pouring into my hands.

Then, her panting breaths reverberate throughout the bathroom, and she collapses against the mirror.

My reflection doesn't look like me.

I look fucking insane, my eyes sharp and hungry, my jaw tense.

I strongly fight the urge to bring my fingers to my mouth and lick her off it like a psycho.

Instead, I turn on the sink and start to wash my hands which are shaking like an addict's.

I wait as realization dawns on her.

"Oh my God." She claps her hand over her mouth, and I school my expression into one of indifference as if I don't care that she just had the sexiest orgasm ever.

"You're mine." My words can't hide the truth, though. They're guttural and possessive and rough with the desire pounding through me. "At least until the contract is filled. No other man gets to talk to you or look at you. Do you understand?"

She blinks at me in horror. And then she shakily gets to her feet, dashing out of the bathroom.

I sigh and lean my head against the wall, wondering how

and when I became a man who could lose control of himself so thoroughly.

By the time I got back out of the bathroom, Dara and her friend were gone. I return to my seat. My steak is cold already, and Nathan likely notes my absence, but he's smart enough not to comment.

I gesture to the waitress, who hurries to my side.

"What can I do for you, sir?"

"Your chef..." I start and pause. What do I plan to do right now? Get the chef fired because he talked to her? Because he touched her?

I have the power to, but I resist my baser urges. Not because of my conscience, which I'm not sure I have. But because of the reason behind my actions.

I'm not doing this because it would benefit me. I'm doing it only out of pure jealousy, and I refuse to be ruled by emotions.

I sigh and shake my head. "Just get me a new steak, please."

CHAPTER 11

Dara

I rush out of the restaurant, and the wind hits me right in the face. There's a line outside the restaurant now, along with the din of several people chatting with each other, but I tune them out. The noise is no match for the chaos within me. My heart is pounding in my chest, my mind a mass of panicked thoughts that have no hope of making sense.

"Dara! Wait!"

I don't obey the voice behind me and continue walking down the sidewalk, narrowly avoiding the bodies in my way. I do bump into one person and mutter an apology as they shoot a dirty look.

"Dara! Where the fuck do you think you're going?"

My mind finally clears enough for me to realize the voice I'm hearing is not Kane's. It's Lisa's.

I immediately stop and pivot to find her jogging towards me, my bag and her jacket in hand. There's a bead of sweat trickling down her face, and she sounds a little out of breath when she says, "What is wrong with you? Why did you just run out of there like that?"

I take a deep breath. Annoyance and worry mix into her

expression, and it only adds to the guilt within me. I shake my head.

"Nothing," I tell her. "I just…" That's where the words end. Because how on earth do I explain what happened?

I just had the best orgasm of my life in the bathroom of a high-class restaurant. And the person who gave me said orgasm, my fake husband, is an unmitigated asshole who likely only did it to prove a point.

The empty look on his face after it was done was like a dagger to my chest. While I was losing my mind in the passion, he looked like it was a regular Tuesday for him, like he frequently cornered women in the bathroom and gave them intense orgasms that had them squirting their brains out. It was nothing to him but a calculated act meant to assert his dominance over me. It was humiliating, and I hated him so intensely in that moment that I wanted to slap the hell out of him.

But I hated myself even more.

"Dara?" Lisa says quietly. She's still standing, waiting for an answer, and I need to give her one that will satisfy her so she doesn't dig deeper.

"Yeah, I'm okay," I say. "I guess I just got…overwhelmed."

"Overwhelmed?"

"Yeah. You know, being there, around those people, with all that wealth and good food, I just…I couldn't help thinking of my Dad…" I hated tainting my memory of my father and using it for selfish reasons, but it was the only way to get Lisa off my back so she wouldn't keep asking questions and uncover the real reason for my temporary mania.

And it works. Sympathy sinks into Lisa's expression, and she says, "Shit. I forgot. The two of you used to go to restaurants together."

"Yeah." It was a ritual for us. Dad and I didn't have a lot of money growing up, but it got even worse after he got sick. He couldn't work as much, and his electrician salary dwindled to nothing.

But we would still save whatever we could, and every month at least, we would try out a new eating spot that opened up in Chicago. Usually, it was a food truck or some mom-and-pop diner.

But I always dreamt of taking him to a place like this, on my dime, and treating him to whatever he wanted to eat. He worked so hard to provide for us and make sure I never had to work for anything. All I ever wanted was to repay him the favor.

But I never got the chance to. He died, and now I'm here eating the food I should have been eating with him.

Damn. Now I'm sad for real.

"It's fine," I tell Lisa and attempt a smile, even though the twin sentiments of guilt and heartache make me feel nauseous. "I just had a mini freak-out, but I'm fine now."

"No, you're not," Lisa says. "And it's okay not to be fine. I don't think anyone would be fine under the circumstances."

Another rustle of breeze punctuates her words, and I have nothing to say to fill the silence.

"Do you want to talk about it—"

I'm already shaking my head before she can finish. "No. I just want to leave." I want to go home, bury myself in bed, and forget the past thirty minutes ever happened. I want to forget that Kane made my body sing and that it meant nothing to him. I want to forget that I'm such a weak woman that I melted into the arms of a man who was so indifferent to me.

If your father could see you now, he would be so ashamed.

It's true, I tell myself as my face heats. Dad was always

proud of me for how hard I worked and how I never took handouts from anyone. But look at me now, leaving my entire fate resting on a man who's as callous as can be.

"I think we need to go back, though," Lisa says. "You left your card at the restaurant."

His card. I swallow past the nausea and shame the thought brings and nod. "Yeah, let's go get it."

After retrieving the card, I come out to find Pope waiting at the entrance with a disapproving look.

"Did you try to avoid me again?" he asks.

"Again?" Lisa parrots, and I shake my head.

"No. I was just having a moment," I answer quietly, and it must show on my face because Pope's expression morphs into something resembling sympathy. I don't want it, though. I'm already getting enough of that from Lisa. I can't stand getting it from him, too.

"Can we drop Lisa off at home first?" I ask, and Pope answers, "Of course."

I got into the car, and Lisa got in beside me.

Thankfully, most of the trip is silent, and she doesn't try to ask me any more questions. She does, however, shoot me concerned looks out of the corner of her eyes, and at some point, she holds my hand and squeezes it.

I send her a weak smile in return. Lisa isn't usually the touchy-feely type, so I know how much it's taking for her to be like this with me. I'm grateful she's trying but I would much rather we go back to the status quo, so I say, "Tomorrow, I'm picking you up for lunch at that brunch place on the fifth."

Lisa shakes her head. "No, can't do. I mean, today was nice and all, but to be honest, I'm not sure how much rich people's food I can stomach. Before you know it, I'll be shitting caviar and red wine."

Pope snorts in the front seat but doesn't comment. I smile and shake my head, although disappointment rolls through me. I was hoping Lisa would help me spend the money on the card so that I would meet the quota every day. Now, how the heck am I supposed to do that by myself?

I suppose I could always just give it to charity.

It's like a lightbulb goes off in my head. *That's an idea.* I started planning ways to do it. Once I get home, I'm going to look up a list of charities around the area and find a way to discreetly donate the money from the card. Discreetly, because while Kane didn't say that I *couldn't* do that, somehow, I feel like it's bending the rules a bit.

But so what? I could at least do something worthwhile with my newfound wealth. Maybe that will prevent me from feeling so guilty about having it in the first place.

When we arrived at her house, Lisa gave me a big hug. "Call me tonight. Alright?"

"I will," I tell her and hug her back. After she gets out of the car, I watch her walk away. Usually, I would go in and say hello to her family before I leave, but if I do that, then her brothers will be all over the fact that I rode up in an expensive car and will demand to know why. And I really don't feel like getting into *that* conversation with them so soon after I had it with Lisa.

I've known Lisa for half my life, and her brothers view me as a little sister as well. And they can be very protective.

Pope begins to pull off, and I rest back in the car, closing my eyes.

Although Pope isn't as inclined to let me wallow in silence now that Lisa's not here.

"It gets better."

My eyes fly open, and I glance at him in the rearview mirror. "What?"

"It gets better. Trust me." His eyes are not reflecting pity. Instead, a deep, pained understanding.

I swallow thickly to keep the tears at bay, then say hoarsely, "Thank you."

He nods and then refocuses on the road ahead.

At the mansion, I'm met with chaos in the form of a crash and an echoing scream.

I'm immediately rushing toward the sound, my heart racing as I run up the spiral stairs.

"Kenny!" I hear someone shout, "Kenny, where are you?"

"This isn't funny anymore," says another female voice.

"It's never funny with that little brat," someone mutters.

I rush into the large room and glance around to see three uniformed women scrambling about the said room.

"What's going on?" I ask.

One of the women glances at me and shakes her head. "Nothing to worry about, ma'am."

"If it was nothing to worry about, you wouldn't be panicking right now," I remark. "Who is Kenny, and why are you looking for him?

"He's the master's son," the red-haired woman announces. It hits me like a lightning bolt.

KANE HAS A SON?

I blink at them in shock, but before I can react much to that, the woman continues, "He's currently missing."

"He couldn't have gotten far," another woman says, wringing her fingers. "I was gone for a second."

"That's all it takes with him," the dark-haired woman snaps. "You know better than that."

"It's fine," I say before the first one can snap back. "I'll help you look downstairs."

And then, before anyone can stop me, I rush out of the room, searching through the curtains, peeping behind every nook and cranny, and trying to think of where a little kid would hide.

So far, nothing.

I keep going until I see a garden with colorful bougainvillea, roses, and tall oaks.

I slowly glance around as I walk through the shrubbery, trying not to be distracted by their beauty.

When I'm near the oak tree, I hear something that sounds like snickering.

I glance up.

Sure enough, there's a child seated in the tree.

He's partway shielded by a branch, but I can see a shock of curly dark hair and blue eyes, bright and brilliant like his father's.

I stand and peer at him with a hand up to shield my eyes from the sun. "You're Kenny, right?"

He brings one leg up on the branch and sticks his nose up in the air. "Yeah. And what about it?"

I grin. I'm sure he meant it to sound arrogant, but he sounds very much like a kid trying to appear grown-up.

"I'm Dara," I tell him. "A guest of your Dad's."

"I know," he says.

"Good. Now that we're introduced, could you do me a favor and get down from there? I don't know how strong that branch is." It's thick but looks a little dry, and there's a crack underneath it. If the crack goes deeper than that, then the branch could snap at any moment.

"It's fine," Kenny responds. "I've been here before."

I sigh. Clearly, Kenny is as unreasonable as his father. I have to find another way to get him down.

"Okay, how about this," I tell him. "We play a game. And if I win, you come down. And if you win, I'll let you stay up there and pretend I never saw you."

He frowns. "What game?"

"The guessing game. It's very simple. We each say three words about something in this garden without mentioning the actual thing, and the other person tries to guess the word we're thinking. Whoever guesses it correctly wins."

He frowns as he considers it for a few seconds. "How do I know you won't cheat?"

Smart boy. "I'll write my word in the ground here and cover it with my foot. So, when you get down, you can check. And I know *you* won't cheat because you're not a cheater."

"I am not." His chest puffs out a little with pride at that.

"Alright, I'll go first." I squat and write the word down in the dirt, hidden from view, then cover it with my feet. "The three words are brown, ants, and hurt."

He thinks about it. "Tree!"

"Nope," I lift my foot. "Dirt. Rhymes with hurt. Now you go."

He thinks about it. "White, fluffy, and windy."

"Dandelion," I say, and his eyes widen in shock.

"How did you get that?" he frowns. "I thought you would say cloud."

Yeah, but I saw his eyes glance briefly at the dandelion bush behind me before he said the word. Nevertheless, I don't tell him that. Instead, I say, "I'll tell you when you get down."

He shakes his head. "Best two out of three."

"Fine."

Ultimately, I win those too, and each time, I can tell that he's reluctant to tell me that I guessed right, but his honor doesn't let him lie. And then, finally, with a mulish look, he starts climbing down the tree.

My heart is in my throat the entire time, and my hand is out to catch him. But he doesn't fall, to my surprise.

And when he's on the floor, he crosses his hand over his chest. "Now tell me how you did it."

"Later." I hold out my hand. "Everyone is going crazy in there. Let's help them calm things down first."

He glances at my hand for several seconds and then takes it.

We walk in together. But we don't get a chance to continue our conversation. When we get back, the other women meet us in the hallway, down the stairs beside themselves, and before I can tell them what happened, I hear a deep voice behind me saying, "What are you doing here?"

CHAPTER 12

Kane

One instruction.

I gave her only one rule about being here. Don't go into the first wing and she couldn't even keep that.

But I don't know why I'm surprised. She probably thought that my uncontrollable attraction to her was a sign of weakness in me, and I should have known she would try to take advantage of it.

Her face pales slightly as I walk forward, letting her see my displeasure.

"You're back early, Dad," Kenny says, but I don't look at him yet. I'll deal with him later after this simmering anger is gone from my chest.

"May, take Kenny to his room. And keep him there if you can manage it."

"Yes, sir." She wraps her hand around his wrist, but Kenny protests, struggling to extract from her hold.

"No," he says stubbornly. "Dara said she would tell me about how she won the game. I'll go when she's done."

"That wasn't a request, Kenny," I respond, finally pinning him with a look.

He gives me a sour one in return. "What? You're going to lock me in my room again?"

"I should. I would if that would teach you to stop causing chaos. I hired these people to look after you, not run around fixing things that you broke." I shake my head in disappointment. "I thought you would eventually grow out of this phase, but you're determined to remain a child forever, aren't you?"

Kenny's face turns red like it does whenever I scold him. His lips press together tightly, and his cheeks blow out. Then he runs off, with May calling after him. The other nannies quickly followed, leaving Dara and me alone.

I let her stand for a few minutes in the tense silence, but to my surprise, she doesn't cower under it. On the contrary, she crosses her hand over her chest as though readying herself for battle. She also meets my gaze head-on.

How nice.

"You're in the first wing," I say softly enough that she can still hear the menace in my tone.

"I am," she says cocking her chin boldly. "I heard a ruckus, and I came to find out what it was about."

"It was none of your business," I tell her. "You should have stayed in your wing like a good little girl and done as you were told."

Her face heats, and her cheeks blow out, not unlike Kenny's. "I don't know if you noticed, but I'm not a little girl anymore. I don't just do as I'm told. And if I was a little girl, then that would make you a pedophile."

The words provoke me in a completely different way than she likely expects. Rather than anger, they remind me of our session in the bathroom and her exploding around my fingers.

That cataclysmic ecstasy. The ambrosia-like scent of her. *Fuck*.

I want it again, and her audaciousness is stoking the desire even more.

Apparently, I like women who challenge me.

"I own this house," I tell her. "I decide where you can go and where you are prohibited from. And I already told you not to come here."

She thinks about it and shakes her head. "No."

"No?"

"Yes," she says. "This is a business deal that benefits you just as it benefits me. I don't see why I should be treated like a second-class citizen."

"Oh, don't exaggerate. And let's be honest now," I smirk, letting the insult roll in my tongue. "This deal benefits you a lot more than it benefits me."

She blushes, and then anger sparks from her eyes, making them glitter in the most arresting way. "You haven't even asked what happened."

"It doesn't matter what happened."

"Of course it does." She throws her hands up. "You haven't asked about what happened with your son or how much danger he was in. You know where I found him?" She points out toward the windows. "He was twelve feet off the ground on a tree branch that could have broken into pieces underneath him. Anything could have happened to him. He could have fallen off and broken an arm or even his neck. Something could have stung him. *I* got him down safely, but you don't care about that. All you want to do is focus on your stupid rules, like a controlling ass."

Her words strike a chord in me, painting a vivid picture.

My fury only increases when I realize that Kenny put his life in danger. God, what am I going to do with that boy?

How do I get him to realize that his pointless actions not only endanger him but also those around him?

I'll figure it out, I decide determinedly.

For now, though, I need to deal with her. "You think I don't care about my son?"

She takes a step forward, a clear challenge in her stance. "Sometimes, I think you don't care about anyone but yourself."

The statement ricochets through me and inflames me more than I thought possible. But so does her gaze, so daring and so damn fearless.

The mouse is finally coming out of her hole.

Or perhaps she was never a mouse after all.

At least not when it comes to standing up for other people. It doesn't escape me that the two times she's gotten mad enough to scold me, the topic partly concerns other people. First, it was the fact that I didn't remember my chefs' names. And now it's about my son.

Does she only get so defensive when she's fighting for others? Are those the only times her eyes spark, that she crosses her arms in a way that pushes her chest out on me?

Is that why she's here now, engaging me in this dangerous game that has arousal spiraling through me? Making me want to kiss the life out of those lips?

I could.

I can probably convert her anger into desire so fast that it would make both our heads spin. Like back in the bathroom, I can grab her and just kiss her and let the flames burn the both of us. I could have her under me, have my cock sinking into her wet heat, and forget about everything that I have to do today.

I want to. And I could make her want it, too.

I take a step back, drawing in a ragged breath. *Fuck*. What is it about her that makes me want to lose control so easily? How does she reduce me to this hungry beast?

I'm a man who has everything at his disposal. Money. Respect. Women. I can have anyone I want.

Yet, this little speck of a woman, way too young to be tempting me, makes me feel like I'm starving for her.

"Thank you," I say, startling her into a gape. "For saving his life. But the rule still stands. No trespassing on the first wing. Not even if you hear the entire world crumbling down. And the next time I see you here, there will be consequences. Understood?"

She presses her lips together and doesn't nod, but I can't stand any longer being challenged without kissing her. So I turn and walk out.

My next stop is to Kenny's bedroom. Adella is doing as I told them and not letting him out of her sight. She's sitting across from the bed, watching him, and only glances away when I arrive.

"Kenny," I say, but the boy doesn't turn to me. He's looking out of the window.

"Kenny," I repeat, firmer, and he turns to me with a sulk.

"What? Come to give me my sentence?"

Brat. "They say you climbed a tree."

"Yeah." He turns away. "I climb a lot of trees. I'm very good at it."

"You do that again, and I will cut down every single tree in that garden. Do you understand?"

He pivots to me, gaping. "You can't do that."

"I can, and I will." I plant my hands on the bed and lean down so that he can see my eyes. "You realize that you could have fallen from the tree and snapped your neck like a twig, right? And all your nannies would have been in trouble for not watching you closely enough."

"I wouldn't have fallen."

"Oh, really. Because from what Dara tells me, the branch you were sitting on was on the verge of cracking. She was scared you would fall."

I guess Dara didn't share this information with him because his eyes flared slightly. But then he schools his features once more into a sullen expression. "So? I wasn't scared."

"You weren't smart enough to be scared. I'm serious, Kenny. I will follow true to my word, and you know it. Don't try me again." I straighten and leave the room.

That threat should hold him for the next few weeks. But then after that...

Perhaps it's time to start considering a behavioral therapist. Or a psychologist. Possibly a psychiatrist. Because clearly, my son is partially out of his mind.

I finally settled into my study and started work, but between the thoughts of Kenny and thoughts of Dara, I couldn't focus.

It's just as well that the phone rings about five minutes into the session. It gives me something to do.

"What is it, Warner?" I haven't heard from the lawyer since we met at the courthouse, but I assume he's filed all the necessary documentation already.

"Hi, Kane. I just wanted to...um... inform you of some new developments."

"Such as...?"

"Well, it's kind of a long story, but essentially, according to my research, a year-long marriage might not be enough to secure the company if your father does will it to her."

"What are you talking about?" I bark. "You recommended the marriage."

"Yes, I did, but I warned you that my family law is rusty,"

he says. He's an older lawyer, and I only got him because I needed someone who my father couldn't buy off. "Inheritance laws are complex and differ by state. If she plays it right, you may not get anything after the divorce."

A rumbling rage starts within me. I'm unable to keep it out of my voice when I ask. "So, what now?"

He is silent for a few seconds. "I mean, the best thing to do would be to get her to just sign the company over to you."

"And how do you suppose I manage that?" I ask sarcastically, but I know he probably has no answer for me.

Fuck, I thought I was done with this. I thought I'd won. But fate always finds a way to attempt to screw me over.

Fate and my father.

Once again, I blame the man for putting me in this predicament in the first place, for forcing me to do the things I have to do.

But even as anger rolls through me, I start to think.

And then I'm hit with a stupidly simple answer.

The best thing to do would be to get her to just sign the company over to you.

The easiest way to achieve that is to make her fall irrevocably, stupidly in love with me.

CHAPTER 13

Dara

I try not to dwell on it the next day, on my anger at Kane.

I need to learn how not to be so mad at him all the time. Sure, he's an asshole, but I doubt that's going to change anytime soon. I'm the one intruding on his domain, so I just need to learn to live with it.

So far, I figure I can do that by simply avoiding him for the remainder of our arrangement. Seems simple enough since he's hardly ever home.

Last night, I had dinner in my room alone, and to alleviate the loneliness, I tried to bribe Faith to eat with me, but she shook her head, claiming she had too much work to do. So did Anna. I wonder if Kane has some kind of rule about me eating with the help. Snob that he is, he probably does.

So, I sighed and Facetimed Lisa instead, but we talked for only a few minutes before she had to go in for her night shift.

Then I went to sleep, managing to overcome my thoughts of Kane by looking forward to the next day.

Today, I start culinary school.

I wake up bright and early, a ball of excitement as I get ready. I dress comfortably in jeans and a t-shirt, knowing I'll probably spend most of the day on my feet, and tie my hair back into a neat bun. Today I have a practical cooking lab, as well as a business lecture after it. I signed up for the business classes, too, because I need help starting my own restaurant.

I already started saving up for it. I donated some of the money from the black card already and siphoned some into a separate account that I will use to start my business. Not that I don't believe that Kane will keep his end of the bargain since the contract seemed pretty binding, but just in case.

"Hey, Pope," I announce as I head outside. The driver is already leaning by the Cadillac, staring up at the sun with his sunglasses on. I don't blame him. The sky is in rare form today, a beautiful kaleidoscope of pinks and oranges that seem more attuned to sunset than sunrise. "Beautiful morning, isn't it?"

"It is," he says and then gives me a half smile as he continues. "You look very cheery this morning."

"That's because I am. I'm restarting school today. Do you mind taking me over to the Kelson's Community College?" It's where the culinary arts school is based.

"Of course not. Not like it's my job or anything," Pope quips, and I giggle a little.

"Congratulations, by the way," he says, then sighs. "I wish my kids were this excited about starting the school year."

"You have kids?" I ask as he opens the door for me, and I head into the seat.

"Two. Twins of terror, I call them. You've never met kids more capable of finding their way into trouble than these." He frowns a little and then adds. "Although the boss's son Kenny gives them a run for their money."

Speaking of Kenny reminds me of yesterday and the

boy's sad expression, which only worsened when his father arrived.

"Is he in a lot of trouble? Kenny, I mean." I ask.

"Oh yes," Pope says. He glances back at the rear as he starts to drive out of the circular entryway and then around the fountain. "Every day is a new adventure with him. He's always trying to get himself or someone else into trouble. He runs his nannies ragged."

I stare out the window at the manor retreating in the distance, giving voice to my quiet thoughts. "I can't imagine it's easy having a Dad who works all the time."

Pope is quiet for a few seconds, too, and then admits. "No, I can't imagine it is."

"What about his mother?" I ask tentatively, hoping I'm not entering forbidden territory. "If it's okay to ask, that is."

Pope has been quiet for so long that I think I have unknowingly stumbled onto something. And then he sighs. "It's kind of a nonstory. Last I heard, she dropped the kid off and hasn't been to see him ever since."

"Jeez," I say, feeling absolute disgust for this woman I don't know and sympathy for the child. "No wonder he's so troubled."

"Before you feel too bad for him, know that that little boy has more than most kids his age have at their disposal. The boss practically gives him everything he wants."

"Yes, but wealth can't make up for a lack of affection." The words ring ironic when I recall what I said to Kane. I had no sympathy for Kane's problems, and I called him spoiled and out of touch because he was rich and treated people with a casual disregard.

Now, here I am defending his son for similar behavior.

But Kenny is a child. It's easier to forgive him for his bad behavior.

Kane was a child once too, my conscience speaks, pricking me once more.

Is that why he's the way he is? Because of how he was raised? Was he also ignored by his Dad and thinks that's how it was supposed to be? Perhaps that's why he's raising Kenny in a similar way.

The thoughts threaten to manipulate my attention, but I force them out of my mind as the campus comes into view.

I remind myself that Kenny and Kane are none of my business. This is what I need to focus on right now. My future.

"Could we not park so close?" I tell Pope. "Maybe we could pull up on the shoulder of the road right here?"

"Why?"

I think of a delicate way to say it. "This car is kind of a lot, and the fact that I'm being driven in it makes me feel...I don't really want to become a topic of discussion on my first day back."

I sense that Pope is laughing at me, but he doesn't make any further comment as he obeys.

"Thank you," I say, opening the door before he can get out of the car. "Um.... you don't have to wait for me. I'm sure you're busy doing other things."

"When is your last class over?" he asks.

"Four-thirty," I tell him.

He nods. "I'll be back by then."

"Okay. Thank you."

I wave at him as he pulls off into the road again, and I start walking to the culinary arts building. I inhale, savoring the fresh air as I get closer. It's exactly like I remember.

KCC is a small campus with neatly cut grass and only about five buildings representing ten majors. It's not much compared to other colleges in Chicago, but for two years, it was my home. It was my ticket to a life I wanted and a life I wanted to give my Dad.

I just wish he was here to see it.

Regret colors my mood as I walk.

Even after he got sick, Dad encouraged me to continue lessons. When I couldn't afford to anymore, he cried for me, even though I tried to pretend it wasn't a big deal. He wanted me to stop his treatments so I could pay my tuition, but I staunchly refused.

His health was more important than my education or any other thing. And even though he died anyway, I'm glad I at least got to make his last few moments as painless as possible.

"I'm back, Dad," I whisper into the air, and I feel an answering rustle of the wind as though he's here right beside me, watching over me. Smiling at me.

I know. And I'm so proud of you.

But would he be proud if he knew that I got back on my feet by marrying a man I didn't know? That I was using his money to fund my education?

I'll pay Kane back, I decide at that moment. I'll make sure my restaurant is successful, so much so that I'll pay him back every last dime spent on me. This will be more of a loan than anything else.

And with that determination, I take a deep breath and walk into the lab, a simulated kitchen with kitchenware and stoves on each table.

The class is about a dozen people, two on each table. I don't recognize any of them, but I'm late by about a year. Everyone I knew has probably already graduated by now.

I spot a friendly-looking girl with bushy hair who doesn't have a partner at her table yet and sidle up to her. She grins when I approach and says, "Hi, future lab mate. I'm Brianna."

"Hi! I'm Dara."

The smile disappears once the door opens, and our lecturer walks into the room.

Or at least, I thought it was our lecturer. But on closer inspection, he looks exactly like the chef from the restaurant yesterday.

I gape at him, and I note that he stops when his eyes fall on me. He blinks a little, and his bemused look furrows his eyebrows. Then he continues.

"Hello, class," he introduces. "I'll be your instructor for today. My name is Max."

"Hello, Mr. Max," Brianna whispers under her breath beside me and when I glance at her, she mouths, "He's hawt."

I smile and nod. She's right. Standing at about six foot two, with curly brown hair and a low-lidded gaze, Max is attractive, even more so without the chef uniform. But I'm not attracted to him.

Not even when I notice our eyes meet several times during the lesson, during which we make a variety of quiches.

At the end of the lesson, Max makes his way to my table as I pack my things to leave. Brianna is already gone, as is most of the class, but I hung back to add a few details to my quiche. Max approaches me, leans against the table, and crosses his hands over his chest.

"Fancy seeing you here again."

"I know, right? What a coincidence," I smile, and he smirks back at me.

"You're in culinary school?"

"Yes," I nod. "I've always loved food and can't imagine anything better than being a chef. And I'm even more excited now that you are here because I know that my training is in great hands."

"You are in great hands in general," he says, and his eyes hold an intensity that makes me a little uncomfortable.

You're a married woman, I tell myself. *That's probably why I feel so weird about it.*

Usually, I would relish the attention of such a good-looking man, but I want to escape instead, even though the marriage isn't real.

"Anyway, I gotta go," I tell him. "I have another lecture to get to." The next lecture isn't for a few hours, but he doesn't need to know that.

"Sure thing," he says and winks. "See you around."

"See you." I wave at him as I leave.

I spend the next few hours before my next lecture hanging out at the campus cafe. I grab a quick lunch and scroll through my phone, looking up more charities that I want to donate to. By the time my business lecture starts, I have a good list and start transferring money anonymously to them.

My business lecture goes well, too, and when I'm done, I head out to the parking lot, walking towards the shoulder where Pope dropped me off.

But I don't spot the Cadillac.

Instead, there's a Rolls Royce Phantom parked there, with Kane standing beside it.

My heart involuntarily skips a beat.

What is he doing here?

Especially looking like that.

He cuts quite a striking figure, leaning against the car with sunglasses and his signature black suit. I try to suppress my reaction to him as I walk closer.

"Is something wrong?" I ask.

He frowns. "Why would anything be wrong?"

"Because you're here."

He doesn't quite smile, but his lips move as though he's going to. "I thought we should get dinner together."

"You did?"

"Yes."

"Why?"

He sighs and glances away before looking back at me. "I've been very harsh with you lately. I'm sorry. It's not been the best week for me, and I took it out on you. I'll try not to do that anymore."

I gape.

As far as apologies go, it's not the best I've heard. But the fact that it's coming from him shocks me.

I have a feeling he's a man that doesn't apologize often.

"Um...okay," I say, still in shock. "I appreciate the apology, but I still don't understand what that has to do with us getting dinner together."

He shrugs. "Why not? I don't want us to continue butting heads over things, and I figure it's best we learn more about each other so we can understand each other."

Or we could simply stay away from each other. But I don't say it. That would be rude and come off as confrontational in the wake of his apology.

At least he's trying. I think. *What harm could it do?*

"Fine," I say. "Let's go."

CHAPTER 14
Kane

The ride to the restaurant is mostly silent, but it's not the tense silence that we're used to.

This one is more relaxed but also speculative. Dara is glancing at me every once in a while as though my change of heart has truly stunned her.

The third time she does it, I meet her eyes in the rearview mirror.

"I haven't suddenly sprouted two heads since the last time you looked," I tease, and after a few seconds, a smile reluctantly spreads across her lips.

"Sorry," she says. "It's just that I didn't really expect this change of heart."

"I understand that," I say. "And you were right about a lot of what you said. And from now on, I'll try to be less of a... how did you put it...controlling ass."

She blushes a little in an adorable way as her eyes skitter away from mine.

"I didn't say it quite like that," she mumbles, and when she looks back at me, I wink at her to show that there are no hard feelings. She blushes.

When I turn to get off the highway and turn into a wide paved street, she finally asks, "Where is that?"

"Well, since you like Italian food so much, I thought I should bring you somewhere that has real fine dining." The tall edifice in the distance is a red brick manor with acres of grass behind it. The orange lights over the awning highlight the Seekers Country Club logo—an exclusive club that only a selected few are ever allowed in. I've been a member since I was an infant, but I only come here when I crave a veal shank.

"Is that a dig at the last restaurant I went to?" she says with a smile dancing at the corner of her lips.

"If you want to take it as such, you're free to," I respond smoothly. The restaurant at Wicker Park didn't have bad food necessarily, but they fall for the trap of so many 'trendy' restaurants in that their presentation is far more important to them than taste. Seekers, on the other hand, strikes the perfect balance, and I will say that the taste even beats the presentation sometimes.

And I'm sure it has nothing to do with a certain droopy-eyed chef who had eyes on your woman.

Of course not, I tell myself. It's not like I'm only introducing Dara to Seekers so that she gets hooked on this restaurant and never returns to the other one, and consequently, she never sees that man again.

That would be crazy.

I drive up, and a valet helps her open her door. I hand him the keys and then place my hand on the low of her back, leading her inside. Even over layers of clothing, I don't miss the shiver that goes through her, nor the corresponding hunger it sparks in me.

But I would need to suppress it for now. That's not what this exercise is about.

Today is the start of the ultimate venture to get her to fall in love with me.

At the hostess stand, we both hand in our jackets, and I lead her through the sliding doors into the cool interior. The boar head on the wall adds a rustic feel to the otherwise traditional clubhouse décor with bespoke leather furniture and burnished wooden accents.

I take her to my usual table in the corner, with a prime view of the acres of grass where a few patrons are playing polo.

"Well, if it's the décor, I'm already impressed," she says as I pull out the chair for her. She turns and sends me a smile. "Thank you."

Her simply stated 'thank you' makes something ricochet through my chest that I don't understand.

"Wait till you try the food," I tell her as I take my seat.

"What would you recommend?" she asks as she turns over the menu.

"Depends on what you like. Everything is good here. But for starters, we can try the chicken salad. Their dressing is irreplicable."

"Alright," she says.

The food arrives soon after ordering and she takes a bite of the salad, closing her eyes and moaning.

Fuck. That moan does something filthy to me.

"Chestnut," she says, eyes opening slowly. "They add finely crushed chestnut to it and a dash of lemon powder. That's what gives it the extra kick."

"You detected that?" I say, and she blushes with pleasure.

"My Dad says I have a tongue for detecting food components," she continues. "I'm like a hound dog with it. If I try really hard, I can taste every single ingredient in food and can even remake it. That's how I started cooking in the first place."

"I imagine that's a skill that comes in handy in culinary school."

"Yeah, hopefully, it will come in handy after that too." She brushes her hair over her ears and takes another bite, then ventures tentatively. "I actually, um...I was thinking of opening up a restaurant once I'm done with culinary school. As ridiculous as it probably sounds."

I frown. "Why would that sound ridiculous?"

She blushes. "Because most restaurant ventures fail. And also, because most people don't open up restaurants right out of school. They work as a chef for another restaurant for several years first."

"Didn't you use to be a chef?" It was one of the things my PI pulled up. I suppose now her making me food makes sense. She clearly enjoys it.

"Yes," she says. "Still, I don't know enough about the business side of it. I'm taking business classes now, but I'm still not quite confident about the business side."

"Most businesses aren't complicated," I tell her. "It's the same thing—finding an underserved market and giving them what they want. Almost all business ventures have a high chance of failure, not because they don't know enough, but because there weren't enough opportunities to learn on the job. Some things you can only understand by doing and making mistakes. People often run out of money before they're done making their mistakes and landing their big break. That's where the lack of success comes in. But I don't see why *you* can't succeed."

"What do you mean?" she asks cocking her head.

"Well," I start. "You're intelligent and talented enough. You've worked enough jobs to learn a few things. Every other thing you can learn while you're running your restaurant. And as for running out of funds...if you need my support in any way, financial or otherwise, consider it yours."

She gapes at me. "Are you serious?"

"Of course," I smirk. "You are my wife, after all."

Her mouth remains open for a few seconds, and when she says, "Thank you," her eyes are slightly teary.

I nod. That entire conversation wasn't part of my seduction attempt. I find that I mean every single thing I said to her.

I do think she can succeed, and finding out about her goals makes me think highly of her.

Some women would be comfortable with everything I was giving them, stashing it away somewhere, planning to live out the rest of their lives in relative comfort. Or they would be plotting to get more money out of me.

But not Dara. She's studying and planning for this dream of hers. And that's a most admirable thing under any circumstance.

"Thank you," she repeats and coughs a little. "For the advice and the compliments. That's the nicest thing anyone has ever said to me."

"I know I don't look like it," I quip. "But I have my moments."

She grins. "You certainly do." And then her expression turns thoughtful. "Speaking of business...this is probably rude to ask, but I figure I should know before we meet with your Dad this weekend. But what exactly is it that you do?"

I cock my head. "We won't be meeting with my father this weekend. But with regards to my business, a lot of what I do is planning and relegating. And our focus now is on cell phones."

"Oh?"

"Yes. We're launching a new prototype for a new phone in a few months that is going to shake the market. I'm talking a hybrid snapdragon processor at a fraction of the cost of a traditional snapdragon."

"I'm afraid I don't know what any of that means."

I grin and think of explaining it in terms she'll understand. "Think about it like this. You can either have your meal fast, cheap, or delicious. Or you can have it fast and cheap or have your meal delicious and cheap or delicious and fast. Most people think you have to choose one of the three. But I think I can find a way to have all three. And that's what I'm trying to create here with phones."

"Ah, I see." She nods. "I don't know much about phones, but I think with the economy these days, most people are thinking in terms of saving money and getting value for less."

"Precisely."

The conversation continues into the night as I explain to her the intricacies of the different processors, and she tells me exactly how they make their creamy polenta.

And to my surprise, by the time the dinner is over, I want to continue our conversations, although there's nothing particularly vital being said. Truly, when I set out on this exercise to endear myself to Dara, I didn't expect to enjoy talking with her so much. She's far more intelligent than she gives herself credit for, asking the right kind of questions and grasping concepts pretty easily, even explaining them in layman's terms.

And by the time I take her home, I find I'm very reluctant for the day to end.

"There's a fantastic brunch place close to my office building," I tell her as we arrive at the mansion. "Would you care to join me tomorrow?"

She smiles and it seems even more radiant in the moonlight. "I would love to."

The next day, at brunch, she's even more lively, excitable, and wholly adorable. She tells me all about her classes and how much she's enjoying learning new things. After we eat, we decide to take a walk toward the park, where a fair seems to be going on. She instantly points at the Ferris wheel.

"I've never been in one of those before," she says. "I've always wanted to, but when my Dad would bring me here, I would always fall asleep before I got to the front of the line."

"I see," I comment noncommittally. I've never been on a Ferris wheel either, and honestly, I have no desire to go on one.

"There's no line now," she says, turning to me with excited eyes. "Let's go on it."

I shake my head. "That thing looks like a death trap. Do they even inspect it every month?"

"No, every month," she giggles. "I'm sorry. I wasn't aware you were afraid of heights."

"I'm not scared of anything."

"Right," she says, but her accompanying smile doesn't lead me to think that she believes me.

"Fine," I say and grab her hand, taking her to the damn thing. We get on it, and by the time it rolls over with us at the top, my stomach is a little queasy, but I tell myself it's from the sweetness of the syrup on my crepes and not the height.

But Dara's hand crawls into mine, and she gives me a kind, sympathetic look. "It's okay. I'm here."

I like holding her hand, but I'm not so sure about the delicate way she's looking at me, like I'm the younger, more vulnerable one instead of the other way around. I don't want her sympathy, so I do the only thing I can think of to get rid of it.

I kiss her.

Once again, the kiss takes me by surprise, hitting me like a drug, but I force myself not to swallow her whole. I don't want to rush it this time. Instead, I savor it, the softness of her lips, the little rush of breath against my mouth, the slight hesitation before she presses her lips back against mine and opens her mouth for my tongue.

And by the time I pull back, her eyes are dark with desire once more. We stare at each other, unable to pull our gazes away until the attendant yells, "Ride over."

That's when I realized that we were back on the ground. But a part of my mind continues to float in the air.

Maybe Ferris wheels aren't so bad after all.

The walk back to deliver her to Pope is quiet. Neither of us knows what to say about that kiss, and I suppose we've mutually decided not to address it like the other thing.

"Kenny," she speaks up suddenly, and I glance at her. "Does Kenny like fairs?"

I shrug. "I'm not sure. I've never taken him to one."

"Can I take him?"

I stop in surprise. "You want to?"

She nods. "I just feel that maybe he might be getting too cooped up in the house all day. Maybe that's why he keeps getting himself into trouble."

"He gets himself into trouble because he enjoys terrorizing people," I say, but then think about it. "But I suppose it's not a bad idea as long as you take the proper precautions. My son isn't an easy child to handle."

"I will." She grins, and I can't help but grin back.

∾

OF COURSE, I SOON COME TO REGRET GIVING HER PERMISSION to take Kenny out. Because the next day, in the middle of my meeting, the phone rang. I let the first one go to voicemail, but it rings again and again until I finally pick up.

"What?" I bark, startling the people at the table.

"It's me!" Dara says, sounding out of breath. "Kenny is in trouble!"

CHAPTER 15
Dara

My heart bounces around my chest as I run across the street, my eyes scanning every quadrant for a little dark-haired boy. Every single second I don't see him, my panic grows even higher.

Now I finally understand what his nannies went through those few days ago. When I insisted that they didn't need to accompany us for this trip, I thought I was doing them and Kenny a favor so that they could take a break and so Kenny wouldn't feel so stifled. So that he wouldn't feel like he was being constantly watched and would finally get a chance to just relax and be a kid.

Stupid. I scold myself. Stupid stupid stupid.

Why did you think you knew the kid better than his own caretakers? Why didn't you heed their advice, and Kane's, about how tricky Kenny could be?

And in typical fashion, I thought I was helping but I've only made things worse.

When will you ever learn, Dara?

"Dara," Kane's voice is a steadying breath in my ear,

speaking slowly and calmly. "Calm down and tell me what happened."

"What happened? Heck, I'm not even sure where to start."

"Start at the beginning."

"Okay," I stop running because I don't even know if I'm running farther away or closer to Kenny. I take a deep breath and press a hand against my heated forehead. "Alright. So… we started off at the fair."

"Is that where you guys are now?"

"No," I shake my head. I took Kenny to the park, expecting that he would be excited by the rides and all the delicacies. That always used to excite me as a child.

But Kenny simply looked over everything with a bored expression and then crossed his hands over his chest.

"I don't want to do it," he said.

I furrowed my eyebrow. "What? But I asked you last night, and you said you would love to visit the fair with me."

"I thought it would be cooler," he said. "This stuff is for babies."

It was a complete eighty from his enthusiasm last night. I couldn't lie—my heart ached a little bit. I was so looking forward to seeing a smile on the little boy's face for once.

But now it seemed I was operating on my own and had underestimated how much it would take to make him happy.

"Alright," I said, smiling to hide my disappointment. "Well, we're here now. Do you want to go home?"

He shook his head and glanced around. "Dad's office is close, isn't it?"

"It is," I nodded. "Just a couple of blocks from here."

"There's another park by his office. They have a great ice cream truck. I want to get that before we go home."

"Um. Okay. Let's go back to the car and have Pope take us."

Kenny pouted. "It's only like a mile away. We can walk."

I started to protest but then Kenny suddenly shook his head. "Never mind. It's a stupid idea. It's just that I used to take walks with Dad all the time, and then he just stopped taking me. I guess he got busy."

Oh no. That pricked at my heartstrings. I knew Kenny's behavior was mostly triggered by his father's distance and lack of affection. He must constantly doubt whether Kane loves him or not since Kane barely spends time with him.

I feel bad. Even though we never had money, I never doubted that my father loved me. He showed me every day and spent as much time as he could with me. Some of our fondest memories were going to the park together. He would carry me on his shoulders, and I would laugh and eat cotton candy till I was sick. Then, I would fall asleep in his arms at some point, and he would carry me home.

Is that why I brought Kenny here, to have him experience that?

But Kenny was not me. And I thought that if I wanted to truly make him happy, I had to start listening to what he wanted to do rather than superimposing my will on him.

"Fine," I said. "Let's go get ice cream."

That turned out to be a huge mistake.

Because somewhere along the line, as I turned to tell Pope over the phone about our new plans, Kenny disappeared.

"Where are you now?" Kane asks again, and it drags me back to our conversation.

"Um...I think we're a few blocks away from you," I say. "Pope is driving around right now looking for Kenny."

"Okay," he says, and I hear him moving. "I'm on my way."

"I'm sorry." Guilt hammers into me. "This is all my fault. I should have known better."

"Apologize after we find him," Kane answers tersely. "Look harder. He sometimes likes to shield himself in the corner of a building and laugh at the chaos he causes."

I spin around, trying to see if I find anything in the shadows. But nothing. I wonder if perhaps this is less about him going missing just to cause chaos and more so that he's looking for something. Perhaps he's heading towards Kane's office building. He was the one who suggested the ice cream place close by, after all.

Maybe this was all a ruse so that he would go to see Kane.

The thought occurs to me distantly as I finally glance in the direction of Kane's building.

Then I finally see him, paces away at the street facing me.

"Kenny!" I scream. He's about to cross the road, and he's looking to one side of the crosswalk. But it's a busy area at a very busy time, and sometimes motorcyclists come hurtling down at inopportune moments.

Like one is doing right now.

"Kenny!" I scream again and dash towards him. He's going to try and cross. I can see his leg moving and can already sense that, at that pace, the motorcyclist is going to hit him. I have to get to him in time.

Everything fades into this moment. I push other pedestrians aside and race across the crosswalk, shoving Kenny back just in time to save him from the collision.

Of course, I don't avoid getting hit by the vehicle myself.

I feel the metal slam into my body, and pain explodes in my side.

It's not a bad hit, all things considered. I'm only flung a

few steps away and slam into the floor, rolling over a couple of times. But I don't feel anything snap or explode.

I do hear a few voices shouting my name, but they may be the disembodied cries of my own imagination as I pass out.

~

WHEN I COME AWAKE, THERE'S A LIGHT FLASHING OVER MY closed lids.

I groan and open my eyes, and the light instantly flicks off, revealing a wizened old man in a white suit above me.

"She's awake," he's saying as he backs away enough for the whole room to come back into view. It's a hospital room. Anna and Kane are both standing beside the bed. Anna is wringing her hands, clear worry in her features. Kane's face is stony, and his expression is a bit harder to understand.

He's probably pissed at me for endangering his son. I turn my eyes away from him, unable to deal with my guilt. *And he's right to be pissed.*

The light comes on, blaring into my eyes again, and I wince.

"Does that hurt?" the doctor asks.

I shake my head. "No, just uncomfortable."

"Does your head hurt?"

I think about it, taking note of my body. Actually, my side hurts more than anything, but there is a mild headache starting at the base of my temples. "A little," I admit.

"Any dizziness, nausea, confusion?"

I shake my head again.

He turns to Kane. "Well, there doesn't seem to be any sign of a concussion, but I would watch her through the night just in case."

139

"Are you sure she shouldn't stay for observation?" Kane asks.

"I don't think that's necessary," he says. "The X-ray showed no broken bones, and I believe she just has the bruising. Change the dressing every day and make sure she takes her meds, and she should be fine." He glances back at me. "Of course, if anything worsens, then transfer her back immediately."

"Of course," Kane says, and the doctor nods as he heads to the door.

"I'll come with you, doctor," she says as she follows him out the door, leaving Kane and me alone.

There's a heavy silence for a few seconds, interrupted only by the beeping of machines and the sounds of his footsteps as he steps closer to me.

"I'm sorry," I instantly blurt out.

He pauses, surprise in his raised eyebrows. "What?"

"I'm sorry for everything. This is my fault."

That only seems to increase his surprise even more. "Are you actually apologizing right now?"

"Yeah," I answer hesitantly. "Shouldn't I be?"

He cocks his head. "My son nearly got you killed, and you're apologizing?"

That reminds me. I sit up a little. "Is Kenny okay? He didn't get hit, did he?" I think I pushed him out of the way in time, but what if I didn't? Or what if I pushed him too hard, and he's hurt?

"Kenny is fine," Kane says, and I sag back into the bed, relieved.

"I'm glad," I say.

And then suddenly, Kane's face is now above mine. He's staring down at me, and intense heat in his eyes.

Before I can ask what's going on, he kisses me.

CHAPTER 16

Kane

The kiss, as always, inflames me instantly.

It assaults me with flagrant heat, incinerating all logical thought and inhibition. Part of my nerves still hadn't settled after the chaos of the accident, and it combined with the blatant crash of desire, mixing inside to set a melting sensation through my body.

My heart pounds and my mind utters her name.

Waves of desire crash into me, taking over my senses as I pluck her lips, tease it open, and taste more of her. I put my hand on her cheek tenderly to keep her there as I kiss her harder, deeper, the familiar urgency beating at the back of my mind.

But it's the way it tugs at something in my chest that worries me.

It informs me that this kiss is different from every other kiss that came before it. I'm not kissing her simply for my ruse and not even just because of the desire that snares me every time I see her. I'm not kissing her with premeditated plots in my mind or to prove my possession over her.

I'm kissing her because I want to. Because I can't stand not doing it anymore.

Because for a second there, when I watched the motor-cycle speeding towards her, hitting her, I was terrified that I might never get to do it again.

The memory of her accident makes the kiss more intense. Something violent and chaotic is squeezing in my chest, not letting go. Perhaps it's because the scene keeps replaying in my mind. I keep watching her push Kenny out of the way and get swiped by the vehicle again and again, and each time I see the collision, my chest gets tighter.

God.

I nearly froze when I saw it. I screamed her name. More so, it burst out of me in a rush of sound and emotion.

And I felt something inside me shatter.

I pull back for a mere second, enough for her to gasp in the air and whisper, "Kane" against my lips.

But that's all I allow before going in for more, deepening the kiss until we're both eating at each other's lips like we're starving things.

Her hand grasps my shirt and clings to it, and my hands are at her waist. I feel naked skin, which tells me that at some point, I pushed up her shirt. Although some part of me warns me to stop, the stronger part of me urges me to keep touching her, to go higher and discover more of her skin.

She makes a tiny sound in her mouth as my hand glides over her belly. She undulates and moves into my touch. My lips brush her cheeks, then lower down her neck. I want to taste all of her. Everything else loses meaning. Nothing matters but tasting her.

It isn't until the door opens that I suddenly jerk back to awareness.

"Oh, sorry!"

I whip around to find Anna standing behind us, her face flaming as she tries to look everywhere but at us.

"I didn't…" she stammers. "I mean, I was just….I'll leave."

With the final word, she spins around and bolts out of the hospital room, shutting the sliding door behind her.

I turn back to Dara, whose eyes are waffling between desire, embarrassment, and some amusement.

"Well, I think we sold the husband and wife thing pretty well," she quips in a husky whisper.

I didn't kiss her to sell anything, but I allow a smile and nod. "I guess we did."

I finally manage to drag my body away from her and note that the bottom two buttons on my shirt are undone. Dara notices me looking, and her face flames.

"Sorry," she says.

"Don't be," I say, smirking as I button back up. I wanted her to do more. But truthfully, if I'd felt that gentle touch of hers on my bare skin, I'm not sure even Anna's interruption could have stopped me from taking her to the hospital bed.

And that would have undoubtedly been disastrous.

My humor dies when I'm hit with a sudden realization.

I can't have sex with her. Ever.

I should feel like a cruel villain even thinking about it, like a disgusting old man.

She's too young for you.

Not to mention, she just got hurt, saving my son's life.

I'm not a good man by any stretch of the imagination. I'm often selfish and vicious, without qualms. But when I held Dara in my arms, barking at the spectators to get back and for someone to call an ambulance, I'd never felt that kind of guilt before coursing through my system.

I caused this.

It was my fault that she was in that position, and it was my fault that she'd gotten hurt.

I never should have involved her in this ruse, never should have brought her into my world.

I never should have let her go with Kenny knowing how dangerous my son was.

And the worst part is that by the time this is all over, I'll have to hurt her even more.

I thought about it for a long time while she lay unconscious. A crazy part of me actually considered giving up on my quest to make her fall in love with me. I wanted to tell her the truth and let her decide how she wanted to move forward with this.

But it was only a brief consideration. Because despite my feelings, I'm still the same selfish, vicious man I always was. And I'm still going to go through with it.

I'm going to sacrifice her soft heart, deceive her, just to get my company back.

But the least I can do is to *not* have sex with her. When the truth gets out about what I've done, and it inevitably will, she's going to feel betrayed. She's going to be heartbroken and feel used in the worst way. The only way I can think of to mitigate those feelings is to at least refrain from sleeping with her. And deny us this explosive passion.

That way, she may be able to leave this situation with some dignity.

However, denying ourselves is easier said than done.

Because even as I help her stand to take her home, I feel every single point our body touches—her palm in mine, the brush of her hip against my thigh, her waist in my hand. Lustful thoughts assault me once more. I suppress them with logic and sheer willpower, but it gets harder to do so each minute that passes in her presence.

"Where's Kenny?" she asks as she hobbles towards me. We slowly make our way to the door, but I note that she winces a little when she steps. So, I stop and swiftly sweep her into my arms.

"Hey!" she cries out, her hands automatically wrapping around my neck.

"If you fall, it's going to be even worse," I say.

"Put me down." She kicks up her heels in protest. "I'm heavy."

I snort. "Please." I could lift two of her on a bad day.

She pouts a little and after about a minute of protesting, she finally sighs and settles in my arms.

We stop briefly for me to sign the discharge paperwork at the ER front desk, with Dara red-faced still in my arms, and then continue on our journey out. Anna and Pope are standing by the hospital entrance, and from the distance, they seem to be having an intense conversation.

"Where's Kenny?" Dara asks again.

"Home," I tell her. During the hustle, I had Pope take Kenny home and lock him up in his room, and then he returned with Anna. Anna was supposed to stay in the hospital to watch Dara while I returned to my meeting, but I found that even when Anna arrived, I couldn't leave.

So we both sat there staring at Dara as she lay unconscious while I tried to fight the overpowering guilt.

As we approach, Pope spots us first and nudges Anna, who instantly glances at us. She falls silent.

"Care to tell us about your riveting conversation?" I asked, even though I could guess what they were talking about.

"Nothing important boss," Pope says and then turns his attention to Dara. "Are you feeling okay, my dear?"

She nods. "Yes. Thanks. And sorry for all this chaos."

Pope's eyebrows furrow like he has no idea what I could be talking about.

"I told you already to stop apologizing," I scold her. "Nothing that happened is your fault."

"Yes, but if I hadn't suggested—"

"You were trying to do something kind," I cut her off. "Unfortunately, you were extending said kindness to a demon spawn."

"Don't say that," she says, much to my surprise. "He's not a bad kid. I think he was just trying to—"

"Don't defend him. Not now."

She opens her mouth, then closes it. She appears resigned as she nods. And then we go home.

∼

KENNY IS GROUNDED FOR THE REST OF THE MONTH, AND TO my surprise, he doesn't protest his punishment when I dish it out. He stands stony-faced and then simply nods.

"Watch him," I tell May as I leave. She nods and turns to my son determinedly.

Meanwhile, I do some watching of my own. For the first few nights when she's at home, I watch Dara sleep from the couch across her bed, making sure there are no signs of concussion. She sleeps the entire night, but I wake her every six hours to sip some water.

During the day, I head to work but ask Anna to look in on Dara and take care of her for the rest of the week. I know I need to catch up on sleep in the following days, but I can't. Instead, I still find myself coming into her room at odd hours during the night to watch her as she sleeps.

Like now.

It's midnight, and I just finished up work in my study. I should be in bed, preparing for another tiring day.

Instead, I'm here watching her.

I try to tell myself it's just to make sure she's healing well, but most times, I stay there for an hour or two, leaning beside the window and watching the moon highlight her features.

I trace my gaze over her face and wonder why she did it. Why did she save him?

Why did she risk her life for a boy she barely knows? The son of a man she doesn't even like?

And why does she fascinate me so much?

I figure out the answer to the last question, pretty quickly.

It's not often I meet people like her.

Actually, I don't think I've ever met anyone like her before.

Tonight, though I'm being naturally silent, her eyes flutter open. And rather than react in shock, she smiles when she sees me.

"I knew it," she murmurs.

"Knew what?"

"That you were here," she says. "Sometimes I would wake up in the morning and smell you. I would feel like your presence was here at some point during the night, but I thought I was being ridiculous. But now I know that I'm not."

"Hmm." I don't know how to answer that. I don't know why I'm here. And I should probably be worried that she caught on to my clear obsession with her.

And she should be worried about my clearly creepy behavior.

But neither of us flinch.

Maybe it's the night and the moonlight casting its spell on

us. But here in this room, I don't feel the need to excuse my behavior and explain myself, and she doesn't feel the need to ask questions. We have an understanding beyond words.

This feels right. Us being here together feels like it's the most natural thing in the world.

And then she pats the bed beside her. "Get in."

I shake my head, but it takes some effort to do it.

She pouts. "Please. I really…" She falls silent. "I really want to be with you right now."

That punches a hole in my gut and chips at my resolve.

"Please," she repeats emphatically.

Her second 'please' does me in entirely. If it had just been my desire, perhaps I could have held off.

But adding in hers, with the plea and the vulnerability in her eyes, I can't deny her.

And before I know it, I'm tugging off my jacket and getting into bed beside her.

She shifts to accommodate me on the queen-size bed. And even though there's ample space for both of us and a priest on the bed, she sidles up right next to me.

She sighs her pleasure once she does.

"I've always wanted to do this," she whispers.

"Really?" Desire makes my voice thick, but I try to keep it out. Still, my hand runs down her back in long strokes.

Keep it platonic.

"Yes," she whispers, but it's more of a moan. Then she glances up at me with that dark-lidded gaze.

And suddenly, it doesn't make any sense for me to hold back anymore.

I kiss her.

It begins with a kiss, but in no time at all, I'm bent over her, and my body flushes against hers. I inhale her, devour her and she consumes me. Her arms wrap around my neck as my hand pushes up her shirt, needing skin-to-skin contact. My cock is a throbbing log, my flesh an inferno. I wrap one hand around her breast and skim my thumb over her nipple. She makes a stuttered sound in my mouth.

More.

I kiss down her neck, sweeping up her tank top so I can lave at her nipple. She bites off a cry as I draw the nipple into my mouth, savoring her trembling response. Her thighs shake and squeeze together, reminding me of the wet heat I felt the last time in the bathroom. The scent of her hangs in the air, and I breathe it in, hypnotized.

I lower myself, seeking it. I push down her sleep shorts, and she helps me, her hands shaking with anticipation.

And then, finally, she's bare before me, so pink and pretty and perfect.

I hold her dazed gaze and watch her kiss-swollen lips part as I finally press my tongue against her clit.

CHAPTER 17

Dara

I'm soaring somewhere high above the clouds.

Something desperate rattles in my throat as the tension balls in my stomach, sending shards of desire splintering through me. Every single stroke of his tongue on my clit is heavenly, and everything feels like it's about to send me hurtling further into space. Kane's hands glide up and down my clit, as he slowly leaves the nub, almost worshipful in his regard.

I focus on breathing and squeeze the sheets below me.

I try not to buck against his face and try to maintain composure. And I do something of a good job at it until his finger shifts right to my entrance.

My breath catches in my throat.

He doesn't push in right away. Instead, he lazily floats his finger around the opening of my pussy, teasing me. A tremble starts in my legs. My toes curl with anticipation, and my pussy gapes and clenches on the air, trying to invite him in.

And then, finally, he pushes in, just the tip of his finger, but it feels so monumental it punches through me.

I moan loudly and lustily, and my body undulates against

my commands. He drives in a little deeper, and a sound comes out of me that is unlike anything I've ever uttered.

God, I sound embarrassingly wet down there. But he moans his approval, and his tongue starts licking faster, making the situation all the worse.

"Oh my God," I exclaim when his finger grazes at just the right angle to hit the right spot inside me. I grab onto his hair. My thighs shake and close around his ears, and I feel him shake his head.

"Open up." His voice is leaden and guttural, the order unmistakable. The dark look in his eyes tells me that he will not tolerate disobedience.

There's no space here for me to even be embarrassed.

I slowly open up my legs again, and he makes a sound of approval before he bends again, continuing. But this time, he uses the flat of his tongue to trail long licks down to my center as he thrusts his finger inside me hard and fast. I scream. My head jerks back against the bed and digs in as a rush of breath leaves me. My thighs threaten to close over his head again, but he gives me a hand, pushing one large palm on my thighs to hold it open. Then suddenly, he's in my face, staring into my eyes as he finger-fucks me.

"Come."

I can't hold back, can't resist his command. The orgasm ratchets through my body and out of it. It spreads and bursts through me, from my core, my toes, and my mind.

I explode.

I don't stop exploding.

The orgasm is protracted, seeming to go on and on as his finger continues to thrust, hitting that hypersensitive spot again and again.

It feels too *good.*

I can't breathe. Darkness threatens the corner of my vision.

I'm going to pass out.

No one can take this much pleasure without passing out.

"That's it," he whispers in my ears, his gravelly voice surging me higher. "Again. Come for me."

I obey, and I come until, finally, my body sags back against the sheet, trembling with aftershocks. I can't give anything more. My body is drained.

But my mind is neither tired nor exhausted.

Instead, I feel more alive than I've ever felt.

"Wow," I whisper into the air.

Kane smiles at me and drops a quick kiss on my lips. But that's not enough. I throw my hand around his neck and drag him back for another one, lustier and wetter. He groans into my lips and wraps his hand into my hair.

For a second, I feel the tremble go through his body as his other hand grasps my waist and squeezes hard. But then he rips his mouth out of mine.

"No," he says.

I don't hear it at first. I don't want to hear it.

I try to kiss him again to keep stoking the desire in me, but he pulls his body completely off mine.

I moan, feeling bereft.

"No," he repeats. And my eyes finally opened to see him. He's seated at the edge of the bed, his expression squeezed into something resembling a tortured animal.

"No?" I ask in a breathy voice.

"No."

"But…" He looks like he's in pain, tormented by desire. A large bulge pushes against his pants, and I felt the impression of it against my thigh just a few seconds ago. I want to touch it, put it in my mouth, inside me.

He just gave me the best orgasms I'd ever had once again. It only makes sense that I would return the favor.

"Please," I ask, and he chuckles.

"You're not healed enough for that," he says and lays back down. Then he does something unexpected. He pulls me into his arms, drops a kiss on my head, and states, "Go to sleep."

I blink, a little stiff in his arms. I wasn't expecting this at all, not the halfway sex nor the fact that he would hold me in his arms after it. And some part of me doesn't want to give up the possibility of a full sexual encounter just yet.

"But after," I whisper, blushing. "When I'm feeling better…"

He's quiet for a few seconds, but I get the impression that he's smiling at me. "We'll see. For now, go to sleep."

We'll see. That could be a yes. I'm optimistic that it's a yes because his erection still hasn't subsided.

I smile to myself and close my eyes.

∼

I EXPECT KANE TO WITHDRAW THE NEXT MORNING AND GO back to his usual standoffish self. Despite everything—the late-night visits, the kiss, the mind-blowing orgasm, and the cuddles afterward—I don't actually expect him to still be here in the morning.

Somehow, I can understand him showing me his tender side under the magic of the darkness of night, but I expect once the day breaks, he'll return to his routine.

But no. Even as the sun rises, he's still here, his arms like a cocoon around me. I wake up just as the day breaks over the sky and watch the beautiful kaleidoscope of colors. Then I glance at him. His eyes are closed, his breath steady.

I analyze his features and notice that this is the only time that I've seen them fully relaxed.

And now that he is, I drink him in nakedly. He looks even more handsome like this, a little more so a prince now rather than a tyrant. For an older man, he appears almost boyish, his hair curling over his brows, his eyelashes that are a touch feminine fanning over his cheeks. In sleep, he looks so much like Kenny. It's uncanny.

Except for the fact that there's a little wrinkle by his eyes that suddenly appears. I move a hand to massage that last bit of worry from his eyes, but I hesitate, not wanting to wake him up.

I have a feeling he's a man who doesn't rest much.

Slowly, I watch his eyes open.

"Oh," I say, startled as they snag mine. I don't know what to say next. His intense look has my words drying in my throat, especially when he picks up a hand and caresses it down my cheek.

It's a soft, tender move that I would never have expected from Kane. And perhaps because of how unexpected it is, it hits me right in the chest, stealing my breath for a few seconds.

"Hi," I finally whisper, and Kane smiles at me.

"Good morning," His voice is sleep-roughened, and that, too, wreaks havoc on my senses. He also sits up and winces a little, stretching out his neck. The queen-size bed is the perfect size for me, but it's a little small for his frame. His legs must have been hanging off it the entire night, and he seemed to be lying in an uncomfortable position.

To accommodate me, I realize belatedly, stunned.

"Sleep well?" he asks as he tries to get the kink out of his neck.

"Yes, but I can see that makes one of us."

"It's fine." He shakes his head and then abandons his hopeless attempt to massage his neck. "It's just a sprain, most likely."

"Lie down," I tell him.

He pauses and gives me a curious look. I gesture again to the bed.

"Lay down. I can massage it out of you."

"That's not necessary."

Stubborn man. "Oh, come on, I'm not giving you a kidney. It's just a massage." And as tempting as it will be to have my hands on his body, I'm not going to jump his bones just because of it.

I tell him as much. "I'm not going to attack you, I swear."

"I'm not saying you will," he says in that deep voice of his. He holds my gaze for so long, and his eyes seem to say, *But I wouldn't put up much of a fight if you did.*

But then he sighs and then rolls over, lying on his front. Before he does, I catch a glimpse of his cock still hard and insistent in his pants.

Damn. Has he been hard since last night? Or is that more so morning-wood?

Get your mind out of the gutter and get to work. No more thinking about his dick.

I straddle his back and try not to admire the slabs of muscle on his frame as I begin digging my hand into his neck, expertly kneading.

He groans into the pillow.

"Feels good, doesn't it?"

"Feels fucking fantastic."

I smile, pleased. I've always given amazing massages, but I truly honed my skill after Dad got sick. Sometimes, a massage was the only thing that could help with the pain.

The thought dulls my good mood slightly until Kane moans again.

"God, you may have missed a calling here," he murmurs, and pleasure shivers through me.

By the time I've massaged out all the kinks, desire has risen inside me again. But I resist the urge to lick his skin, and I roll back next to him. He turns his head to meet my eyes.

"Thank you," he says.

"No problem. It was truly my pleasure." I love touching him, and I also love that I made him feel good, even if it's just this.

"I haven't seen Kenny around lately," I mention, remembering what has been on my mind. I've tried asking about Kenny's whereabouts, but neither Anna nor Faith will say anything, likely under Kane's strict instructions. "Has he been banned from seeing me or something?"

Kane is quiet for a few seconds. "He's under punishment."

"Oh." Although it's understandable for the boy to be punished, I still feel sad at the thought. Caution warns me to stay out of it this time, but I can't. "I know you're going to think I'm defending him—"

"Then don't."

"But I really don't think he ran away from me just for the heck of it."

He sighs. "You don't know Kenny."

"I agree. I don't know him. But before he ran away from me, he specifically asked where your office was. I think he wanted to go there and see you."

"Then he should have asked you to take him."

"Maybe he didn't think I would. His nannies wouldn't

have done it without checking in with you first, and maybe he thought you would say no."

I can read the clear conflict on Kane's face, so I push on. "He misses you."

"How?" The furrow in his brows is true confusion. "I see him nearly every day."

"Yes. You see him in his room for five minutes while his three nannies stand watch. You ask him one or two or three questions or bring him an expensive gift to make up for your absence. And then you disappear for another twenty-four hours." I don't know for sure, but the fact that he didn't correct the statement means I was right. "Do you really think that's enough for him?"

"He's getting more than my father gave me."

That explains so much. "And do you want you and Kenny to have the same relationship you share with your Dad?"

That silences him.

"I don't want to tell you how to parent, and I don't want to pretend I know anything about your lives because I don't. But kids typically act out for a reason. Isn't it worth it to find out why?"

Kane is quiet for a few more minutes, but the silence is contemplative rather than defensive. And then he says, "I'll try to spend more time with him."

I try not to smile. "That's all I can ask."

CHAPTER 18

Kane

Later that morning, before I head to work, I approach Kenny's wing. It's quiet. It's the most quiet I've ever heard of it. Usually, when Kenny's grounded, he passes the time by blasting loud music or playing video games or something.

But nothing.

I push open the door and find that May and the other nannies are in the living room. They seem to be whispering about something, but they stop the second that they see me.

"Sir," May greets, getting to her feet.

"Is he in his room?"

"Yes. He's been there the entire day. I check on him every five minutes."

I nod and head into the bedroom, opening the door. To my surprise, it isn't locked. Of course, I have a spare key just in case, but I thought he might have shoved his closet against the door to keep me out.

But the door opens easily to reveal that Kenny is sitting on his bed, scribbling something on a pad.

He glances up when I walk in, and apprehension fills his face.

"Dad."

"Kenny," I say, closing the door before leaning against it and crossing my arms. His apprehension grows underneath my gaze. I don't blame him. The last time we'd spoken, I was furious at him.

Kenny sits up on the sidewalk, his face pale and eyes wide. He appears stunned after the near collision with the vehicle, his eyes trained on Dara's sprawled body. He rises and runs to her. We reach her at the same time.

"Dad."

I draw my eyes away from Dara to the horror on Kenny's face.

I don't know what expression I'm making, but it has him paling. Luckily, Pope drives up at the moment and grabs the boy's hand, dragging him away.

"Take him home and keep him there," I order Pope, who nods.

I didn't have to explain further because Pope understood what I wanted. I didn't speak to Kenny that day. I was sure I would say something wrong with the amount of anger that was boiling through me.

But now that my fury has settled, I can see that Kenny doesn't look surly as he usually does when I punish him, and neither does he have all his usual defense mechanisms up. The eye roll and the sarcastic comment are noticeably absent.

He simply draws his eyes away from mine as though ashamed.

"Why did you do it?" I ask now. This may be the only time he'll feel guilty enough to tell me the truth. "You were out in the park on a great day. Dara wanted to do something nice for you, taking you to the theme park. So why did you punish her for it?"

Kenny's eyes don't meet my eyes, and his face reddens. He shrugs weakly, but he doesn't answer.

That's not good enough.

"It's not like I want to restrict you, Kenny," I say. "Neither do I enjoy punishing you. I want you to be out and about, have all the things a normal kid your age has."

"I'm not a normal kid," he says suddenly and then glares up at me. "I may not have been to school in a while, but I know that much. Normal kids don't live in giant mansions like this and get locked up in their rooms all day. Normal kids go out and have friends and have school and they get to be with people their age."

"Is that what this is about?" I ask. "You miss school?" Kenny had attended school up until a year ago. But he just kept getting suspended due to one trouble or another. At first, it was petty things like skipping class. But his crimes became increasingly concerning. He'd somehow caught and released a snake on the school compound. He'd pulled a fire alarm and caused chaos. And then, when it came out that he was picking on another kid, a young boy on scholarship, who Kenny nearly beat up, I knew it was time to pull him out. The principal thought I could pay off the boy's parents to keep it quiet, but I figured it was to teach my son the consequences of his actions.

Perhaps some time alone at home will be enough to teach him the merits of good behavior.

But so far, he's only been getting worse.

"No," Kenny says tightly. "I don't really miss school."

"Right. Because you've been acting out since way before that," I say.

"I'm cooped up in this room all day, Dad."

"It wasn't always like that," I say. "At first, I gave you free rein. You could do whatever you wanted. And what did you do with that privilege, Kenny, besides making everyone else's life difficult?"

Kenny retreats to silence, pulling it like a protective shroud around him.

I sigh. "You kept doing it over and over, one-upping yourself each crime. There have to be consequences. You have to understand that you can't just do bad things and get away with it. Dara could have died yesterday, saving your life."

That has some of the defensiveness, leaving his posture and shame returning. Still, his shoulders remain raised.

"I never asked her to do that."

"No. She did it because she's a kind person, and she cares about you."

He looks up at me with an accusation in his gaze. "Is she really your wife?"

I raise an eyebrow. I'm not surprised that Kenny found out about my marriage. He probably overheard someone talking about it and went from there.

"That's not important," I say, leaning forward and holding his gaze. "What's important is this, us, how we move forward. Kenny, I need you to give me something. I want us to rebuild that trust again, that relationship we once had. You hate being cooped up in your room? Fine. You want to go back to school? We can work on that. But I need you to give me a guarantee that you'll change. For real, this time. I don't want to have to keep doing this with you."

He glances away for a few seconds and then ventures in a quiet voice. "And if I say I won't, what then? You'll get rid of me like Mom did?"

The statement exposes far more than he probably would have liked, and then suddenly, a realization hits me.

Perhaps all of this delinquency is a belated response to his mother's abandonment.

It would make sense that as he's rapidly approaching his teenage years, he starts to question why she left him behind.

I lean forward. "Kenny. Look at me."

He's reluctant to obey, but then, after a few seconds, he draws his eyes back to mine.

"You're my son," I tell him. "I'll never get rid of you or leave you. Ever. Even if we fight for the rest of our lives. We'll do it together."

His eyes widen. There's a tentative emotion dancing in his gaze, something that looks aching and vulnerable.

A part of him that's scared to trust.

It's a feeling I understand well. But I wait, staring into his eyes with certainty until he nods.

"But I don't want to have to keep fighting with you either," I continue. "So, tell me. What's it going to take for you to give me your word and keep it?"

"You never keep yours."

I frown. That's another unexpected statement. "What are you talking about?"

Kenny crosses his hands over his chest. He looks out the window. "You always say you'll have dinner with me, and then you don't show up. Or say that we can go somewhere, and then later, I find out that I'm going with May and Sophia instead."

Ah. So, Dara was right. Part of why Kenny is like this is because I don't spend enough time with him.

It's confusing to me because I spend far more time with him than my father ever spent with me at this age. I was raised mostly by a nanny and Anna, and my mother when she was in her right mind. I saw my father on special occasions, like birthdays sometimes or Christmas.

I suppose I used to be resentful, too, about the lack of contact, but as I grew, I understood that it took a lot for him to run a multi-billion-dollar company.

"I'm busy, Kenny," I tell him. "I never mean to lie to you, but sometimes, things happen. Work happens."

"And work is more important than me."

"That's not what I said," I say automatically, but I stop myself before I say anything else. Now *I'm* getting defensive. I hate to say it, but whatever my excuse is, Kenny does have a point. I haven't been doing a good job of keeping my promises to him. "You're right. I shouldn't cancel on you just because of work. I'm sorry."

Kenny blinks as though he doesn't expect it.

"But all that's going to change," I tell him. "In fact, from now on, we'll have dinner together. Every night. No matter what."

"You're just saying that."

"No, I mean it," I say. "I promise I will always have dinner with you. Always. Unless there is a last-minute emergency, in which case, I will make it up to you the next day. Understood?"

He hesitates and then nods slowly.

"Good. And now I've given you my promise. You give me yours. To behave. If you want something or want to go somewhere, ask me and I'll let you. But you need to show me I can trust you, the same way I'll prove to you that you can trust me. Okay?"

He nods. "Okay."

"Good." The conversation is concluded, so I get up to go, but Kenny stops me with a hesitant, "Is she…Is she okay?"

I don't have to ask who she is. "She's doing better. You want to see her?"

He nods rapidly. "Can I?"

"Of course. She'll probably be glad to see you, too."

And Dara truly is.

Kenny hesitates by the door for a little after I open it. Dara is sitting up on her bed and on her phone, but the minute she catches sight of Kenny, a smile spreads across her face. "Kenny!"

He walks in awkwardly and waves. "Hey."

"I'm so glad you're okay," she says, pulling him into a hug when he gets close. His body is stiff at first, but then he relaxes into her hold.

"I'm sorry," he says. "For…you know…"

She beams and waves her hand. "Water under the bridge. And I'm sorry I took you to the theme park without checking if it was somewhere you actually wanted to go."

He shrugs. "I didn't hate it. Some of those rides looked fun."

"They did?" Excitement glitters in her eyes. "I knew it. Listen, I feel like we didn't give it a proper chance. What say the three of us give it another try and go to the theme park today? I feel much better, and I want to get out of the house. I've been cooped up too long."

Kenny shrugs again. "Sure. I'm down."

Dara gives me a questioning look. I'm about to say no, but her eyebrow cocks, and I remember the promise I made to her yesterday.

"I suppose I can cancel my activities for the rest of the day," I tell her. Luckily, there are no meetings today, and I can probably do some work on my phone while I'm there.

As Pope drives us to the theme park, Dara begins telling Kenny all about the rides he can get on. I can see the excitement building in his eyes the more she talks about it.

The moment we get there, he demands to go on the Ferris wheel first. Luckily, Kenny doesn't inherit my fear of heights because his eyes gleam with excitement as our booth climbs higher and higher.

"Wow," he says. "It's just like being on top of the tree."

"Right?" Dara says, then gives me a teasing look. "The first time I brought your Dad here, he was scared out of his mind."

"Really?" Kenny's head whips to me.

"I was not," I tell him.

"Sure, dear," Dara says, but I see her whisper something out of the corner of her mouth to Kenny that makes him giggle.

I shake my head at both of them, but a random smile spreads across my lips.

It's just an overall pleasant afternoon.

And this time, reaching the top doesn't make me as queasy, and that might be because of Dara's hand in mine. She sits between the two of us on the ride, and I know she's holding Kenny's other hand. Kenny doesn't question it, and neither do I.

It feels natural.

After we thankfully reach the ground, Dara and Kenny insist on going on three more rides before they're happy.

"That was fun," Kenny says after it's done, his face gleaming with sweat and excitement.

"I'm glad you enjoyed it," I say, then give in to the urge to ruffle his hair. He reacts in surprise and then smiles shyly.

"Disney World has better rides," Dara says. "I've never been there, but my Dad would tell me about it, and I watched videos and stuff. Maybe your Dad can take you one of these days."

"Maybe," I say noncommittally. But in my head, I'm already planning the trip. Not just because Kenny looked excited by the idea of it but it's also the way her eyes glittered when she talked about it.

I want to make her happy.

I hang back as Kenny and Dara go on the Ferris wheel for one last time before we leave. They wave at me, and I wave back, but I'm distracted by the phone ringing.

"Yes," I answer without glancing at the caller ID.

"Kane dear," says a familiar female voice. "I'm back."

CHAPTER 19

Dara

Over the next few days, we fall into a kind of routine. During the day, I have breakfast with Kenny before I head out. Sometimes, Kane joins us. Usually, though, Kane is gone pretty early, so it's just me and Kenny.

Given that we just met, you would think it would be awkward, but it usually isn't.

In fact, Kenny, contrary to what I initially thought, is very talkative. And especially when it comes to talking about the thing he enjoys most—art.

"You drew this?" I gape at the sketchbook he handed me that morning. He blushes at my shocked look.

The sketch is of a bird perched on a branch, and he's shaded it in blue ink. It's beautiful, balancing perfectly between cartoonish and realism.

"Not like it's hard," Kenny says, shrugging. "Drawing is basically like taking a photo in your mind and then recreating it."

"Yeah, but you know not everyone can do that, right?" I ask him. "You know that makes you special."

He shrugs again, but I don't miss his pleased smile. "Whatever."

He tells me all about how he started drawing. Apparently, it started during his first of many tree climbs. He thought the view from up there looked pretty neat, and pretty soon, he wanted to recreate it.

"Everything looks so much better from up there," he says. "And smaller. Like we're all living in a giant dollhouse. You know?"

"Yeah," I tell him. "I know. But no more climbing for now. At least not until you learn which branches are safe and which ones aren't."

"How will I know?" he asks.

I wink at him. "One of these days, I'll teach you." I have to ask Kane for permission, of course.

After breakfast, Kenny's home schoolteacher arrives, and he typically heads over to his wing for a lesson.

Then, I catch up with Lisa while I get ready for my culinary lessons. On days when I don't have class, I hang out with Pope, Anna, or Faith and try to figure out a new way to spend my money, mostly by finding a new charity to help. Pope and I sometimes just drive around, and he shows me his favorite ice cream spots and where his kids like to go eat. While Pope talks about his kids a lot, I notice he never mentions his wife. I never ask. I have a feeling it's a story as painful as the one I share with my Dad.

But my favorite part of the day is typically at the end. It usually culminates in a dinner with Kenny and Kane.

Kane told me about his promise to have dinner with Kenny every night, and he has kept his word so far.

The first time, the dinner was filled with awkward silence and stilted conversation between two males who aren't very good at talking to each other. Contrary to how Kenny is with me, he tends to be very closed off whenever his father is around and more careful with his words. And Kane is simply quiet by nature. He doesn't seem to realize the reason for his son's silence, though. He likely thinks Kenny is just naturally distant like him and not that he's intimidated by his father.

So typically, I try to facilitate conversation between the two, asking them individually about their day and forcing them to elaborate. At first, it's downright painful. But, then eventually, the conversation starts to become more natural.

"I'm thinking of enrolling you back in school," Kane says unprompted during one such dinner at the end of the week.

Kenny's entire face brightens up. "Really?"

He nods. "Yes. I've already spoken to the principal, and they'll be happy to have you when the next quarter starts in a couple of weeks."

"Oh. That should be fun," Kenny says, and then he ventures tentatively. "Thank you."

Kane smiles wryly. "I was never this happy about school when I was your age."

"Try being locked up every single day for months," Kenny shoots back, and Kane chuckles.

"But," Kane says, and his face suddenly gets serious. "You have to continue to behave, alright? I don't want to get calls about you at work. I especially don't want to hear anything about you bullying a kid."

This makes Kenny bristle with indignation. "I never bullied him. It wasn't like that at all."

Kane opens his mouth to say something, probably the wrong thing, so I interject and ask, "Then what is it like?"

They both glance at me, and Kenny looks relieved to finally be able to tell his side of the story.

"Harry Tennyson stole something from another friend of mine," he says. "I saw him do it. But then, when I told on him, he tried to pretend that I was picking on him because he was poor or something. As if I ever cared about stuff like that. I tried to get him to admit what he did and give it back, but he wouldn't, so we started fighting."

"Oh," I say. I can see the sincerity in his gaze, and I already know enough about Kenny to know that he doesn't lie. He plays pranks and misleads sometimes, but he never outright lies and never so emphatically.

"Yeah," he continues. "It was Caleb—my other friend's—Dad's Rolex. He wanted to show it to us, and his Dad would kill him if he didn't get it back. I saw Harry take it, but he refused to admit it."

"And before that?" Kane challenges. "Because your teacher said there were several incidences prior to that where you made fun of Harry."

"That wasn't like that either," Kenny refutes. "We used to be friends, all three of us. And we used to make fun of each other all the time. We would laugh at Harry's hand-me-downs, Caleb's stupid red hair, and my skinny legs." He ducks his head, avoiding my gaze, and blushes slightly. "I know it sounds stupid, but it was just how we talked to each other because we were friends. I guess it made it easier to handle when we said it out loud. Made it feel like it wasn't so bad if we could joke about it."

Kane shares a look with me and then says, "Fine."

Kenny blinks as though stunned by his father's acceptance. "You believe me?"

"Of course," he says. "I used to be the same way with my school friends. But you guys should probably tone it down. Wouldn't want it to be misconstrued."

"Oh, I'm not going to be friends with Harry anymore," Kenny says darkly. "He's a snake. He let everyone think I was just bullying him for no reason. And Caleb just believed him."

Kane nods. "It's good to be careful of people in general. Remember, you're a Leon. People will always try to find your weakness and use it against you. You must always be smarter than them."

Kenny nods and puffs out his chest, feeling important. I shake my head at both of them and cover my smile with broccoli.

It continues like that for weeks. Until I notice Kane starts getting busier. He started leaving earlier and coming by later. Usually, he would drop by for a quick dinner with us, but then he would head back out, presumably to the office.

And then, once, I get a text in the middle of the afternoon.

Hey. I don't think I'll be able to make it for dinner today. I know I promised Kenny, but there's an emergency, and I need to take care of it. Tell Kenny I'm sorry and I'll make it up to him.

Without missing a beat, I text back. *It's okay. I'll explain it to him. But you need to rest, too. Have you even slept?*

He didn't respond to the last text, which told me everything I needed to know. I sigh. And I also dread having the conversation with Kenny once his lessons are over.

In the late afternoon, Kenny emerges from his wing and walks into the kitchen while I'm cooking with Harold.

"Hey," he says as he walks in.

"Hey Ken Ken," I ruffle his hair and he lets me. He also frowns at the nickname but doesn't comment.

"Watcha doing?" he asks.

"Just making dinner," I say, then decide it's best to rip the Band-Aid off immediately. "So, Kenny, um...your Dad texted me. He wanted to tell you that he may not be able to make it to dinner today. But he says that he'll try to make it up to you."

Disappointment flashes across Kenny's expression.

His lips tighten. I see him struggle with the emotion as it churns within him.

And then he nods, setting his face in a determined expression. "Alright."

"Alright?"

"Yeah. Dad told me this might happen because he's super busy and whatnot. He says he'll make it up to me, and so I'll trust him..." Then he cocks his head and sniffs. "What are you making?"

"Um..." I distractedly glance at the dough in my hands. "Some gnocchi with some salsa verde for your dinner. And then a cheesecake I thought we could have for dessert. Wait, you're really not upset?"

"No," he says, and as though to prove it, he grins slightly. "I don't know if you noticed, but I'm very mature for my age."

I snort. "That you are. And you're also an awesome little man, you know that?"

He ducks his head. "Whatever."

Suddenly, I'm struck with an idea. "Hey. What do you say, we make your Dad a dessert to add to the gnocchi? What does he like?"

Kenny thinks about it. "Nothing too sweet."

"Yeah, I noticed he doesn't like sweets much." *The creme brulee taught me as much.* "How about a blueberry pie? With a little bit of cheese in it?"

He narrows his eyes. "Are you sure those two go together?"

"Yup. Here I'll show you. You can make it with me."

Kenny hesitates. At first, I thought he was going to say no, but then he shrugged. "Why not?"

He told me about his lesson as we cooked. I notice we're getting curious looks from the rest of the staff, so I assume this must be an unprecedented event—both Kenny cooking and Kenny being generally helpful rather than destructive. But I ignore it, focusing on Kenny. His artistic skill comes through in decorating the blueberry pie with thin strands of fluffy cream cheese. He outlines a lion on it and smiles when I tell him how amazing it looks.

After we're done, we send it off with Pope and retire to his wing to watch some TV. At some point, Kenny dozes off against my shoulder, and I rearrange him so he can be more comfortable.

I should probably get him to bed, but I feel far too comfortable like this.

And for the first time in a long time, I feel like life maybe hasn't been so bad to me after all.

CHAPTER 20

Kane

I stare at the older man sitting before me quietly. I stare for so long that he shifts uncomfortably in his seat, and his eyes begin to skitter across the room.

Like me, Percy is a large man, although most of his girth seems to be concentrated around his mid-section. He's been the head of the project management department for years now, and he's one of my most trusted employees.

But now he sits and fidgets like a boy who has been called to the principal's office.

I suppose it could have something to do with the expression I'm making. But I can't help it. Business-wise, it's been a terrible week.

I slide a folder across the desk toward him. Apprehensively, he draws it closer and opens it up.

"What do you see?" I ask.

He frowns, and then his eyes travel across the page, clearly searching for the error.

"This looks like our plans for the new X3," he responds.

"Wrong," I say. "Look closer."

He flips a page and peers at the next one, bringing it

closer to his face. Even after a few seconds, he can't tell me what's wrong.

"Look at the letterhead," I prompt.

Finally, his eyes glance to the top of the page. They widen.

"This is—"

"Textra electronics," I finish. They're our largest competitors, launching affordable phones to the public yearly. Although their phones aren't half the quality of ours, they sell well, just because they're so cheap.

Still, Textra has trailed behind Leon for many years in terms of both reputation and gross profit.

But now, they're holding our patented design in their hands, a design for affordable, high-grade phones. The pendulum could swing very quickly in their direction.

Which is bad news for us.

"How did they get this?" Percy asks, as the horror quickly draws on his features.

"That's what I would like to know," I ask. At the beginning of the week, the mole I planted at Textra found out that they were planning on releasing a whole new line of phones, and they managed to get me some information. I thought a few features sounded familiar, so I had him get his hands on their design files, copy them, and send them over to me.

Then I confirmed that their new phone was not just similar to our design.

It *was* our design.

It's basically standard procedure in our industry for us all to keep an eye on each other. I already know who the mole they have at our company is, some low-level employee in HR. But that mole would never have been able to get a hand on our designs especially not in such intimate detail. The only ones who would have such knowledge are the creators of the design, the technology innovation department, and the project management department.

And so here I am, working my way down to see who the fuck is this new mole I don't know about. The second I find him, I'll crush him like a bug.

Percy catches the direction of my questioning almost immediately.

"It wasn't me," he says, shaking his head rapidly. "I've worked at this company for many years without fault. I've been here even when it looked like everything was going to shit. Your father and I have maintained a loyal friendship for many years. Heck, I changed your diapers at one point."

I wince at the reminder and hold up a hand to stop his tirade. "Relax. I know it's most likely not you." It's the only reason why I brought this issue to his attention because he's the only one on the project management team whom I implicitly trust. Nathan is performing a private investigation on his own by going through all the communication logs to find out if it's someone on his team leaking the information, which leaves me to tackle Percy's.

Percy himself has always been notoriously bad at lying, and he's also been sentimental to a fault, even when it would have been in his best interest to sell us out.

"I know you're not the one who leaked the information," I say. "But I need you to think of anyone on your team who could have done this."

He thinks about it and then shakes his head. "No one. None of them will have this much information anyway unless they have access to my computer and have downloaded the file. But the tech team might. Have you asked Nathan about his team?"

I nod and feel a headache starting at the base of my neck. I haven't slept much this week, and the stress is catching up to me. But I can't rest now. I need a name, and this might take a while.

It would be easier if Percy could give me a few clues, and we could narrow it down. But even after asking several times, he still insists that no one on his team is guilty.

Which means I will inevitably miss dinner with Kenny and Dara.

At least I warned them, but I hate that I'm disappointing my son this early after my promise, especially when I notice how hard he's been trying lately to stay on his best behavior.

"I need you to get everyone's personal files on your team," I tell him. "Bring them, and we'll go through it together."

"All of them?"

"Did I stutter?"

Percy shakes his head. "Right away, then."

I lean my head back against the chair after he leaves, thinking about how much I'd rather be home right now with them, watching Dara smile at Kenny's endless chatter. Oddly, work used to be my solace from home before.

It has quickly become the other way around.

Either way, work needs to be done. The quicker we can find the mole, the better we can mitigate the damage done.

For the next few hours, Percy and I meticulously go through hundreds of files, trying to narrow them down. He makes comments here and there about each employee, most of it random things, like who just had a baby and who got drunk at the last holiday party.

Nothing that would implicate any of them.

It's still not enough to vindicate them, either. I would likely need to look deeper and get my PI involved.

It's a little past nine, and I finally let Percy leave. He hurries out before I can change my mind.

I sit in the office, massaging my temples, when the door opens again. I glance over at Nathan, who is standing there.

His face looks as weary as mine.

"I suppose you didn't have any luck?"

He shakes his head. "No. If it's anyone on my team, then they did a very good job hiding their tracks."

I sigh. "That's what I was afraid of."

"There's something to consider, though." He appears reluctant to share this last part, but he pushes on anyway. "I mean, it's a long shot but...let's assume for a second that the leak isn't from my team or the project management team. Then that would mean…"

"That one of the senior partners did this," I finish and smile wryly at him. I've already considered the possibility, although I'm praying that isn't the truth. Because that would make this a lot more complicated and messy than it needs to be.

What would be the motive behind it? Will it even matter? Those vultures are only as loyal as their bottom line, and backstabbing is expected in my line of work. Perhaps Textra offered them a better deal, one worth discarding decades of work and unity.

Nathan pulls up the chair that Percy vacated and sits. "So what do we do now?"

I sigh. "We need to push forward. If we can't isolate and eliminate the problem, then we need to release our product before Textra beats us to it. That way, we can control the narrative and drown out their release with ours."

Nathan's eyes widen. "But we're not ready to release for another year."

"The product itself is ready. We're only waiting for funds to invest in marketing correctly?"

"Yes. And the board will need to approve it, which will take them God knows how long."

Nathan has a point and also introduces a separate problem. If this problem was caused by someone on the board, we can't let them know that we moved up the release date, or they will tell Textra.

"We have to make it a surprise drop," I say. "Even the board can't know about it."

Nathan gapes. "How are we going to manage that?"

I say nothing, but an idea starts to form in my head.

There's a knock on the door interrupting our conversation.

Melissa, my secretary, sticks her head in, and I nod at her, allowing her to speak. She holds up a basket.

"Sorry to interrupt, sir, but Pope dropped this off for you a few hours ago. I would have brought it in, but you requested no interruptions, so I kept it in the fridge for you."

I gestured to her to bring it in, and she laid it on my desk. It's a basket holding a plate of food and some dessert covered with a glass dome.

"I didn't order anything," I murmur but then notice a piece of paper at the side. I pick it up and read:

Hey. I told Kenny you couldn't make it, and he seemed to be okay, so don't worry. He understands. Hope everything is okay, but I know it probably isn't seeing as how you're working more now. Don't forget to take care of yourself. You need a vacation, seriously, so hopefully, when you've dealt with whatever it is, you can take one. Anyway, we made these gnocchi. I saw how you liked the ones at the country club, so I tried to replicate them. Also, Kenny and I made a blueberry pie for your dessert. It's not too sweet, so please take a bite and let me know what you think.

Love,

Dara and Kenny.

PS: Kenny drew the lion.

A warmth crawls over my heart, easing the tension in my neck.

When I look up from the note, Nathan stares at me oddly. "What?"

"Nothing," he says. "I've just never seen that look on your face before, especially given our current situation." He peers at me. "Are you smiling right now?"

"No," I say, although I suddenly realize that I am.

In fact, there is a big stupid smile on my face.

I instantly wipe it off. "Let's get back to work."

〜

WHEN I GET HOME, DARA AND KENNY ARE ASLEEP ON THE sectional in Kenny's wing.

They make an endearingly domestic image, leaning into each other. Kenny is curled up into Dara, and she has her hand thrown around him protectively.

The image does unimaginable things to my chest.

I gently extract Kenny from her arms and carry him into his room. When I lay him on the bed, he stirs a little but doesn't wake up.

I hesitate, then kiss his forehead before I leave.

Back in the living room, I stare at Dara for a few seconds, wondering at the aching in my heart.

Then I pick her up in my arms and carry her to her room.

To my surprise, she sleeps the whole way there. I shut the room door with my feet and head to the bed. I lay her down slowly and hesitate to let her go completely.

That's when her eyes flutter open.

She doesn't say anything. Neither do I.

We stare at each other silently for several seconds.

And then suddenly, we're kissing.

Once again, her taste explodes through me, and I curl my hand around her hair as I taste her. She wraps her hands around my neck, dragging me into bed. I'm on top of her, and she's holding me there with her legs wrapped around her waist. Her fingers flutter down my chest over my pounding heartbeat, and I'm too busy eating at her lips to notice the direction in which they move.

At least until she wraps it around my cock over my pants.

I tear my lips away from her lips and grit out a "Fuck."

Her eyes are misty, and she slowly pumps my cock through the fabric. I throw my head back and let out a groan from my chest. Her light touch feels so good that reason flees.

It attempts to come back a split second as she struggles to unbuckle my belt, but then she squeezes the mushroom tip a little, and the top of my head nearly flies off.

"Shit. I can't—" The words stutter in my chest as she moves up and down, pumping slowly. Disintegrating me.

"Can't what?" Her sultry voice teasy knowing fully well that I can't even respond to her. I can barely remember my own name.

She twists her palm around my stalk, and the desire arcs through me. My brain tries to fight back. *Don't do this. Don't fuck her.*

Her soft lips pluck mine. "Please." She takes my other hand and places it on her pussy. I groan. Even through her panties, I can feel the wetness against my palm. "I've been dreaming about you. I want you so bad. Please don't leave me like this again."

The words are an assault on my senses, but it's the way she moans that does me in. With a final groan of defeat, I throw her legs open and settle in between.

I give myself over to the madness.

CHAPTER 21
Dara

Kane is a caged animal suddenly unleashed.

His jaw is clenched hard, his cheekbones stark against the skin, like something is pushing out of him. His eyes are crazed on mine, the passion in them out of this world.

He wraps his hand around my beck lightly but with an obvious command in the move.

He's in charge now.

And then he kisses me.

Never have I been kissed like this before with such bone-shaking intensity. It's like all his fire and determination, that dogged drive that he uses to conquer the world, all that is now concentrated on me.

And my body just moves under his command, following his lead. I let him take full control of the kids, my tongue dancing as he plunders and licks at my lips. At the same time, his hips are between mine and subtly driving against me, as if he's barely aware of doing it.

The rhythm, the feel of his hard cock so close to my pussy yet so far away...all of it is getting me in a space of mind where nothing exists but bone-melting lust. Where I don't know my own name or where this is headed, only the temptation that climbs within me so quickly that it makes me lightheaded.

I want to relax and let the drugging feelings take over me completely.

At the same time, there's haste grating my nerves, urging me to go faster to get him inside me as fast as possible before something horrible happens and he changes his mind.

I can't let him change his mind now. I need to ride this madness to the end.

He rips his mouth away from my lips, allowing me a single breath as his hand travels down the front of my shirt again. My nipples are already engorged and waiting for his touch, but I still jerk slightly when one of his fingers finds them, plucking them expertly.

"Easy," he says, and his baritone runs through me like syrup. It's oddly relaxing and stimulating at the same time, but combined with the easy movement of his hand plucking lazily and kneading, it's an incredible sensation.

My toes curl, my pussy aching for him. But he stays with his teasing caresses and drops kisses on my heated neck, murmuring words onto them. I'm not sure what he's saying. Perhaps litany or praise. Or softly uttered curses about how I'm going to kill him.

And each one of them drives me higher.

I was already dreaming about him, about this, when I woke up and found him leaning over me. I've wanted this for so long, and now it's in my grasp, and I almost can't believe it's going to happen.

But it needs to happen soon, or I am simply going to pass out from the combined sensations shooting through me. His hand finally leaves my nipple, plucked to a point and pushing rudely against the material of my shirt. He pulls back, and his dark gaze is enraptured onto that point even as his hands trail down my stomach. I'm already moving against him, undulating and pleading with my body with every single gasp.

But then my breath leaves me in a whoosh when he takes the nipple in between his teeth.

I release a choked cry. Electricity arcs through me.

"Delicious." The words are the only precursor before he rips open my shirt, leaving the breast bare for him. I didn't wear a bra today because the shirt I was wearing had an inbuilt bust, and now I'm bare for his gaze, the flowery shirt fluttering open for him.

And in the next breath, he's sucking my nipple in his mouth

The move steals all my breath. All my strength flees.

He takes everything.

His hands massage over my pussy, and I splay my legs open for him wantonly. But he doesn't rush any part of the process, even with the hunger boiling in his eyes. It feels like this is almost an experiment to him like he's testing and trying which parts of my body are most sensitive and which parts make me squeal out my pleasure and shake and promise him everything if he lets me come.

"Please," I give in to the desperation. "Please, I'll do anything. Just fuck me. Just let me come."

"Anything?" His voice has temptation and is low and sultry. I imagine this is what it was like when the serpent tempted Eve.

"Yes. Please."

He leans in, and his scent surrounds me.

"Touch yourself," he whispers in my ears.

My eyes widen, jerking as the image assaults me. But nothing compares to the look in his eyes. He wants me to…

but I've never done anything like that before in front of another human being.

He smirks a look that's half pain and half amusement. His cock grows thicker against my thigh, and I bite my lip from hunger. I don't even know how it's possible, but it's nearly the size of my forearm now.

And pretty soon, it will be inside me.

I shiver with anticipation, pussy leaking.

"Please." The words are thick in my throat. I reach out and grasp his shirt weakly. "I need you."

His eyes boil over, and he rolls over me, his body flush on mine. I moan and struggle to wrap myself around him, but he keeps me in place.

"Anytime, anywhere," he whispers against my lips. "I will take my due, do you understand? It means I will ask you to touch yourself for me, and you will do it, no matter what. Understood?"

It's a risky bargain, but I'm already nodding. Anything. I'm ready to promise him anything.

Finally, one hand shifts, and he shuts his eyes, groaning heavily as he takes himself in hand. I glance down, watching as he wraps his fingers around the thick stalk underneath his pants, pulling it out and groaning.

Fuck he's larger than I thought. His mushroom tip with angry veins stands out on his cock.

I swallow.

His face is a mask as he aligns himself to his entrance, his eyes two navy obsidian pools, shivering as the sensation rushes through him.

Then he starts pushing in slowly, gradually.

My mouth falls open, but I can't take a breath. Electricity shoots through me. My body jitters and tries to escape itself.

It's too much,

It's all far, far too much.

And he's not even halfway in yet.

I bite my lips as he pushes in incrementally, moaning at the sensation of it all. It's pleasure and pain combined, so intense I want to scream. He groans, too.

"Fuck!" He shouts and lets his forehead lean down against mine. "Too good. Too fucking good."

I open my mouth to agree, but no word comes out. It feels like all my nerve endings are being touched at the same time. And then, he pushes in again, finding new dimensions to the madness.

God.

"Dara."

I don't answer. I'm floating somewhere in space, and my name sounds like it's coming from far away.

"Dara! Fuck."

The expletive comes with a slight, hot squeeze on my throat, and I tune back to his almost angry-looking face.

"Are you alright?" he grits out. "Please tell me you're alright."

I open my mouth to tell him that I'm more than alright and that this is the best thing I've ever felt.

But all that comes out is a throaty "More."

"Shit." That seems to be more than he can take. He shuts his eyes, and his body shudders. His shoulders flex, and he freezes, holding himself still for a few precious moments.

And then he pushes in again.

By the time he's fully seated, we're both sweating and panting at the end of our ropes.

Then Kane pulls out and groans jaggedly like he's on the edge of his control.

I want him to lose it completely.

So, I wrap my legs around his waist and squeeze. His body goes ramrod straight.

"Don't—" he starts, but I cut him off by doing it again.

The next time when he pushes it, he does it hard.

I screamed. He swallowed it in his mouth. He does it again and again fucking me into the bed. Each time, I beg for more.

His tongue replicates the rhythm in my mouth, one hand tightening in my hair, the other squeezing my breast.

The true animal is now at the forefront, and I can't hold back anymore. I come, violently, and it shakes through my body. He rides me through it so hard that I come again.

"Fuck," he screams again, his entire body jerking as he squeezes his eyes close. "Fuck."

And then, once his orgasm is done, he collapses over me.

Silence reigns for several minutes and seconds.

I can't catch my breath. It seems like all I can do is lay here, splayed and weak. I would be embarrassed about it, but he seems to be in the same state, his chest pumping with each drawn breath.

"Wow," I gasp.

Slowly, he pushes himself off me, and it's a little bereft without his weight on top of me. But then he draws me against this body, and I feel the pressure of lips on my hair.

"Thank you," he says

I raise an eyebrow. Did he just thank me for sex?

"Um...you're welcome," I say awkwardly. *What do I say to that?* "It was my pleasure."

He gives me one of his sideways grins.

"Not for the sex," he says. "For the food. It was delicious."

"Oh," I nod, but pleasure rolls through me at the compliment. "Well, if the sex was a reward for that, then I should probably never make you my world-famous mousse. It's even better than my blueberry pie, but I think your reward for that might literally kill me."

Kane is silent for a second, and then he does something glorious.

A rich, throaty sound escapes him, his chest rumbling with it. He huffs into my hair, too.

It takes me a second to realize he's laughing.

⁓

A ROW OF FLOWERS WAITS FOR ME OUTSIDE IN THE SCHOOL courtyard.

I'm escaping my calculus class when I see the first bouquet outside the glass doors. I don't know who put it there or how they did it without us noticing. But then I realize it's not just one bouquet.

There's a line leading out to the courtyard, where there's an even more elaborate display.

Someone went overboard. I raise an eyebrow at it and almost walk past it until I spot Pope standing at the edge of the display.

He greets me with a shrug.

Oh no.

Curious, I get closer and see the roses spell out my name.

And it also says *This is the real thank you.*

Warmth and embarrassment war in my brain. I stare at the words, wondering why they make me feel all fuzzy inside.

The courtyard is getting busy, too, with people coming out of the classes, whispering about the flowers.

"Is that for you?"

I turn to find Brianna walking up to me.

"I think so," I say, blushing. "My...boyfriend did it."

"Wow." She looks amazed. "He must be a real sweetheart."

A week ago, I would have laughed out loud if anyone said that about Kane.

But now, I smile. "He can be."

After I meet up with Pope, I decide to head to the office to say thank you. And maybe I can pick him up some food on the way there.

Pope parks across the street to order the food while I head to Kane's building.

But when I get close, I'm slightly intimidated by the high rise, and I pause a few steps away. *What do I say when I get inside? Do I introduce myself as Kane's wife?*

How laughable. It's incredulous that I'm married to a man who owns this building. No one would buy such a story.

But it's true.

"Are you looking for someone?"

The question comes from a well-dressed gentleman walking up to me with a Kane in hand. I'm not sure where he comes from, but when I turn to him, he pauses and pales.

He stares at me for a few seconds while I blink at him.

"Dara," he whispers.

He knows my name?

"I'm sorry," I say politely. "Have we met?"

He shakes his head. "No. But I suppose you must be Dara. You're prettier than your pictures."

"Thank you," I blush and cock my head. "And you are?"

"Samson Leon. Kane's father."

I gape. That's not at all what I expected to hear.

For starters, he looks nothing like Kane. While Kane is darkly colored, his father is light and has a slighter, slender build.

"Oh my God," I say and stick out my hand. "It's so nice

to meet you. Kane has been meaning to introduce us, but I think he hasn't had time."

Samson hesitates and then takes my hand, peering at me. I can't read his expression very well, but there's something sad in his gaze.

"We'll talk soon," he says. "I have a meeting that I have to get to, but I do want to converse some more. In lieu of that, I have a piece of advice for you."

"What is it?"

He lets go of my hand and takes a few steps closer. His eyes are a bright hazel color, nearly iridescent.

"Never under any circumstance trust my son."

And with those cryptic words, he walks away toward a Cadillac parked a few steps from us.

I'm left stunned and blinking after him.

What was that about? What does that mean?

But as I turned to continue to the Leon skyrise, I'm stopped again.

This time, by the picture of a beautiful woman walking hand in hand with Kane out of the building. Their backs are turned to me, but it seems she says something, and he chuckles.

My stomach knots. The warning echoes in my mind.

Never under any circumstance trust my son.

CHAPTER 22

Kane

"Okay." Anastasia blows out her breath from her lips and purses her lips. Her shoulders bump into mine, her hand laced in my elbow as we stroll toward the park near my office. Her favorite hobby is mindlessly walking through structures and occasionally entering shops to pick at the items. Although I would rather be doing just about anything else, I usually accommodate her now for the several years of friendship we've shared.

And also because I need her help.

"Explain it to me like I'm five," she says. "What do you need my Dad's company to do again?"

I sigh and think of how to simplify it. "Essentially, I need a small advance, a loan if you will. I would need it by the next two weeks, and it would be paid back in full next year."

"But it's not a loan for Leon? Correct?"

"No. This would be a private loan, and no one else can know about it."

"Not even your Dad?"

I shake my head. "It has to be kept secret strictly."

"Why?"

I hesitate. As much as I trust Anastasia with a lot of things, this isn't one of them. At least not until I've caught the mole.

That's another reason why I'm having this conversation out in the park and not in my office.

The idea struck me first when Anastasia informed me of her arrival days ago. It was serendipitous timing because I needed a source of funds urgently, which is why we had to rush the release of the X3. And I can't withdraw that much money from my personal assets without raising suspicion.

However, a private loan from Anastasia Coleman would do the trick.

Anastasia belongs to the illustrious Coleman dynasty, a family that has a hand in everything from diamonds to oil. Her father owns a string of jewelry stores, and as his only daughter, Anastasia enjoys a life of luxury and relaxation. She's spoiled rotten, but overall, she's not a bad person. In fact, she's one of the few people I can stand for lengths of time, even when she's behaving childishly.

Like now, when she purses her lips. "I don't know. I would have to tell my Dad about it first."

"No problem," I say as we stroll. "Or you could set up a meeting, and he could tell me himself."

"That would work," she says and stretches her neck. "Now, onto more fun things. What good parties are happening around here?"

I snort. "I wouldn't know. I haven't been to a party in forever."

"Really?" Her eyes widen. "You live in the party center of America. How can you not know any good ones."

I shrug. "Most of my life is business now. My rebellious partying days are far behind me."

She pouts. "I know we're older, but I never thought you

would get so boring with age. I remember when you used to be so much fun. We would go to all the cool parties, and you would pretend to be my boyfriend to keep the assholes away from me." She smiles wickedly. "We should do that again."

"No." I take her hand out of my elbow, which is suddenly uncomfortable.

"Why not?"

"I'm married."

"Yeah, right." She starts laughing in that tinkling way of hers, but it fades as soon as she realizes that I'm not laughing along with her.

Her amusement slowly turns to shock when we reach the street where the famous Berlin Sky bar resides.

"What?"

I don't repeat myself, simply nodding to the hostess and entering the sleek building, heading to the elevator.

She's still silent as I press the button and wait for the elevator to open up. Once it does, we both walk in and the doors close behind us.

Only then does she seem to rediscover her voice.

"You're pulling my leg, aren't you?" She narrows her eyes. "Tell me you're pulling my leg."

"Nope." I grin at her suspicious expression.

Her eyes flicker down to my fingers.

"You're not wearing a wedding ring."

"It's not necessary to wear one to get married. You know this, right?"

She lets out a sound of indignation, throwing her hands up dramatically. "Well, excuse me for not being an expert. Who did you marry?"

"No one, you know."

"Well, I need to know," Her nose goes up in the air. "I'm

your best friend. How can I not know your wife? Are you keeping her a secret from me?"

"More so, I'm keeping her safe from you." The elevator opens and allows us onto the top floor. There are already a few patrons there, but it's scarce enough for my liking. A waiter immediately strides to us with a perfunctory smile and a practiced welcome.

The conversation continues after we're seated.

"Well, she should at least know what she took from me."

I raise an eyebrow. "And what would that be?"

"We promised that we would marry each other if we were still thirty and single," she says. "Remember that?"

"When we were thirty, you were already engaged."

"Yes. And look how well that turned out. Wait..." It's like a sudden, horrific thought occurs to her. "This has something to do with your Dad, doesn't it?"

I glance over the menu. "The seabass is good here. You should get it."

"Kane..." Her expression is suddenly serious. "Be honest with me for a second. Did you marry some girl because your father wanted you to?"

I cock my head. "Not entirely."

She sighs and rubs her forehead. There's not a single wrinkle on there, courtesy of the best aestheticians in Malibu.

"Kane," she starts. "I'm going to say this as gently as possible, so don't get defensive. But you need to stop letting that man control your life."

"No one controls me," I say.

"Really?" She raises an eyebrow. "You live, eat, and breathe for his company. You basically worked yourself sick to earn his approval. And now you've stuck yourself to a woman probably because your Dad asked you to."

"I wouldn't say stuck." Although, I do remember that we had been sort of stuck last night, with her body on mine. The memory spurs a host of pleasurable sensations through my body. "I don't mind being married to her."

"Are you smiling?" Anastasis gapes in shock. "Wait a second. Are you in love with her or something?"

I nearly choke on the air. "No, nothing like that. But I do like her, and there are worse people I could be married to." At this point, I'm ready to change the subject. "But enough about me. How are things with you?"

"Nice pivot." She rolls her eyes but ultimately caves into changing the subject. "Well, things are good, I suppose, except I'm just now finding out that my best friend is married, and I'm not even allowed to meet the woman."

I sigh. "You'll meet her. When the time is right."

"Promise?"

"Yes. Because if I tell you not to, you're just going to try and meet her anyway without my knowledge, and that would be even worse."

Anastasia grins. "Ah. You know me so well."

~

WHEN I ARRIVED HOME LATER THAT AFTERNOON, POPE WAS on his way out.

"Hey, boss," he says. "Do you need me to pick up something? I was just heading to the pharmacy to get some medication. Your missus isn't feeling very well."

"What's wrong with her?" Alarm instantly spirals through me.

"She says it's just a headache, but I want to get her some Advil just in case it gets worse," he says. "She went to rest."

"Alright. Hurry back then. And thank you for letting me know."

As Pope gets into the car and drives out, a feeling of guilt pops up inside me.

Shit.

Is her headache because of me?

Perhaps we went too hard the other night and now she's suffering for my selfishness.

I need to do something.

I immediately head into the kitchen. The chefs are standing around chatting until I catch the attention of one of them.

Oscar and Harold. That's what Dara says their names are.

"I heard Dara is sick," I say. "What are you making her?"

They share a look. "Um, we were just preparing a regular lunch, sir. We didn't know she was sick."

"Well, now you know." I have a thought. "You should make chicken soup."

"Chicken soup, sir?"

"Yes," I recall one of the few times I spoke with Carter when he had fallen sick in our home. He'd mentioned his father's famous chicken soup and how it always made him feel a lot better. He'd described it in such great detail that I bullied him into making it for me once, just to see what the fuss was about.

I wonder if Dara also likes her father's chicken soup. "Get me a pen and paper. I'll write down the recipe."

"Oh...okay." One of them runs to do my bidding while the other one starts getting the ingredients out of the fridge.

After leaving them with my instructions, I head upstairs to Dara's bedroom.

She's asleep when I get there, and she seems peaceful

enough. She also looks achingly beautiful, like a fairy fallen on earth. I stand and watch her, resisting the urge to touch her. I don't want to wake her up.

I just hope this headache is nothing serious.

It can't be serious because the thought of her sick has panic ricocheting in my chest for reasons I would rather not explore.

The turmoil inside me remains, teasing out some of the guilt from last night.

I keep promising myself that I'll stay away from her, and I keep breaking that promise.

I can't help myself. She's an addiction I never learned to fight, and I am now powerless to resist, not even for her own good.

I guess I must be more selfish than I thought.

In a few minutes, a quiet knock announces that Faith has arrived with the chicken soup. I direct her to bring it to me first, taste it, and then wince.

"What is this?" I ask.

"Chicken soup, sir," she answers nervously.

"Did they follow the recipe?"

"Exactly, sir," she says, but I shake my head. This tastes good, but nothing like the soup I remember.

"Give that to someone else or put it aside," I say. "We're going to try this again."

CHAPTER 23

Dara

I come home with a headache at the base of my temples, probably triggered by overthinking and stressing out about seeing Kane with that woman.

I keep waffling between whether or not to ask Kane about her when he gets back. The questions plague me, and I probably need answers for my mind to settle down.

Who is she, and why does he look so comfortable around her? They had an easy camaraderie as if he'd known her for years.

As if he's shared secrets with her, and shared parts of himself that he's never shared with me.

God, don't be ridiculous, I scold myself, as Pope drives in through the gate and comes into the distance. *And don't be delusional, either.*

It's probably not my business to know who she is. This arrangement of ours has a time limit, after all, as much as I hate reminding myself of it. The fact that Kane and I had sex doesn't change that, and I'm not going to be one of those women who equate great sexual chemistry with feelings.

But at the same time, a part of me insists that his laughing with another woman is dishonoring our contract, too. After all, the entire reason that we're doing this is to convince his Dad that we're together. How is he going to manage that if his Dad catches him flirting with another woman?

Was he actually flirting with her, or was that just my jealousy talking?

I groan, and Pope shoots me a curious look from the rearview mirror.

"It's nothing," I tell him. "Just a headache."

He nods silently but glances at me a few times while we drive. He appears concerned, but still, I can't keep my thoughts from drifting back to Kane and that woman.

I didn't particularly like the way he was touching her and smiling at her, the familiar way she rested her hand on his arm. Plus, the fact that she was sickeningly beautiful, tall, and statuesque with flowing blonde hair in perfect curls, just made the entire thing worse.

And by the time I get home, I'm not in the mood for anything besides sleep. Thankfully, the hallways are pretty empty, and I hurry up to my room, hoping no one sees me before I get there.

Then, I lay in bed and let the thoughts run through my head until they eventually exhaust me enough to fall asleep.

Only to wake up to Kenny at the base of my bed, his warm palm pressed against my forehead.

It takes me a second to orient myself to his presence so I don't jerk in shock.

"Ken Ken." I reach out tiredly and ruffle his hair while stretching and yawning. "What's up?"

"They said you were sick," he says. "I was checking if you had a fever."

I smile fondly. "I don't have a fever. I had a headache, but it's all gone now. I just think I needed a little sleep."

"Oh," he says, but he's still frowning. "It's not from the accident, is it?"

I shake my head. "No. I'm all healed up from that." I know that the little boy still feels some guilt about the fact that I got injured because of him. I don't want him to feel that way again. "And even if I wasn't, it wouldn't be your fault. Understood?"

"Yeah," Kenny says, but the ensuing silence makes me think he's not exactly convinced of this. "Dad's making some chicken soup for you."

I blink at him. "What?"

"Yeah. Sophia mentioned she saw him doing it in the kitchen, so I had to go check for myself. And yeah, he is cooking. But I don't think he's doing it right because he keeps frowning and muttering under his breath."

I'm tempted to think Kenny is teasing me, but his facial expression is deadly serious.

Although it doesn't make any sense. Why on earth would Kane be cooking for me?

I get out of bed immediately, and Kenny backs up.

"I have to go back and finish my lesson," he says. "Glad you're okay."

He waves and then runs off, leaving me waving behind him.

Then, I make my way down the silent hallways and downstairs to the kitchen.

Kane's back is turned to me, and he's bent over the pot, turning a ladle.

His sleeves are rolled up to his elbows, and he's wearing a black apron over his clothes.

"Kane?"

He turns and immediately frowns at me. "What are you doing out of bed? I thought you weren't feeling well?"

"Yeah, I wasn't," I murmur distractingly. "But I'm better now. Are you cooking?"

He nods and then brings the spoon up to his mouth, blowing. "Yeah,

why?"

He sips the soup from the ladle and then smacks his lips together, consideringly. "They weren't making it right."

"Who are they?"

"Oscar and Harold. Someone told me to learn their names." He smirks. He gestures to the bowls on the side of the table. "They made the chicken soup three times, and they still couldn't get the perfect consistency or taste. So, I decided to do it myself."

"Oh," I say, still as confused as ever. "I wasn't aware chicken soup was that hard to make."

"This one is. Surprisingly."

I wonder what's so special about this chicken soup that it took three tries. I also wonder where he banished Oscar and Harold for their crime of not making the perfect chicken soup.

"Relax." His gaze is teasing, as though he can tell what I'm thinking. "I only gave them a break to go buy some more ingredients, just in case I fuck up this one too. But I don't think I did." He finally puts down the ladle and then gestures to the oven. "The grilled cheese should be nearly ready."

"How did you know I liked grilled cheese with my chicken soup?"

"I'm good at knowing things about you."

I gape. I wonder briefly about how he could have found out such a minor detail like that. And then I remember. Carter. I sent him a letter a long time ago detailing how I was sick, but at least I was happy that my Dad made me soup with grilled cheese.

Did he tell Kane about it? And Kane remembered, after all that time?

An intense warmth starts in my heart and rolls through me. My emotions are so strong that they feel nearly achingly tangible.

He's cooking for me. *He went through all that trouble of making three different plates of chicken soup for me.*

"Come here," he says suddenly.

I'm prompted forward, and he puts the spoon on my lips. I sip the soup and tears water my eyes.

It tastes exactly like my Dad's.

I choke up, but I cover it with a whisper, "It's perfect."

He smiles and then reaches out, drawing his hand over my lips and wiping off the stray piece of liquid there. "You're perfect."

I don't even think about it. I stand on my tippy toes up and kiss him roughly. Emotion flows through me, pounding in my chest as he kisses me back, one hand skimming my cheek tenderly.

Then he groans and grabs me by the waist, drawing me closer. The food is forgotten as he hoists me up onto the counter, and the kiss grows more intense and passionate.

"That's disgusting." A sudden voice interrupts, and we break apart in time to see Kenny frowning at both of us, a look of disgust stamped on his face. "Ew, guys. Get a room."

Kane and I share a look and chuckle.

"Technically, since I own the house, all the rooms are mine," Kane points out at his son, but he sets me down on my feet and takes a step back to face him.

Kenny rolls his eyes and comes closer, eyes trained on the pot. "That smells good, Dad."

It does. "And it will taste even better with all the other

things I ordered. Including a key lime pie from that restaurant you like on Martha's Vineyard."

Kenny's eyes widen. "That's super far away."

"I know," he says. "But it's your favorite pie, and I owe you. Pope is on his way to get it right now."

Kenny grins widely and ducks his head like he does when he's embarrassed by his own emotions. "Thanks."

"You're welcome," Kane says and pats his son's shoulder. I smile, my heart blooms with affection for both of them.

The phone suddenly rings, and Kane slides it out of his pocket, answering without looking at the number. "Hello?"

The voice at the other end is too light to hear what it says, but Kane frowns. "No, I can't meet you right now. I'm with my family. Is it important?"

Kenny's look of dread at the phone call turns into pleasure at Kane's statement. Our eyes meet briefly, and I smile. I'm guessing it's the first time Kenny has seen Kane choosing to be at home over business.

"I see," Kane says, and I can't tell from the expression on his face whether this is good news or bad news.

He listens for a few more seconds and then nods. "Give me some time to work out the dates. It will need to be soon, but I have a few other priorities to take care of."

Kane removes the phone from his ears, about to hang up when we hear: "Alright, but don't take too long. You know I don't like to wait."

I freeze. The voice on the other end of the line is unmistakably female and her laugh is a high tinkle. A familiar sound.

It's likely the woman from earlier today.

My stomach tightens in my belly.

Kane hangs up and then drops his phone on the counter, turning back to the soup. He turns off the gas.

"Who was that?" I venture, trying to sound casual about it.

"No one," he responds. Then he looks up as though he suddenly has an idea.

"By the way," he says. "What do you guys think about a last-minute trip to France?"

"What?" Kenny says.

"A friend just invited me there," he says.

"A friend?" I inquire, and this time, he catches the note in my tone.

He smirks. "Are you jealous?"

"No," I answer too quickly for it to be the truth.

He shakes his head and wraps an arm around my waist, drawing me closer and kissing me on the lips again. Kenny makes gagging noises.

"I think you are," Kane teases when he draws back. "But there's no reason to be. Anastasia has been an old friend of mine since we were kids. There has never been anything romantic between us."

Relief flushes through me, but I still can't stop myself from asking. "Not even a little bit?"

He shakes. "No. Stassi can be flirtatious, but she doesn't have any real interest in me, and I don't have any interest in her." His eyes grow darker as they drop to my lips again. "There's only one woman around that I'm fascinated by."

I gape. I don't know if this is a part of his scheme, but there's honesty in his eyes when he says, "You're the only woman for me."

My heart thumps in my chest. The words fall out of my mouth. "You're the only man for me too."

He smiles gently. "It's a good thing we're together then."

I don't know what to say to that. Is this for real? But

there's no one around us to perform for, so it has to be some-what real, right?

Heat fills my face, and lust thrums through my body. My saliva dries up, and I open my mouth to speak, but the words don't come out.

"If you guys kiss again, I'm going to throw up, I promise."

Kenny's claim has Kane snorting as he faces his son. "What do you think about a trip to France, Kenny?"

He shrugs, feigning nonchalance. "France is cool."

"Good. Then it's settled."

~

IF ANYONE HAD TOLD ME THAT WE COULD PLAN A TRIP TO France in only a day, I would have called them a liar.

But that's exactly what we managed to do.

"Don't bother about packing much, except essentials," Kane tells me that evening during dinner. "We'll do most of our shopping there."

"Okay, but I don't have a passport," I tell him. "Or a visa, for that matter."

"That will be taken care of, too," he says.

And he really does take care of everything. And on Saturday morning, we're driven to the airport by Pope, except we don't go to the usual parking lot where everyone else does. Instead, we're driven around to the tarmac, where a sleek black plane is waiting for us.

It takes me a second to figure out what's going on.

"Wait," I say as Pope opens the door for me. "We're going in a private jet?"

"Duh," Kenny says, smiling at my astounded expression.

"Of course," Kane says. "How did you think we were going to get there?"

"Well, I guess I didn't have much time to think about it." Twenty-four hours ago, I didn't think I would be in France either. "This takes a lot of getting used to."

"Get used to it," he says as he brushes his mouth over mine. This time, Kenny merely rolls his eyes.

But it's hard to get used to it. I don't know much about private jets, but this one must be the elite of the pack. It's very fancy, with leather seats, golden hardware, and dotted lights on top that remind me of a constellation. The plane also comes with a very kind-faced air hostess, who's offering us wine, coffee, and hot chocolate for Kenny. Kenny falls asleep as we lift off in the air, but I can't. My body is buzzing with too much excitement. I admire the view from the clouds.

"This is amazing," I point out, and Kane grins at me.

"You haven't seen anything yet."

After we touch down at the Charles De Gaul airport, we're met at the tarmac by a stretch limo with a suited driver standing in front of it.

As we step down from the airplane, with Kane carrying a sleeping Kenny, a driver opens the door of the limo, and the blonde woman steps out.

"Kane and family," she says, grinning. She strides confidently towards Kane, opening her arms for a hug.

He only manages to give her a side hug while holding Kenny, but still, I have to tamp down the slight jealousy in my stomach.

She says something to him in French, and when he replies, she throws back her hair and laughs.

God, it's like she stepped out of a hair commercial.

While she greets Kane, I glance around the tarmac, noting

that it seems empty. I wonder if it's natural or if it was emptied by our arrival.

A few guards stand back, talking to each other, and then one of them gestures towards us. The other one nods and heads to the back of our plane, presumably to take our bags. I watch him go, and then I blink as he gets closer.

Shock hits me.

Familiarity shoots through me. There's just something about his stance, the way he walks, and the brief glimpse of the side of his face…

He looks like Carter.

I don't know. Maybe I am imagining things.

"Hi," the woman says, distracting me from my thoughts. She's turned to me now. "You must be the new wife."

"I am," I say. Something about her tone has a little bite to it, even though her smile is pleasant enough.

She runs her eyes down my body and gives me a scan.

"Hmm," is all she says.

"Anastasia," Kane says and there's a warning in his voice.

"Oh, Kane, come off it. It's just not what I expected to see you with. Plus, she looks very young."

"I'm in my late twenties," I feel the need to clarify.

"Yes. And Kane is nearly double that," she says and then adds. "By the way, I hope you don't mind that Kane and I are so close. There's going to be a lot of inside jokes during this visit that you don't understand. We've known each other forever, and you're kind of the odd one out here."

"Oh," I say as embarrassment spirals through me.

"That's enough," Kane's voice is suddenly dark as he walks closer to me.

He fixes the woman with a cold look. "Apologize. Now."

CHAPTER 24
Kane

Both Anastasia and Dara turn in shock at my words. But without missing a bit, I take Dara's hand and draw her closer, pinning Anastasia with a look.

"Dara is my wife, and you will treat her with respect," I say firmly. "That means no more backhanded comments and no more flirting. She doesn't know you well enough to know that you're joking. Is that understood?"

Anastasia purses her lips stubbornly. "I wasn't giving her a backhanded compliment. Just because she doesn't look like your usual type doesn't mean she's ugly. And I do think that her outfit is adorable, just a little…simple."

"Am I understood, Anastasia?" I say firmly. Stassi is not generally unkind, but her playfulness can sometimes go overboard, veering into rude territory.

And she can also be very territorial, particularly regarding me. I've allowed it for so long because I didn't have a reason to protest before.

But I won't allow it anymore. Especially not after seeing that embarrassed look on Dara's face.

That infuriated me.

Anastasia brushes her hand over her hair flippantly. "Fine. I get it. I won't say it again."

"Good. Now apologize."

Her back goes ramrod straight the way it always does whenever her pride kicks into high gear. Anastasia is very driven by her ego, even when she's in the wrong. Perhaps, especially when she's in the wrong.

She is her father's daughter, after all, and she absolutely loathes to apologize.

But she has to pay for the hurt on Dara's face.

"That's not necessary," Dara immediately interjects. "I didn't take offense at what she said. Plus, she was right. I know the two of you have been friends for a long time and I am the outsider here, so I may misunderstand—"

"You're my wife, not an outsider," I cut off whatever she's about to say because I have the feeling that it's only going to piss me off even more. I can't believe she's defending such behavior. She thinks that she deserves to be treated how Anastasia just did? She thinks she's not worthy of being stood up for?

Or is she intimidated by Anastasia? She shouldn't be. Though Anastasia is older, I find Dara far more mature.

And far more intoxicating.

But I resent her overly gracious nature. It makes me feel like a mad, protective bulldog who wants to raze everything in the world that could potentially hurt her.

"Apologize, Anastasia," I say. "Or we can forget about this business deal and our friendship altogether."

Anastasia's eyes widen, and even Dara gasps a little, but I'm dead serious. I may need this deal with her father badly, but I'll find another way. If she disrespects Dara, then that's the end.

Three decades of friendship down the drain. You're willing to give that up for a woman you met a few weeks ago?

Yes. There's no question about it, not even a moment of hesitation. I won't forgive Anastasia for hurting Dara.

Now, that should concern me. It should concern me a lot because I've never felt that way about any other woman I've been with.

You're in love with her, my conscience warns.

No, I deny it vehemently. *I can't be in love with her. It's simply the principle of it. I won't have anyone disrespect my wife, even if she's just my pretend wife. That is basically the same as disrespecting me.*

Anastasia finally releases a sigh to end the tension.

"I'm sorry," she says to me and then repeats it to Dara. "I'm being a brat for no reason. Maybe it's some leftover jealousy because he turned me down for you, but it's also my anxiety about meeting new people. Especially pretty young women. I get mean so I don't feel so intimidated by them."

Dara blinks at the blatant honesty and then offers a weak smile. "It's okay," she shrugs. "If it makes you feel better, I find you intimidating too."

"Really?"

"Have you seen yourself?" Dara gestures to her. "You're like a walking centerfold. You probably trigger like ten of my insecurities every time you breathe."

Anastasia slowly grins at her, placing a hand in the middle of her chest.

"Thank you for that," Anastasia says, then turns to me with a teasing smile on the corner of her lips. "Okay, now I see it. I like her."

"I'm glad," I respond wryly, at which point Kenny starts to stir.

He lifts his head and blinks for a few seconds, glancing around with his eyebrows furrowed.

"Hey, my little friend," Anastasia beams at him. "Do you remember me?"

He considers her and then nods slowly. "Dad's friend Stassi."

"Correct, my love. It's nice to see you again."

"Nice to see you too," he mumbles sleepily and then wriggles for me to let him down, which I do.

"Come on," Anastasia remarks, gesturing to the limo. "You don't want to keep the old man waiting for you?"

I nod and direct Dara and Kenny to enter first before I do.

The drive to the Coleman estate is fifteen minutes, during which Anastasia and Dara get into a conversation about designers and Paris Fashion Week. I can tell Dara is lost during most of the conversation, but she's great at listening, and that's really all Anastasia wants most of the time.

We finally arrive at the Coleman estate, which is about twice the size of mine and is decorated in a French Gothic style.

"Dad is in the garden having tea," Anastasia says as we walk down the cobbled walkway, surrounded by statues of the other ancestral Colemans who previously owned the estate.

We finally arrive in the perfectly manicured gardens to find a white-haired man in a robe, reading brown leather-bound books with his legs crossed.

He looks up at our approach.

"Kane," he comments and then peers over his glasses at me. "What a domestic picture you make."

"James," I acknowledge him with a nod and say, "This is my wife, Dara, and my son, Kenny."

"Hello," Dara says, and then she signals Kenny to do the same.

But instead, Kenny frowns. "Why are you reading that book upside-down?"

James seems intrigued by the question, shifting his gaze to the little boy. "It's an ancient script," he says. "I'm reading it how it's supposed to be read."

"Isn't that hard?"

James shrugs. "A little. I have to translate every word myself. But it's good because I get the true meaning of the text and not some second-rate translator's opinion."

"Does that take a lot of time?"

James nods. "It does. Sometimes it takes me all day."

"You must not have a job then," Kenny says.

Anastasia snorts a little, and I crack a smile. Dara looks mortified, but James smiles too and then glances at me. "He reminds me of you."

I lay a hand on Kenny's shoulder. "Well, he is my son," I quip.

Kenny grins, and Anastasia claps her hands.

"Well, let's leave the men to talk about business." She gestured to Kenny and I. "What do you guys think about us heading out and getting some ice cream? Montfort can take us to the Eiffel Tower too."

"Sounds good," Kenny says, and Dara nods.

"Are you sure?" I ask Dara. I know she's trying to be polite, but I don't want her to subject herself to Anastasia's company just for me.

Stassi rolls her eyes. "Come on, Kane. I'm not going to bite your wife."

"I don't trust that," I tell her and Dara says.

"It's fine, really." A twinkle appears in Dara's eyes. "I

kind of also want to spend some time alone with her. So, I can get some real dirt on you and your childhood."

"Oh," Anastasia remarks. "Believe me. There's so much dirt to have."

Stassi laces her land through Dara's and leads her away while she holds Kenny's hand.

I sit and face James in the meantime.

"So," he says. "You're married."

"Yes, but that's not what I came here to talk about." I've already had enough conversations about my marriage this week, more than I would like.

"Oh?" James raises an eyebrow. "You're here for business, then?"

"Yes. Did Anastasia not explain it to you?"

James winces. "You and I both know that explaining business concepts is not Stassie's strong suit."

I nod, and then, in the next few minutes, I give him an abbreviation of what I told Stassie.

He frowns while I speak but doesn't interject, waiting till I'm done.

"So, what you're saying is, you don't trust the board of directors at your own company."

I should have known James would pick up on what was happening without me telling him.

"There have been some leaks," I admit. "And I need to find where they're coming from."

He rubs his beard and leans back in his seat. "I seem to recall there was a time I tried to convince you to leave Leon and work with me. You turned me down."

"I worked with you long enough," I tell him. During the summer of my eighteenth birthday, I interned under James, and I learned a lot of things about running a business from him and not my father, who was busy most of the time and believed I should have just been born with business skills.

"I appreciate everything you've done for me and everything you've shown to me."

"But it's not enough to overcome your loyalty to your father." He points out wryly. "And now he is surrounded by traitorous vultures."

"It's not his fault."

"Everything is his fault." A hard look enters James's eyes, but it only lasts for a second. "But that's beside the point. Do you want my help? Then you have it."

"Thank you," I say, relieved that I've solved one part of this equation.

He smiles. "That's a beautiful family you have there, by the way. I can't say I'm too happy about your marriage, though. I always thought you would make a great son-in-law and husband for my Stassi."

"We would murder each other in the first week," I tell him. "She would bore me with tales of shopping, and she would poison my coffee the first time I tell her I'm too busy to accompany her to Milan."

"Mmm." James grins. "You know my daughter will perhaps be better than anyone else."

"Yes. I know her enough to know that we're better off as friends. Besides, I'm happy with my current wife."

And it shocks me, once again, to find that it's true. Somewhere along the line, the pretense wasn't really a pretense anymore.

I genuinely enjoy being married to Dara.

Jesus. When did that happen?

And why aren't I more worried about it?

"Yes, I can see that," James responds. I stand, ready to escape the conversation.

But I can't escape the uncomfortable realization that I've gotten far too comfortable in my fake marriage. And I have no clue what I'm going to do about it.

"By the way," he says. "My offer still stands."

"Offer?"

"Yes," he says, and some of that hardness returns to his gaze. "If you ever want to abandon that sinking ship that is your father's company, I'll be ready to welcome you with open arms."

∽

WITH THAT SETTLED, FOR THE REST OF THE WEEKEND VISIT, I try to spend as much time with my family as possible.

After resting at the Coleman estate—where Anastasia and Dara spend a suspicious amount of time together talking—I take my family out on private tours and explore the architecture in Paris. We also go to so many museums, which Kenny is fascinated by. I learned recently that my son is quite an artist, so I take him to a few galleries, too. At the Louvre, we meet Martin Rousteing, one of the most prolific modern artists in France, and he invites us for dinner so he can show Kenny his art room. Kenny is over the moon about it.

Then, the next day, I took Dara shopping, and we had brunch at a quaint French restaurant sitting atop a hill in Versailles.

Dara can't stop smiling as we sit to eat.

"I've always wanted to own a place like this," she says, her gaze drinking it all in eagerly.

"You will," I tell her, and she glances at me in surprise.

The firmness with which I say it is a surprise to me as well, but I mean it. No matter what, I'm determined to make her dream of owning her restaurant come true.

And the fact that it's become so important to me draws me short.

Until she smiles, and it melts any resistance I have.

Her smile is quickly becoming my kryptonite.

So is her body.

Every time that we're skin-to-skin having sex, I stare into her eyes and feel a sense of completeness, of overwhelming connection.

Her kiss is becoming an addiction.

I draw her body close to mine and shudder at what she does to me. Being inside her is heaven. Being with her is also hell.

And it's unlike anything I've ever felt.

That night, after we have sex, there's a heavy silence. I don't feel inclined to break it. I don't want to crash the dream space we've created just yet.

"I think I saw someone who looked like my brother," she states softly, suddenly, and I glance at her in surprise.

"At the airport when we arrived," she continues, then shrugs. "I know it probably wasn't him, and I was just imagining things, but it's just...I don't know. I guess I miss him."

Her softly uttered words make me ache, make me want to promise her the world. I want to find Carter and bring him back, not to make him pay for what he did to my family but to make her smile again.

Only then does it hit me.

Fuck. I really am falling in love with her.

The realization jerks me back into reality. The dream world crashes around me, and I rip down whatever fantasies I've formed in my head.

A future between Dara and me isn't possible. It can't be.

A young, beautiful ray of sunshine like her will not fare well in my world. It will destroy her. I will destroy her.

This needs to end.

CHAPTER 25

Dara

I sigh as I turn the spoon, mixing the sugar in my coffee.

"What seems to be the problem, madam?" Lisa asks in a fake British accent. I glance up sourly as she grins at my irritation.

"I told you to stop calling me that," I say.

"Sorry, it's hard not to." Lisa giggles and gestures around the room. "You live in a literal castle with servants. I don't know what else to call you."

"It's not like it's *my* castle," I mutter grouchily. She's been teasing me since we sat in the patio to eat. I almost regret bringing Lisa here, but she insisted that it was about time she saw where I lived. So, when I picked her up for brunch, we decided to have it at home instead.

Of course, Lisa's eyes went wide as saucers the minute we drove up to the estate.

"You live here?" she exclaimed. "This looks like a house off Downton Abbey."

"Not you, too," Pope groaned, but Lisa ignored him, too busy gawping at everything. She reminded me of myself, the first time Kane showed me his home and I had to smile.

Of course, her reaction only got worse when she walked in and was greeted by all the servants in the hallways as we strolled through. Anna smiled warmly at us and waved while talking to Sophia upstairs.

And then finally, when we settled in the kitchen, and she met Oscar and Harold, they immediately bonded over her love for food and Downton Abbey. Their conversation lasted for nearly an hour before they had to return to work.

Right now, we're on my bedroom balcony, and Lisa hasn't stopped calling me madam. I stare out at the sun, wondering where Kane is. He and Kenny went off somewhere earlier today, but neither of them clued me in on where they would be going. That's been happening a lot lately, and I get the feeling that it might be on purpose. And while I appreciate the fact that they're spending solo father-son time, being left behind feels a little isolating.

"Okay, seriously, tell me what's wrong," Lisa asked, drawing my attention back to her. "Because you've been happier than a clam for the past few weeks, but that's the third time you've sighed in the last ten minutes."

"It is?"

She nods and picks at the scones on her plate. We've already pretty much demolished the tarts and sandwiches Oliver made. They were delicious, and so are the scones, but we can't bring ourselves to stuff any more down our throats.

"For the past few weeks, you've changed," Lisa says. "You know that?"

"I have?"

"Yes. You've been almost glowing. I haven't seen you that happy in a *long*, long time, and that's part of the reason why I've accepted this little arrangement with your husband, even though I'm not crazy about it. But today, you're down."

"I…I don't know why," I respond. Although I do have some idea, and it has to do with Kane.

I can't figure him out. Lately, I can feel him pulling away from me, and I don't know if it's just in my head or if it's real. We haven't had sex since our last night in France four days ago, and even though he still has dinner with Kenny and me, it's not the same. He's not as chatty with me or as friendly as he used to be. It's like there's an invisible wall that has been erected between us, one that can be insurmountable.

And I can't figure out why.

Was it something I did? I wonder. Or did his France trip not go as planned? It seemed to have. He appeared happy in France and relaxed. And we spent a lot of time together. He took me to places I'd never seen and showed me beautiful things. I'll never forget the experience of sitting in that cozy restaurant with him and Kenny, laughing and talking like a real family.

And then he just pulled back, like all of that never happened, leaving me bereft and confused.

I'm so tired of being confused about Kane.

Interestingly enough, Anastasia and I have become friends since the trip. We've been texting back and forth, and she tells me all about how Kane used to be as a kid.

Apparently, he used to be a little rebellious.

"You can't tell him I'm telling you any of this," she said. "He's going to kill me. I tell you because I like you."

"I like you too," I told her, smiling because it was true.

But hearing stories about Kane only made his current coldness hurt even more.

"It's nothing," I tell Lisa. "Just thinking about the school-work I have to complete. But tell me, what's been going on with you?"

Lisa gives me a look like she doesn't quite buy my

excuse, but she doesn't push the issue. Instead, she launches into a story about two of her younger brothers and how they're pissing her off and the recent fight they had with her Dad about staying out too late. Lisa's family is super tight-knit, so when two people fight, the rest of them are inevitably involved.

I try to pay attention and not let my mind wander to where Kane and Kenny might be. Are they coming home anytime soon? Lisa has been wanting to meet them and now would be the perfect opportunity.

The phone dings distracting me momentarily and I glance down at it. I just got a message from an unknown number.

I scan through the message and initially think it's for the wrong person until I get to the end.

My chest seizes.

Hi Rabbit. I'm back in town. Meet me at the coffee shop opposite where you used to work. I'll be waiting there.

Love,

Tiger.

Oh my God.

I haven't gotten a message like that in years. Could it be….?

But it has to be. No one else calls me Rabbit except my brother. And only he knew I called him Tiger.

It used to be our codenames for each other when we would send letters back and forth. At a point when I was about fifteen, my brother stopped texting me and only delivered letters for me at the PO Box.

Eventually, the letters stopped coming.

I immediately rise. "I'm sorry, Lisa, but I have to go," I tell her. "Um…I just forgot I needed to pass by the library and get a textbook to complete my homework. I'll have Pope take you home."

"Um, okay..." Lisa also stands looking bemused. "Why don't I just go with you?"

Shit. My mind searches for an excuse, but then she snaps her fingers. "Oh shit. I forgot I have work later."

"Bummer," I say, secretly relieved. If the text is really from my brother, then I want to meet him alone first. I need him to explain where he has been all these years, and I need space to explore my tumultuous emotions about his disappearance.

We head to the car, and I try to act normal during the ride, conversing and making all the usual responses. Pope drops me off at a library a few blocks away from the restaurant before continuing with Lisa. I wave to them, making sure the car is out of sight before I walk away.

Once I'm in the restaurant, I text back, "I'm here." And then turn, searching for someone who looks like my brother.

In a few seconds, I receive a tap on my shoulder.

I try not to yelp as I spin around, but he says, "Easy, Rabbit. Don't hurt yourself now."

I peer at the man wearing a black cap that covers most of his expression. Upon closer inspection, the twinkling green eyes and the sideways smirk appear all too familiar.

It's my brother.

"Carter." The words escape me in a gasp. A flood of emotions hit me all at once.

I don't think. I throw myself into his arms, hugging him tightly.

A part of me never thought I would see him again, and now I'm so happy I am.

He holds me even tighter, lifting me off the floor and pressing his nose against my hair. "God, I've missed you so much."

"I've missed you too." My voice is hoarse with emotions,

and I pull back and smack his chest. "Where the heck have you been?"

He smiles weakly. "It's kind of complicated." He shakes his head as he scans me from head to toe. "Man, you've grown up. Last I saw you, you were a little bit of a thing."

"Well, it has been nearly fifteen years since then," I commented wryly, and he finally let me down on my feet.

"Come on," he says. "Let's sit and talk."

I follow him to a booth at the back, noting that he's wearing all black to match his hat. Although he's tall and broad, his outfit does a good job of making him appear nondescript and indetectable.

Is that on purpose? Is he trying to hide or something?

There are so many questions I have for him, I realize as I slip into the booth. Where has he been all this time? Why did he stop replying to my letters? Why didn't he come by when Dad was sick?

"Was that you?" I ask the minute he sits. "In France? I thought I saw someone who looked like you?"

He hesitates, considering the question. Then he nods. "That was me."

I swallow the information, digesting it. "So. That's where you've been all this time?"

He sighs, "Dara—"

"They have cell service in France, you know," I tell him. "They also have a post office, so you could have written a letter. Or texted. Or, heck, sent a fax—"

"I couldn't, Dara."

"Dad's dead." The emotions churn inside me, switching between anger, sadness, and happiness seamlessly. "He died about a year ago."

Pain ripples across his expression. "I heard."

There's a moment of silence. "That's all you have to say? You heard? And yet you didn't bother coming home?"

"Dara, it's a long story."

"And I look forward to hearing it. But I need to get this off my chest first." The anger that I didn't know I had boils to the surface now. "You left. Not so much as a goodbye or anything. You just stopped answering my messages. Half the time, I didn't know if you were alive or dead. Didn't know if you were even getting the messages. And when Dad was sick, you never bothered to check in. Look, I don't care what differences the two of you had, he was your Dad. And I'm your sister. I needed you, and you weren't there."

The words seem to hit him like blows and the pain in his expression magnifies. I wait for him to talk, but he only shakes his head.

"I don't have any defense," he says. "Only that…things got very complicated on my end."

"Right," I scoff and lean back, crossing my arms. "That's why you sent Kane to find me?"

At the mention of Kane's name, every other emotion disappears, and his expression goes cold.

"Look, I'll explain everything that has to do with Dad and me later," he says. "But for now, I need you to know something. Kane isn't a bad guy, but he is incredibly selfish. And he can hurt you. I don't want you falling in love with him and getting your heart broken when he abandons you."

"That's rich coming from you," I retort because his words sting.

He looks guilty again. "I said I'll explain that later."

"I want to hear your explanation now."

"It's not the time for that."

"Are you kidding me?" I rise to my feet, uncaring that we're drawing attention. "I was nearly homeless, Carter. I had

231

to drop out of school to take care of Dad, which I did without your help. I'm not a kid anymore, and you're telling me that I'm not ready to hear the reason why you abandoned us?"

"Listen, I'll tell you," he says. "But for now, I want you to be careful of Kane."

"Oh, God. Again, about Kane." I blow out a frustrated breath. "I'm going to go now. Otherwise, I'm going to say something I regret."

"Dara—"

But I don't wait around to see what he has to say next. I'm already out. At least walking back to the library gives me something to do to get rid of the bubbling energy within me.

I hear my phone ding again, but I don't look at the text. Probably going to be another useless apology and warning about Kane.

And my thoughts fly as I walk.

Why the fuck does everyone seem to distrust Kane, especially those closest to him?

Why do I feel like they all know something I don't?

Something is very wrong here.

The suspicion builds inside me until my indignation overpowers my reservation.

Well, no more. If there's something shady about Kane, I need to find out ASAP.

I'm done being a clueless pawn.

CHAPTER 26

Kane

I t's an unusual lunch date.

My son's eyebrows are furrowed over his eyes as he cuts me a glance and then looks away again. He stops madly scribbling at his canvas for two seconds and leans back, biting his lip.

"Are you done?" I ask.

He shakes his head. "Not yet." He turns his pencil and rubs the eraser end on the sketchbook for several seconds, then carefully draws the curve again.

A smile kicks up the corner of my lips as I shake my head.

He's been at this for the past hour already. I brought him out to eat during the middle of the day and thought perhaps we could visit a few art museums once we were done. I saw how much he enjoyed the ones in Paris, so I thought that might be a good way to spend our time together. I blocked out a few hours today to spend with him despite my busy schedule.

Of course, the minute we sat down in the restaurant and began waiting for our food, Kenny started fidgeting. And a few seconds later, he pulled out a sketchpad and started drawing.

I thought at first he was drawing the charming scenery from outside, overlooking a lake. But I noticed his eyes would flicker to me several times during the exercise, enough times for me to figure out that he was, in fact, sketching me.

After I learned that, I tried not to move too much. I drank my coffee and ate in five-minute intervals and made sure to return my body to its original position after so I didn't interrupt his process.

I simply watch him as he watches me, observing him in his element.

And it turns out my son is every bit the crazed artist when he draws.

He runs his hands through his hair enough that it now sticks out at angles. He also mutters to himself several times. Occasionally, he talks to the sketch itself and then falls into long stretches of silence, completely absorbed with what he's doing and uncaring of the outside world.

I don't mind. I'm glad that he's found something he's passionate about at such a young age and that it makes him happy.

Out of the corner of my eye, I see the waitress approaching with the food, but I hold up a finger to stop her. I don't want her to disrupt him, so I gesture for her to give us a few minutes.

She nods and walks away with the tray.

It takes Kenny fifteen more minutes until a pleased smile spreads across his face. "Done."

"Excellent." I finally bring the coffee to my mouth and take another sip. "Can I see it?"

"Yup." He passed the sketchpad to me, and I analyzed my likeness.

He's drawn a man with a stern face and intense eyes, staring back at the artist. His legs are crossed underneath the table, his arms reaching out to his coffee mug.

"Impressive," I comment, tracing the lines with my fingers. My son truly has a unique way of drawing. His style is somewhere between a caricature and true to life. He's emphasized the slant of my eyes, giving me a draconian flair, but he also managed to perfectly capture the smile at the corner of my lips.

It's like looking into a surrealist mirror.

And I can't help but be proud of my son for his exceptional talent. "You're incredible at this."

Kenny's chest puffs out a little, but he shrugs. "No biggie. But now I'm hungry. Is the food coming out soon?"

I nod and gesture to the waitress behind the counter. She instantly disappears into the kitchen doors, and less than a minute later, the food is in front of us.

"Why didn't Dara come with us?" Kenny asks after he starts eating his medium-rare steak burger. "I wanted to draw her too. Was she busy or something?"

I stiffen a little at the question. I've been trying my best for the past few days not to think too much about Dara, but it's near impossible. And even for brief moments when I manage to convince myself she's not on my mind, she always inevitably comes up in conversation. If it's not Anna telling me about how Dara's tarts are becoming famous with the staff, it's Pope singing her praises.

Or Kenny asking about her.

It seems she has fully ingratiated herself in my household. Everyone loves her.

Bringing her into my home was my first mistake.

"Perhaps," I answer Kenny's question. "But I just wanted to spend time alone with you today." Although a part of me feels guilty about leaving Dara out of our hangouts, I must start detaching from her instantly.

What happened in France was a wake-up call.

I already feel way too much for her, and every moment I spend with her, it's easier and easier to deceive myself into thinking that this little fling of ours is real.

And I can't do that. This has to end sometimes, likely sooner rather than later.

Warner has already provided me with the document for Dara to sign over her inheritance to me. He gave it to me the day before we left for Paris. It's a document that gives me full control of the Leon, but it reads like a post-nup. It is written in confusing language, but I'm pretty sure that at this point, I have enough of her trust to get her to sign it without much thought.

She trusts me.

Perhaps that's why self-loathing strikes me every time I think about betraying that trust.

Try as I might, but I can't muster up the will to do it. I have it shoved in a drawer, gathering dust. I could have given it to her in Paris after I kissed her. Or when we came back, still in our romantic mood. I could have done it and then ended our relationship once and for all.

But no. I'm holding off on it for reasons beyond me.

You know why a voice whispers, but I ignore it.

"Did you two fight?"

I tune back into the conversation to find Kenny frowning at me. "What?"

"You and Dara? Did you fight? Is that why she's not at lunch with us?"

"No, we didn't fight," I say.

Kenny is quietly introspective for a few moments and then turns back to his food.

Then, out of the blue, he goes, "What was my Mom like?"

The question, once again, surprises me.

"I mean, I don't really remember her much," he continues. "Just flashes here and there. I think about her sometimes, though."

My first instinct is to shut down the conversation there and change the subject. As a father, I want to protect Kenny from painful truths.

But as someone who lost their mother at a young age, I can sympathize with Kenny. At least I knew my mother well, and we were very close up until her death.

Kenny's mother abandoned him. That has to be difficult to get over.

I think about how to answer the question in a way that spares his feelings.

"She was..." I don't know what to say because, try as I might, I don't remember Rachel much either. "She was beautiful. Very charismatic. And I suppose she was a nice enough woman, too."

"And so why did she leave me?" Kenny asks tentatively. "Did she just not want me anymore?"

"That's not the case," I say firmly and reach out my hand over the desk. Kenny hesitates for only a few seconds before placing his palm in mine. "She wasn't cut out to be a mother. She didn't have it in her, and so rather than have you suffer, she gave you to someone who could take care of you. And though I'm not exactly doing the best job at that, I'm trying."

"I think you're doing okay," he says simply with a smile. "And then Dara...is she going to be my mother now?"

My heart pounds.

"I like her," he says. "I don't mind if she wants me to call her Mom or whatever."

This is very bad. I never should have involved my son in this ruse.

I tried to keep them apart, but it didn't work.

His heart will be broken when she leaves, and there's nothing I can do about it.

"We'll see," I say. "Do you still want to go see museums after this?"

"No," he says. "Maybe we can just check out the art stores on the way home so I can pick up some more pencils. But I wanna go home soon. I miss Dara."

I sigh, then finally admit the truth in my heart. "Yeah, me too."

≈

I LAST FOR ANOTHER TWO DAYS.

Two days of torture, not allowing myself to so much as talk to her. Two days of awkwardness at the dinner table and stilted conversation.

Dara has caught on because she's starting to treat me with the same cool disregard that I treat her with. She's still affectionate with Kenny, but she only addresses me briefly and only out of necessity.

And even though I know I deserve her scorn, I also despise it so much.

And then, finally, I can't take it anymore.

I miss her badly.

So one day, on my way home, I detour and head to her school instead.

My mind isn't working enough to convince myself not to do it.

Maybe if I just watch her from afar, it will be enough.

Maybe I can just have one conversation, just to make sure she's okay.

Or maybe I can finally admit to the feelings tearing through my chest and admit that I fucking miss her badly and that I want to be with her.

She's Carter's sister.

She's too young and innocent for you.

But that's not enough to stop me as I turn into the near-empty parking lot.

I'm about to head out of my car when I see her.

But she's not coming out of a classroom.

Instead, she emerges from a Subaru, laughing. Another man is getting out from the other side.

It's the chef from before.

I see red.

CHAPTER 27
Dara

"You look down."

I glance up to notice Max standing right in front of me. Glancing around shows that the rest of the class has slowly filed out, leaving just me and him loitering around.

I guess I was so lost in thought that I didn't realize I was moving slower than normal as I packed up.

Max is still waiting for an answer, staring at me with that sympathetic, low-lidded gaze.

I attempt a weak smile. "Yeah, I'm fine. Just thinking."

"A penny for your thoughts?" he says with a smile. I'm sure it would have set Ashley's heart ablaze.

But tonight, I just don't have it in me to even admire it. I wish I could, if only to prove to myself that I can be attracted to someone other than that asshole.

That asshole in question being my husband.

I don't want to think about him, so I cut that thought short. Thinking about him inevitably leads to equal parts anger, sadness, and confusion.

But lately, the sadness is overpowering all the other emotions.

It has been nearly a week, and I still have no answer about what is going on with Kane and why he suddenly cut me off. The only thing I know for certain is that it's not in my head.

I guess I was warned. I should have seen this coming.

My brother's message remains unanswered on my phone.

Be careful. I'll tell you everything when the time is right. I'm sorry I wasn't there. And I love you.

It stung even more because I'm sure somewhere inside, he meant it. He did love me, but he still hurt me without a care. He still abandoned me when I needed him most.

But try as I might, I can't hate him.

He's the only family I have left.

How ironic that I'm stuck here angry at the two men I love.

Wait. I pull up on the thought.

Love?

No way.

There's no way I love Kane in that short amount of time. I just met the man, and these silly fantasies are just because I've never been wined and dined like that before.

Yeah.

"Hello?" An amused voice intrudes my thoughts. "Have I lost you again?"

"Sorry," I say and shake my head to clear it. "I guess I'm just tired. I've been doing a lot of homework lately."

"Yeah, sorry about that," he shrugs. "But it should help you reach your goal quicker."

I blink.

"You know. Starting that restaurant."

"Oh," I remember we had a conversation about that.

"Speaking of which, I heard from someone that you've been searching for a location."

I nod. "I have." I'm trying to speed up my dream, so I have something else to focus on apart from *him.*

"Well," he says. "I just so happen to know someone who has a fantastic space for pretty cheap. And I could probably get him to give you a discount on top of that. It's right on SoHo, near Oxford Street."

"Oh." It's a pretty trendy area, and a location might be perfect. "I'm definitely interested."

"Excellent," he says with a wink. "I can take you there right now if you want to see it."

"Ummm." I think about it. "Yeah, that sounds great except...um..."

I don't know how to clarify if this would count as a date or not. For some reason, I feel vaguely guilty, given his flirtatiousness, and I don't want to give off mixed signals because I'm married.

Although not really, because my marriage is a sham, and my husband is an ass.

But as luck would have it, I don't have to voice it out loud. Max gets the message without me saying it.

"Don't worry about it," he says with a wink. "I already know you're seeing someone."

"You do?"

"Yeah. Hard to miss that display your boyfriend put on the other day."

"Oh." I blush, embarrassed at the memory of the flower arrangement. Tough to think that he did all that, and then a week later, it's like nothing.

Love bombing. I'm pretty sure Lisa mentioned one of her exes did the same thing to her. I sympathize with the confusion that she felt during that time because I'm feeling the same thing now.

What is this all for?

"So," Max checks his watch. "Now that we've cleared that up, are you too busy to check it out or...?"

"Oh. Sure thing." It's Monday, which means I have a few hours before my business class. "Let's go."

The location of the store is ideal, but that's about it. It's too small to accommodate much besides a takeout or delivery system. Plus, I can hear the faint buzz of electricity echoing in the empty space, and the bulb flickers twice when I'm there.

As the daughter of an electrician, I already know that's bad news.

Not to mention the fact that it would take too much money for renovations and additions I want to make.

The owner of the space, a small, curly-haired man who spends most of the time on his phone, gets increasingly annoyed the more questions I ask. And then, by the time I tell Max that I'm not interested, he's red-faced.

Presumably, he thought I would be falling over myself to buy it. So, his shock when I walk away with Max is satisfying.

Max finds the whole thing hilarious. He chuckles to himself the entire drive back.

Still, when we make it back to school I'm grateful for the experience. At least I know a little more about what I don't want now.

"Thank you," I tell Max as I step out of his car.

"No problem," he says, grinning. "And thank you for unintentionally taking Chris down a peg for me. I don't think he expected you to be quite so picky."

I shrug as I shut the door. Perhaps, a few weeks ago, I wouldn't have been. I probably would have been impressed by the place or too intimidated to note the flaws. But now, I feel confident enough to walk into expensive locations and not feel that immediate sense that I don't belong.

I suppose I have Kane to thank for that.

He's shown me true luxury and given me unbelievably VIP experiences. So, things like this no longer intimidate me.

Max walks over to my side of the car and lays a hand on my shoulder. "How about we do this? In a few weeks, I'm going to be going on a trip to East Village. How about you come with me? They have beautiful locations up there, and I have a few people who owe me favors."

I open my mouth but don't get a chance to answer.

The heavy stamp of shoes is the only warning we get before chaos ensues.

It happens so fast. One second, I'm staring at Max, and the next, he's slamming against the car hard enough to make a dent, driven there by a fist to the face.

I scream a little and jump back, but then I'm paralyzed with shock when I recognize the man advancing on Max.

"Kane!" I exclaim, shocked, but my husband isn't looking at me.

He's staring down at Max like he wants to kill him.

Max recovers and attempts to swing back, but Kane dodges the blow easily before delivering another to the gut. Then he yanks Max back up to his feet by his jacket and whispers in the darkest voice imaginable.

"Keep your fucking hands off my wife, you bastard."

"Kane!" I finally grasp his shoulders, which feel like steel, and attempt to pull him off. "What on earth are you doing? Let him go."

"What the fuck is your problem, man?" Max snarls, trying to extract Kane's hand from his jacket.

"Stay away from her. Do you understand?" Kane says,

getting in Max's face even more. Max's eyes are spitting with anger as well, and the fight looks like it's going to escalate.

I step in between them, facing Kane. I wait until his eyes meet mine and then finally say firmly, "Let. Him. Go."

Kane's jaw clenches, and his nostrils flair. A vein throbs in his forehead, and rage exudes from every line of his body.

But I'm not scared of him. I know physically Kane won't hurt me.

My heart is another matter, though.

Without warning, Kane finally releases Max and then grabs my arms, dragging me away.

"Let me go, Kane," I say, but he doesn't listen. I have to jog lightly to keep up with his stride and I look back to see Max is following us.

Oh no. The last thing I need is another fight.

I shake my head at him, and he stops in step.

Kane stops in front of his Corvette, pulling open the door.

"Get in," he orders.

I want to defy him. I'm pissed that he thinks he can just order me around, but if we stay longer, Max might come over, and I'm trying to avoid another fight.

I bite my tongue and get in the car, crossing my arms and staring out the window as he shuts my door. I don't look at him as he enters the car and tugs my seatbelt over to buckle me in. I don't look at him as he drives off, either.

Neither of us says a word.

All we do is seethe.

The arrival at the house is quick enough, and I'm tearing open the car door, ready to run out of there and up to my room. I'm so mad I'm ready to spit, and I want to rage alone.

Unfortunately, Kane isn't about to let me do so.

The minute I get a few steps into the living room, he grabs my wrist and spins me around.

"What the fuck were you doing with that man?" His voice is not quite a yell, but it's trembling with anger. "Why were you getting out of his car?"

"Why do you care?" I spit.

"You're my wife! Of course, I care."

"Oh, now I'm your wife? Was I your wife when you ignored me for the past week?"

He runs his hand over his face. "This has nothing to do with that."

"It has everything to do with that! He's my teacher. And you're my husband who ignores me for days and then comes over and humiliates me in school! Do you have any idea how embarrassing that was? And poor Max...you just acted like an animal with him."

"Poor Max?" His eyebrows slant over his eyes. "You're on a first-name basis with that asshole."

"You're the asshole here," I tell him and then turn away. "God, I regret ever agreeing to marry you."

I try to walk away again, but he grabs me and spins me around.

This time, he doesn't talk. He kisses me instead.

The kiss is fire and fury. It's not sweet, it's bitter but drugging like aged wine. I fight it first, but his hands are around my waist, his hair in my hair holding me in place.

And desire swiftly replaces the anger.

Or at least it mixes in with it, forming a dangerous cauldron of explosive energy between us that I've never experienced.

I don't care where we are or who's watching. I don't remember what we were arguing about.

Only this need inside me that threatens to swallow me whole.

I don't know how we make it to the bedroom. One second, I'm standing, and the next second, my legs are wrapped around his waist, and he's walking.

We slam into walls on the way there, and he holds me there, kissing me like his life depends on it, groaning into my mouth.

And as he continues, every step drives his cock closer to the part that needs him the most.

And once we get into bed, there's no more patience left in us.

There's no space for gentleness here. We're both losing our minds, ripping off clothes, dragging us back for another bone-melting kiss.

His finger finds me wet and ready, and I scream my passion into the air as he quickly drives me to the peak.

I wrap my arms around his neck, and his palm goes around my neck. He fucks me hard and fast, his voice in my ears.

"You're mine," he rasps as I tremble and explode around his fingers. "Mine."

And then, when he replaces his fingers with his cock, spreading me apart slowly, his head falls against my shoulder in a surrender groan.

This time, his voice is lower as he says, "And I'm yours."

CHAPTER 28
Kane

We know it's a mistake the second it's over.

Dara recovers first, pushing at my body with mere breaths after our joint explosive orgasm. The second she does, I roll off her, and she jumps out of bed, storming out with her in disarray.

I release a breath I'm holding as I hear the door slam.

Self-loathing fills me.

I throw my arm over my face, battling with a vague sense of regret.

That was not at all how I wanted or expected any of that to go.

Everything became a red blur in my mind the second I saw her with that man. He had his hand on her shoulder, and she was smiling at him.

Even the memory of the image is still enough to spur some rage inside me.

Mostly because I realize how well they fucking fit together.

I put a hand on my chest, wondering at the vague ache in there. The torturous thoughts continue.

I'm sure if I had never come along, Dara would have ended up with a man like that. A man around her age who was nice and uncomplicated and who would give her the nice, happy life that she deserved. They would probably open up some restaurant together, and even if it were only mildly successful, it would bring them a lot of joy to work together daily.

They would wake up together every morning, and she would bake him scones and tarts. He would eat them because he likes sweets, and they're tasty. He would tell her how delicious they are while they share a sweet kiss, and then at night, he'd make her some Italian nonsense, and she would fucking love it.

Such a cozy scene shouldn't make me so enraged, but it does.

It also makes me feel strangely guilty.

I robbed her of that. With my plan and my selfishness, I robbed Dara of a life like that. Instead, she's here having mad, angry sex with me.

You can end this quickly.

Those fucking papers are damn near burning a hole in my drawer. I haven't even touched them since Warner gave them to me, but it hasn't been too far from my mind. It's been the bane of my existence.

I can solve this very easily. Once she signs those papers, I don't have to be married anymore. I can set her and myself free.

It would be the commonsense thing to do, the only choice we both have at this point.

But I still don't want to do it.

Which tells me everything I need to know.

Fuck.

I finally rise out of bed and attempt to redo the shirt she ripped open, only to note that several buttons are missing.

That nearly gets a smile out of me.

She was a wild cat today and gave every bit as good as she got. The hickey on my neck is a testament to that, and a part of me delights in having it. The sting is a sign of my link to her—a brand for everyone to see.

It's also a sobering reminder of the consequence of the animalistic lust we shared.

I wasn't as gentle with her as she deserved. It was all raw and rough, and I need to apologize to her for that. I never meant to hurt her in any way, and if I did, I wouldn't forgive myself.

At least I knew she came hard from it, but that was beside the point.

I slipped off my shirt and chose one of the cotton tees in my dresser, pulling it on. But as I leave the room, I have another thought.

My son.

Thankfully, I had enough presence of mind left to take our lovemaking to the bedroom, but hopefully, Kenny didn't hear us arguing. I didn't think we were that loud, but Kenny has always had good hearing, and I never want this to be his reality, hearing his parental figures arguing.

I remember how traumatic that was for me as a child. I loved my mother, perhaps more than my father, and hated seeing her upset. I especially hated after my father stormed off, how she would break down on the couch and just sob.

I would escape from my nannies to comfort her, but nothing I seemed to do would be enough to stop the tears.

"I'm sorry," she would say over and over. "I'm so sorry."

I feel a strange pang, the way I always do when I think of my mother. She's been dead for years, but sometimes I still miss her. Sometimes, I stare at her painting in my hallway and think about her and how things would have been if she were still alive. Would she be proud of me?

I doubt it.

I've become a copy of my father, the man she both loved and loathed at times.

And now I'm treating my wife the same way he treated her.

On my way to check up on Kenny, I stop by the painting again.

Her blonde hair falls in perfect curls around her shoulders, and her smiling eyes glitter, but there's something dead about them. My mother used to be a happy woman, but as the years passed, she became less and less so. Before her death, she was beset with a deep depression that I never quite understood.

When she died, my father took all her belongings and locked them away, and the only thing I had left was a brooch she gave me a few weeks earlier.

A brooch that Carter stole when he left. He left just days before my mother's death, and the brooch went missing on that day, too.

That was perhaps the worst thing he did to me.

With everything else, I could understand. He needed money, so he stole.

Perhaps he needed even more, so he leaked the smart TV model to our competitors.

But he did not need that brooch. He knew how much it meant to me, knew it was my mother's gift to me.

And he stole it anyway.

That felt vindictive.

And for that, I can never forgive him.

Kenny isn't in his room when I get there. I frown but note

that neither are his nannies. I immediately head downstairs to the gardens to see May lounging on a loveseat at the entrance. She notices me first and stands tentatively. "Can I help you, sir?"

"Where's Kenny?"

She points at an oak tree, and I spot him immediately, lounging back in one of the lower branches.

The grass rustles around my ankles as I approach him. "What did I say about climbing trees?"

"This one is a good one," he responds. "Dara already showed me." Without looking up from his sketchbook, he gestures to his nannies. "Plus, I came with them, so it's not like I'm going to get hurt."

"Kenny..." I can sense his tension even though he doesn't look at me. But his shoulders are stiff, and his frown deep.

He must have heard at least some of our argument when we stormed in.

"Come down for a second. I want to talk to you."

He hesitates and then closes his sketchpad, jumping off the top and landing nimbly on the ground.

"What's up?" he asks as he avoids my gaze.

"I'm sorry," I say, and he finally meets my eyes, anger and surprise warring in his gaze. "You heard us arguing, didn't you?"

He shrugs. "Adults argue all the time."

"Yes, but we shouldn't have done it so loudly. And not with you at home. It was my fault."

"Yeah, I know that," he says with an eye roll. "You picked a fight with her. You were jealous of some guy, weren't you?"

I sigh. He *heard far more than I would like*. And now I'm being given the disappointed look by my ten-year-old. "Yes, I was. It was unreasonable of me and very childish."

"She likes you, Dad, but I'm not sure she's going to keep

liking you if you yell at her and act mean to her all the time. Eventually, she's going to get sick of it."

I nod. "You're right. Once again, I apologize."

He peers up at me and then shrugs. "It's fine. I get it. Sometimes, when you like someone, you get jealous when they hang out with other people. But you really shouldn't be jealous of Dara. She loves you, Dad."

I smirk at my son. He's far more mature than a kid his age should be.

I ruffle his hair. "I'll keep that in mind."

After I visit Kenny, my next stop is to go check on Dara.

I knock on her door after, readying myself for a fight and fully expecting her to tell me to get lost.

But instead, she says, "Come in."

I open the door, unsure what I'll find.

I wouldn't be surprised if she was packing her things to leave.

Instead, she's sitting on her patio in a robe and staring out into the garden.

She doesn't spare me a glance as I approach her. Her expression is cold, but there's a hint of hurt behind the cold distance.

"I'm sorry," I say.

She glances at me. "For what?"

"For...everything." I have too much to apologize for, even things that I'm yet to do.

A bitter smile curls her lips, and she turns away. "I think, for Kenny's sake, we probably shouldn't fight like that again. It's important that we cooperate successfully however long this arrangement lasts."

"I agree," I tell her, touched that she would think of Kenny rather than herself.

She cares about him. Another thing that's my fault.

"And we also shouldn't sleep together anymore." Her voice is flat when she says it. "It's not good for either of us, and it's setting up an unhealthy dynamic."

I agree with that as well. But for some reason, I can't say the words.

Even though I know what she's saying is true, it's a hard pill to swallow.

It's hard because I still want her so badly, and not just the sex. I want our conversations. I want to hold her hand again.

I want to cuddle and laugh with her, smell her after we have sex, and talk about a whole lot of things that don't matter.

I want to see her eyes smiling at me again.

But I don't deserve any of that, not after what I've done.

What I'm going to do.

"That's for the best." The words feel like gravel coming out. "But I wanted to make sure you're okay and that I didn't hurt you."

"I'm fine," she says shortly. "You didn't hurt me."

I watch her for longer until she starts to get visibly uncomfortable under my regard.

And then she twists to face me again, "Are we done?"

"Are we okay?"

It's a weak question because I already know the answer to it.

She stares at me and gives me a smile that doesn't reach her eyes. "We're okay."

I don't sleep well while the night is tormented with thoughts of that smile. Tormented with guilt for everything I was doing wrong.

So it's only fair that the next morning begins with the world imploding on me.

I wake up to the phone ringing incessantly. When I open

my eyes, it's still dark outside, but I reach over and grab it from my stand anyway.

"What?"

"We have a problem, sir," Melissa's voice is panicked. "A very big problem."

"What is it?"

"Someone leaked our financial documents. Our stocks are crashing."

CHAPTER 29
Dara

After Kane leaves, I let out a breath.

I don't cry, which is a good thing at least. I don't think I have tears left inside me, and I refuse to waste them on him and a situation like this.

It's all so stupid.

Here I am, hurt and stressing out over a marriage that's ultimately going to end in less than a year anyway.

And Kane, displaying jealousy when we don't owe loyalty to each other is *hilarious*. Even though I wasn't doing anything wrong with Max, it wouldn't matter even if I was just as Kane was free to start a relationship with Anastasia if he wanted to.

Kane and I mean *nothing* to each other.

And the fact that we were both jealous of each other's opposite-sex friendships didn't imply that we had feelings for each other.

And even if we did, it doesn't change much.

We were still very wrong for each other, and that wouldn't change no matter what.

So, the only thing I can do is accept my current situation. It isn't bad, all things considered.

I'm getting two million dollars for doing virtually little work, not to mention, I've been able to help a lot of people out in the meantime. Just recently, I secretly cleared out Lisa's loans—going through a proxy loan forgiveness non-profit—and saw the way her eyes lit up when she told me all about it. I'm trying to figure out how to do the same for her brothers without raising suspicion.

Not to mention the other charities I've been able to help.

I can do so much good with the money and comfort Kane provides.

And it has been worth every tear I've shed.

There's a tentative knock on the door.

It's not Kane, I know that for sure. Kane knocks with confidence as he does everything else, even when he's about to apologize. I assume it's Sophia or someone else coming to check in on me, so I say, "Come in."

But when the door pushes open, it's none other than Kenny who's standing there.

"Ken Ken." I beckon the boy closer as a smile spreads across my face, a little shred of happiness spurred by his appearance. He walks closer to me, his gaze slightly guarded.

When he gets close enough, he surprises me by taking my hand in his.

"Are you okay?" he asks as he shuffles his feet. "I heard you and Dad arguing."

Regret lines my nerves. Oh God. I thought he would be in his room. "You heard that?"

He nods and I draw him closer into a hug. He hugs me back without hesitation this time.

"I'm sorry, baby. I didn't know you heard. Your Dad and I

fought, but it's settled now. He actually just came here, and we apologized to each other."

Kenny nods into my shoulder.

"Dad's really bad at apologies," he says, the sound muffled against my shirt. "He gets really awkward with them."

"That's true." I smile. "But I accepted his apology and made one of my own. And now I'm offering you an apology. We shouldn't have argued, and I'm so sorry."

Kenny finally drops his hands, and I release him from the hug.

He avoids my eyes for a little bit after we do, and he is probably feeling awkward now.

"I know my Dad can be difficult sometimes," he starts. "And he's bad at talking about his feelings, and he's bossy and thinks he knows everything all the time."

"He's not so bad," I say, smiling. "He's just...him."

Kenny winces. "Yeah. But he's getting better, trust me. You just have to be a little patient with him. Okay?"

I give Kenny a bemused look. "Are you giving me relationship advice about your Dad?"

He blushes and shakes his head. "I guess, even though it's kinda gross. I'm just saying...he's a lot better when he's with you. And I know that he really, *really* likes you. So, I think for this to last, you gotta be patient with him."

And then suddenly, it hits me.

Kenny is actually rooting for this relationship to work out.

We've formed a pseudo-kind of family here, and he likes it.

It's going to break his heart when this all ends.

Oh God.

Guilt spirals through me. I didn't even think that far of

259

what it would do to him when I eventually have to leave. I don't know if Kane will let me continue my relationship with Kenny, but I doubt it.

And even if we do, it won't be the same.

Kenny is going to be hurt.

I want to tell him the truth now, to stop the pretense, but I can't say it. How on earth do I explain to a little boy that my relationship with his father is nothing more than a contract I have to fulfill?

It's so fucked up to even talk about.

And Kenny is going to become collateral damage in this ruse of ours.

Now I understand why Kane tried to establish that distance between us. He was right to do it.

I sigh and draw Kenny into another hug. I hold him tight. At least for now, I want to show him how much I love and appreciate his company.

"You're an amazing kid, Ken Ken," I say. "And I love you very much. Never forget that."

Kenny hesitates. "Why are you telling me this now?"

Because I want you to remember it when I'm no longer here.

"Because I need you to know it."

～

IT'S NOT EASY GETTING INTO CONTACT WITH KANE'S father. I can't exactly ask Kane for his number, and I have a feeling that it's going to be difficult to ask Pope, too.

His information is not readily available online either. Very little is known about the personal life of the elusive billionaire Samson Leon.

I'm left cracking my head, trying to think of a way to set up a meeting with him.

But in the end, it's all for nothing.

Because the mountain comes to me instead.

The next day, I was on my way out to meet up with Lisa when I noticed an Escalade parked outside my home. It's black, but unlike Kane's, it has a cream interior.

"Is someone here?" I ask Anna, who is turning the corner, seemingly returning from the garden with a basket full of cherries.

She glances at the car and visibly stiffens.

"Master Samson is here," she says, a grim look on her face. Before I can ask more, she hurries inside.

I head inside, too. I suppose he's probably here to meet with Kane, but Kane has been out since yesterday. But this is the perfect opportunity for me to talk to the man.

I find him halfway down Kane's hallway, staring at the painting with the woman on it.

"Um..." I cough a little awkwardly, and he turns to look at me.

"You again," he says and smiles. I can't help but smile back at his welcoming expression.

It once again strikes me that he doesn't look like a man with less than a year to live. My Dad, deep in the throes of his disease, had lost so much weight he was almost skeletal.

This man, while slender, looks healthy.

Then again, he's probably rich enough to afford an end-of-life care that I could only dream of.

"It's nice to see you again, dear," he says as he walks closer, his cane echoing on the ground.

"It's nice to see you too," I say, then suddenly feel awkward. He's the CEO of a multibillion-dollar company, after all, and Kane's father.

And now I'm going to ask him questions about Kane. "I wanted to talk to you if you have time. If you don't mind, that is."

"For you, darling? I can make time." He gestures. "Come. We'll talk on the patio, and you will tell me what's on your mind. Hopefully, the boy is not there."

The boy? Does he mean Kenny?

I don't know what his relationship is with Kenny. Kenny never talks about his grandfather. It just strikes me how odd that is.

Does Samson not like Kenny?

It would be impossible for me to like the man if he didn't.

The thought niggles at the back of my mind as we settle at the table overlooking the gardens. The minute we sit, Faith appears from seemingly nowhere with her shoulders hunched and her hands folded in front of her.

She avoids my eyes and gives an unusual amount of deference as she says, "Welcome, sir, madam. May I get you some coffee?"

"Um..." I'm taken aback by her tone. Faith isn't usually this formal with me, and she looks damn near terrified of Samson.

He flicks his hand casually. "Nothing, dear. I'm not in the mood for coffee."

"Um, I'm fine too. Thanks, Faith."

She nods but still doesn't look at me when she leaves.

Samson looks after her with distaste and says, "It's good that the servants haven't forgotten their training. Kane usually lets them get away with their bad behavior."

"What?" I blink in surprise.

He smiles, humor in his eyes.

"In America, they call it classism when servants know their place," he says. "But that's just the way the world works. In certain countries, they can't even look at our faces."

I nearly gape at the man but then remember that this is the man who raised Kane.

Now it makes sense why he's how he is.

I want to retort but remind myself that I'm not here to give the man a lesson about egalitarianism. It's not my place to, and I don't want to accidentally get Faith in trouble.

I swallow and get straight to the point. "I wanted to ask you about Kane. And my brother."

He nods as though he expected it.

"Kane said they were friends."

Samson gives me a sardonic look and chuckles. "Friends? That's not the word for it. Can there really be friendship between two people as different as them?"

I shake my head. "I don't understand."

"Your brother came to me when he turned eighteen. At that point, he had dropped out of high school months prior and was looking for work. Your parents and I had been close friends in the past, and I suppose your mother probably told him about me." He smiles. "You look so much like her, by the way."

"Wait?" I cock my head. "You knew my parents?"

"Yes. I would say I invested in a few of your Dad's business ventures. Though they were unsuccessful, we remained friends. I also got him a lawyer during his trial."

"His trial?" I knew that my Dad had served some jail time before becoming an electrician, but I never knew the details. It happened before I was born, and he never spoke about it; he only mentioned it briefly.

Samson doesn't go into it either.

"He had too much pride to ask me for any more help even after he got out of jail," Samson continues. "I suppose he was embarrassed, but I didn't care. I would still have helped him get back on his feet, but he insisted on doing it without me. Anyway, his son eventually came looking for me. Bright, hardworking, ambitious man. I saw a lot of myself in him." Samson smiles wistfully. "He became my understudy. He lived with us, and I groomed him for a role at my company. That's how he met Kane. But a friendship..." He shakes his head. "I don't know if I would call it that."

"Why not?" My heart is racing now. Part of me is scared of the truth.

Scared of finding out that truly everything I know about Kane is a lie.

"My son is a lot like me," Samson says. "I raised him that way. And in some ways, he's worse. While I can recognize the humanity of the working class, he can't. Kane always saw Carter as inferior, sort of like a pet. An errand boy. Someone he could use to amuse himself, but when it came down to it, Kane never saw them as equals. They could never be friends." He laces his fingers together and leans forward. "And so, once Kane saw that I was getting closer to your brother, his entitlement kicked in."

"What?"

"Carter was a very intelligent man, far more than Kane was. He was doing everything he could to help his family and had been from a young age. On the contrary, Kane was spoiled and wanted everything to be spoon-fed to him. At a point, I worried about how the company would fare under just Kane. I considered adding Carter to the will, giving him some of my shares."

My eyes widen. "You did?"

Samson shrugs casually in a move that reminds me of Kenny. "Your father helped me a lot in the past. It was the least I could do. Since he refused to accept my money, I thought perhaps his son would accept it on his behalf."

My head is spinning. There's so much I'm finding out. "And?"

"And Kane found out. He was furious. He threw a tantrum and drove Carter away, told him never to come back."

I swallow and shake my head. "That doesn't sound like Kane."

"You think so?" Samson cocks his head. "There's a lot you don't know about my son."

There's a lump in my throat. I open my mouth but can't say anything to deny the knowing in his eyes.

"What did Kane tell you to convince you to marry him?" he suddenly says. "Did he tell you that I was going to put you in my will, give the shares that I meant for your brother to you?"

My mouth falls open.

The statement completely floors me.

Samson nods. "I told him I would. And then the next thing I know, he marries you."

"What does that have to do with anything?"

Samson shakes his head, a little like he's disappointed in me. Then he pulls out his phone from his pocket, presses a few buttons, and turns it to me. "These are pictures of documents I found in Kane's dresser. Send this to your lawyer and find out what it says. Then you will truly understand the evil that is my son."

CHAPTER 30
Kane

After Melissa's announcement that morning, I head straight to the office. She explained what she could do to me on the phone as I drove, but what she knew wasn't a lot.

The second I arrived, I headed to the finance department, where the CFO could tell me what I needed to know.

"Give me the update," I say the second I storm into his large, conference-style office. About a dozen people are milling about, and they all stop when I enter and blink at me.

Ian Chan, my CFO, immediately rises to his feet.

"They got their hands on our financial dockets," he says, straight to the point how I like it. "And they're claiming that we've been manipulating our stock market prices for years now."

"Bullshit," I claim.

"I would say the same until I saw this." He hands me a folder and docket. "We're being audited, but so far, it seems that everything they claimed is true."

I briefly scan through the document he just gave me, my tension rising with every word.

It truly looks bad.

A lot of switching hands and arbitrary buying and selling. Insider trading.

And it's a lot of it, so much so that only the major shareholders would have the power to pull off something like this.

Including and possibly directed by my father.

The reason why is obvious. Leon stocks had been sinking for years and would have fallen even more if they knew how close to the red we were.

I understand why they did this, even though I disagree with their methods.

What pisses me off is that they were so careless with it to get caught.

"Who approved this audit?" I ask Ian. To his credit, he doesn't avoid my gaze.

"I had no choice," Ian says. "The press were eating us alive, and apparently, the information was leaked to the authorities anyway."

I brush my hand over my face and feel the frustration biting at me. I'm no stranger to handling crises at Leon. But I hate it when I'm blindsided by them.

"Find out where the leak came from," I say. "I don't care what you have to do to get it. I need someone's neck on the chopping block by the end of the day…Today! Understood?"

"Yes."

The rest of the day is spent putting out several fires. The first thing we do is to release a statement alerting the public that an investigation is underway and that we're getting to the bottom of it quickly. Of course, that does very little to appease our core stakeholders, who are all threatening to sell.

I have a private conversation with each of them, promising them that we have everything under control. That seems to be enough to keep their hands steady in the meantime.

But that doesn't entirely stop the bleeding.

By the time night falls, we're all still in the office, and I guarantee everyone will be here at daybreak, too. Luckily, the funds from Anastasia's father cleared.

Percy, Nathan, and the marketing department are all preparing to announce the new X3.

Percy wants us to do it by the end of the week.

"We can do it now, at the height of our controversy," he says with a shrug. "It's easy marketing."

I cock my eyebrow. "You think it's good to market off this kind of controversy?"

"Perhaps. As they say, all publicity is good publicity."

I'm not so sure about it, but I do agree to prepping an announcement of the new phone by the end of the week.

I also wait to hear news from Sam, the PI I hired, about finding Dara and investigating the mole. I told him the situation and ordered him to find out who had leaked our financial documents.

He doesn't have any news for me until the next day.

"You know, you're going to need to increase my pay for all these hours I'm putting in for you," he says wryly when I answer the phone.

"You can have whatever you want," I say. "Now, do you have something for me?"

"Yes. Mostly because the information I have for you already coincided with the separate investigation I was doing for you about the mole who leaked the phone information."

So, the mole is the same person. Excellent. "And?"

"The leaked X3 designs passed through a few hands before it reached your competitors. It was cloaked using dummy PO boxes and mailing addresses. But it was actually held in a private storage center for some time. When I went there and looked through their records, the last person to hand in the document was Taylor Pierson, the roommate of a Josh Tyson. You know who that is?"

"Yes." The name sounds very familiar. "It's my Dad's former PA."

"Yup."

I can imagine what happened. My father fired Tyson months ago, and this is probably his way of getting back at him and the company.

But the fact that he was able to get so much information and do this much damage meant he had help.

But all that would come sooner.

"And you should probably know that the so-called Josh Tyson also bought a ticket for Fiji out of O'Hare. His flight leaves tonight in two hours."

"Oh no, the fuck he won't," I say and hang up. My next call is to the Governor of Chicago. He answers on the third ring.

"If this is about the golf tournament, I'm not giving you a break just because you're having a bad day," he says.

"This isn't about that. I need you to have a man detained at the airport. His name is Josh Tyson. He's flying out of O'Hare in a few hours."

There's silence on the other end of the line for seconds as the governor swallows the information.

"Is there a reason you're going to give me that will allow me to bypass his constitutional rights?" he asks quietly.

"Corporate espionage."

"Okay, that will do it."

As he gets it ready, I call Sam back, and he gives me everything he has on Josh Tyson.

Much later, I'm at the airport, heading to the security post.

It's relatively crowded, but the crowd parts for me as I walk, like Moses through the Red Sea. Probably a good thing.

The way I'm feeling, I'm liable to take someone's head off.

The security post is at the corner of the sixth gate. When I get there, I see Josh Tyson sitting with his head lowered, surrounded by three TSA agents.

He glances up, and his eyes go wide for a second before he looks away.

"Oh, don't do that now," I say as I approach him and squat. "Be bold. Don't be a coward after your spectacular betrayal."

"I betrayed no one," he says, lips pressed together defensively.

"Did you not?" I say. "Tell me who it was then. Who did you do this for? Because we saw the money in your account, and it doesn't make sense for someone unemployed to casually withdraw three million dollars from his account."

Josh's lips press together. He says nothing.

"Alright. Since you won't tell me, perhaps your sister will."

His head snaps to me. His eyes widen in horror. I give him a humorless smile.

"Here's what's going to happen. You're going to be punished anyway for what you did. But what you do next determines how far that punishment extends. Because it could end with you...or it could extend to the rest of your family. Your sister. She wants to be an actress, correct? How would you feel if she never ever got a role in her life? If your brother got kicked out of his little prep school and if your father got fired and could never find a job in the government ever again." I smile at him. "I can make all that happen very easily."

Fear and loathing battle in Josh's expression. "You're a monster."

"Correct," I say easily. "A monster you never should have fucked with."

He battles with himself, his eyes widening in shock that he's been caught this easily, trapped like a rat. I can see the information at the tip of his tongue, but he fights to swallow it down.

But then, he finally tells me what he knows.

And it's my turn to be in shock.

～

MY FATHER IS IN MY OFFICE WHEN I GET BACK, PRESUMABLY waiting for me.

He's relaxed against the sectional, without a care in the world. I'm sure one of his spies alerted him that Josh had been caught, and he knew I would get the truth out of Josh.

So, he's here to mitigate the damage. Or to gloat. I never know which it's going to be with him.

"Do you want to explain yourself?" I ask, closing the door behind me.

"Do I have to?" he responds.

My anger threatens to explode, but I suppress it. I can't lose this game now. Not when I'm so close.

"You sabotaged my company," I say. "Our company. The one we've worked so hard for. You made Josh leak that information to the press and the new cell phone designs too."

He doesn't deny or admit it. He simply shrugs.

"Why?" I grit it out, heat spearing through every bone in my body.

He smiles. "Did you really think I was going to let you have all this?" He gestures around the room.

I hate this. I hate how he thinks everything is a joke.

How it reduces me to a desperate child again, begging for his approval.

"You've done well so far," he says. "But you, as always, have been far too greedy. Wanting what's not yours." He cocks his head. "None of this is yours, Kane. Because you're not and never will be my real son."

Heat shoots through my body, and pain arcs through my chest.

Yet, the announcement doesn't shock me. I've long since wondered about my lack of resemblance to either my mother or my father.

The way my father sometimes treated me, like he loathed me. He only gave me affection on the few occasions I achieved something.

So, I assumed it wouldn't matter if I was his biological son or not if I worked hard enough and if I could earn Leon's name.

"Who is your real son then?" I smile, a monstrous smile spreading my lips. "It's Carter. Isn't it?"

"No," he smirks. "But Carter is closer to me than you will ever be."

CHAPTER 31
Dara

I tear into Kane's bedroom, searching around wildly. Breaths escape me in horrified, panicked little pants.

Where is it? Where did Kane keep those documents?

The drawer. That was where Samson said he saw it.

Ever since he left, his words have been ringing in my ears like a cursed mantra. A warning that I should have heeded long ago.

Send this to your lawyer and find out what it says. Then you will truly understand the evil that is my son.

My heart thumps in dread.

What could the contract possibly say that's so bad? I already sent the photo of the documents to Lisa's brother, Logan, but I couldn't sit around waiting for him to review them. I wanted to see for myself if it was true. If the papers were in Kane's dresser.

My mind is splintering from the thought alone.

As I approach the bedside dresser, I take a second to drink in Kane's decor. It's exactly what I would expect from him: a lot of blacks and grays and spartan decorations.

In most ways, the room is similar to mine, with the stone etching on the walls and the large Moroccan rug on the floor. But it's bigger, and his patio doesn't overlook the garden.

Instead, it gives him sight of the vast forest and a hint of the glittering lights of the city in the distance.

Over there, he can stand and imagine he's the king of the world.

It's occurring to me that this is the first time I've been in his bedroom. Every other time we had sex, it was always in my bedroom, in my wing.

Probably because it makes it easier for him to keep things separated and not get attached. Like I'm just his lover rather than his wife.

Also, so he doesn't have to worry about me snooping around his space.

I do so now. I tear open the dressers by his bed and ruffle through the properties, uncaring that he'll know I've been here. I immediately found the document wrapped in a brown folder and sandwiched between two leatherbound notebooks. I retrieve the folder and open it, skim over the title POST NUPTIAL AGREEMENT, and try to make sense of what it's saying.

As I read, I recall the end of my conversation with Kane's father.

"He said you were sick," I remember whispering to Samson. "That's why he wanted to marry me so quickly. Because it was your dying wish."

Samson smiled indulgently and then let out a little chuckle. "That's ludicrous. Now, I know my son despises me, but I never thought he would be trying to kill me off so easily." He shook his head. "I'm not sick. I'm a picture of excellent health, as a matter of fact. Kane likely only said that to prey on your soft heart because he knew it would make it easier for him to manipulate you once you fell for his sob story."

That statement shot through my heart, sharp and painful.

But I had to accept what he was saying.

All of a sudden, things started making sense. That was why he never ended up taking me to his Dad for dinner. He never even introduced us.

Did he plan on keeping us apart for the rest of this marriage? Because he knew Samson would tell me the truth?

Was Samson telling me the truth now?

I flip through the document. Samson has to be telling the truth. He has no reason to lie or even plant the document here.

Besides, the day before we left for Paris, I recall Warner coming over to meet with Kane briefly. He was holding this folder. I assumed it was something business-related, so I didn't pay attention or even talk to him much besides offering a brief hello.

But then I also recall the side look he gave me as he went into Kane's study, an almost pitying expression.

Now, I finally understand what the look was about.

I sink to the floor by the bed as my heart threatens to beat out of my chest. The ringing of the phone pierces the atmosphere, but it takes a few seconds for it to penetrate my despairing thoughts.

I bring it up to my ears.

"Dara? Are you there?"

"Yeah, Logan," I say, clearing my suddenly hoarse voice. "Did you read it?"

"Yeah. Sorry, it took so long, but I also sent it to a friend who specializes in family law and told him to do a stat read because you said you needed it urgently. But essentially, he said the same thing I had already thought."

"Which is?"

Logan sighs. "The contract is written in overly confusing language, and there are a lot of things hidden in the fine print. But essentially, it's not so much a post-nuptial agreement as it is the transfer of inheritance."

"What?"

"Yes. Person A is transferring their inheritance to Person B. That's the gist of it. It also gives certain powers of attorney to Person B and a few other details that we'd need more time to properly dissect."

A gasp flies out of my mouth.

It's like a punch in the chest, the painful explosion of energy inside me.

It cracks my heart into two.

Samson was right.

I just realized at this moment that I was hoping he would be wrong. Despite everything, I still held out stupid hope that Kane isn't who they say he is.

My mind works fast, putting the pieces together. *So that's what all this was about.*

Not about a dying father.

Not about my brother or looking out for me.

This marriage has always been about gaining access to...no, stealing the shares of the company that Samson was going to transfer to me.

Kane married me to do it. All his romance, his affection, heck, probably even his sleeping with me, was just to earn my trust, so I wouldn't question it.

So, I would sign the documents without even thinking twice.

And then he would have discarded me.

A sob tears out of my chest then, and I slap my hand over my mouth to subdue it. The heartbreak pierces, sharp and painful, and now I finally understand what my brother meant.

Be careful of Kane.

"Are you okay?" Logan asks, his voice suddenly concerned.

"Um, yeah," I say, trying to hide my despair as much as possible.

I need to leave. The next thing in my mind is escape. I need to get out of here before Kane returns, and somehow, he convinces me that this is all a dream. I only need to trust him and not what I've just discovered.

"I'll talk to you later, Logan," I choke the words out as I rise off the floor.

"Umm…okay, sure," he says, sounding uncertain. "Tell me if you need anything else."

"Yes. And thank you." I hang up before he can answer because I feel like I'm about to start crying. But I move even as the tears flow down my cheeks, walking determinedly to my room.

I need to leave now. I can feel the weakness inside me that still wants to remain and wants to give him a chance to explain himself.

"He's a master at manipulation," I whisper to myself. "If you stay, he'll manage to twist everything around and convince you to disbelieve your own eyes and your own instinct."

I need to leave.

Luckily, I don't run into anyone on the way back to my room. I don't think I could deal with anyone questioning my current emotional state right now.

Once I get there, I grab a large shopping bag that I got at the grocery store and start packing. I only pack everything that I came here with. Clothes. My parent's treasure box. I don't like any of the gifts Kane bought me.

It would feel too much like I was taking a piece of him.

I want nothing of him.

Even though, inevitably, pieces of him will remain imprinted in my heart

"Are you going on a trip?"

I spin around and see Kenny standing at my doorway, eyeing me curiously.

"Kenny."

"Were you crying?" he says, walking forward and then frowns sternly. "Don't tell me you fought with Dad again. What did he do this time?"

I shake my head, but I can't form words to voice my denial. "I have to go, Kenny."

"Where are you going?"

I don't know yet, but then the answer comes out anyway. "To my friend Lisa's place. I need to go stay with her for a few days."

"When will you come back?"

Once again, the words escape me. I don't want to lie to him, but I can't tell him the truth.

Nevertheless, a heartbreaking realization dawns in his eyes as he says quietly, "You're not coming back, are you?"

The pain in my chest magnifies at the reflected hurt in his eyes. Hurting Kenny is like stabbing myself in the heart.

Now, we're both torn open and bleeding once more.

I swallow my sob as I walk to him and hug him tightly. He's stiff for a few seconds, and then his own hands wrap around my waist like a vice.

"I'll come with you," he says, the words muffled against my stomach.

"You can't," I say."You have to stay here with your Dad."

He shakes his head. "No. I hate him. He drives away everyone."

"Don't say that." I squat and take his precious face in my hands, forcing his suddenly teary eyes to mine. "Your Dad and I...we could never work. But I know he loves you, and I love you too, and we both want you to be happy."

"Then why are you leaving?" The words carry accusation, and I accept it. I share some blame for this whole fiasco. I kiss Kenny on the cheeks, tasting my tears and his.

"I love you, Kenny," I whisper and hug him again. This time, his arms go around my neck, and I feel the wetness of his tears on it, too.

"Will I ever see you again?"

God, I hope so.

"Yes," I answer. I'll figure out a way, maybe a deal with Kane, so that I can see Kenny again. "I'll come see you soon, alright?"

When I pull back once more, Kenny reluctantly nods, looking so miserable that I almost change my mind.

Especially when he asks for a third time, "But why can't you stay?"

I muster up all the willpower I can to shake my head. "I just can't." That I know for sure. If I stay here, I'm going to lose myself.

Somehow, I manage to extract myself from the hug and pick up the shopping bag, hoisting it over my shoulders.

Then I ruffle his hair one last time and walk away from Kenny, feeling his eyes on my back.

Never have I felt the distance of a few dozen steps so heavily as I do now. Never has existence felt so damn heart-breaking.

I also managed to make it back out through the gates and up the street without anyone else stopping me. Anna does spot me leaving but I pretend everything is normal and tell her that I'm taking a few clothes to a friend.

I hate that I won't get to say goodbye to all the friends I've made here, but I can't risk any of them questioning me or telling Kane where I'm going. I don't want to get them in trouble, too, because once Kane finds out that I left and no one stopped me, he's going to be furious.

So I scurried out of the gates and to the top of the road before I called an Uber to take me to Lisa's place.

Luckily, it's one of her days off, and she opens the door a few seconds after I knock.

"Dara?" Her puzzled look has it all going.

And just like that, I burst into loud sobs.

"Dara." She's shocked for a few seconds and then draws me into a hug, and her hands rub my back up and down. "Okay, you're scaring me. What's going on?"

I shake my head. I can't talk yet until I let all the pain out. Over her shoulder, I see her Dad in an apron and her brothers playing video games on the couch. They all turned to watch me with puzzled expressions.

"I had to leave," is all I can choke out.

Her eyes become firm, and she nods. "Come in. Tell me everything."

I nod miserably.

Lisa takes my hand and leads me to her room, shutting the door. And then I sit on her bed, and the entire sordid tale comes flowing out in between bouts of sobbing.

I tell her about Samson's visit and everything I discovered. I also tell her how painful it was to leave Kenny behind.

By the time I'm done, she shakes her head.

"I knew it," she says. "I knew something stunk about this."

"Lisa." But before I can continue I hear commotion outside. And then I glance out her window and gasp.

There's a man outside in the driveway, facing off against Lisa's large brothers.

It's Kane.

CHAPTER 32
Kane

My Dad says nothing for several seconds.

I don't break the silence even as the rage pulses within me, like a growing darkness that has been seething for the past hour.

I've been furious since I found out that my father was the one who ordered Josh to do what he did.

The wrath is truly alive in me, clenching my hands into fists, tightening the air in my chest.

I want to scream at him. I want to curse him.

But I suppress the urge, reminding myself that I left the tantrums behind me years ago. I'm not a child anymore.

And no matter how furious I am, I know Samson doesn't care.

On the contrary, he enjoys seeing my rage. I won't give him the satisfaction this time.

Vaguely, I wonder if my father is suffering a psychotic break. He could have put everything we worked for in jeopardy, our entire company. Why the fuck would he do this? Merely to teach me a lesson? To hurt me?

That was what his last comment about Carter was about. It's also why he suddenly announced that I'm not his blood.

All his words are targeted specifically to piss me off, to get me to lose it.

Why?

I have no clue if it's even true or not, but in the wake of everything he's done, I find I no longer care.

"What did I do this time?" I ask, leaning against the wall and crossing my arms. My voice is steady but commanding, heated but restrained. "What offense did I commit that was bad enough for you to risk sinking your company just to punish me?"

Samson smiles humorlessly. It's the same smile he gave me whenever he doled out his sick punishments. As a child, when I would do something my father didn't like, he wouldn't mention it. He wouldn't scold me or even give any indication that he was upset.

But he would always make me pay in far crueler ways.

He would take away whatever I loved most at that moment.

He has destroyed many of my friendships, going as far as to ruin their families to do it. As a teenager, he once locked me in my room the night before my ski competition, knowing how much my team relied on me.

And the worst was when he kept me away from my mother in her final moments.

But he has never gone this far before. Never has he hurt himself just to hurt me.

I wonder why he didn't just throw my stock holdings in jeopardy. He has done it before and also nearly jeopardized my friendship with Anastasia by fucking up her father's stocks too.

That was because of Carter.

Everything he has done thus far has also been about punishing me for letting Carter take advantage of my friendship to gain access to company files and steal from us. He blamed me for letting Carter get away, and he was still making me pay the price of that.

I thought I would eventually win his trust back once he was done making me atone for my sins.

I thought when I took Leon Inc. to the top once more, I would prove that, despite my mistakes, I was worthy of being his son.

But now, as I look into my father's eyes, I note something that I didn't let myself see before.

I notice the madness gleaming in their depths.

And I wonder for a moment if my father is truly insane.

Samson stands and takes slow, measured strides to stare out the window overlooking Lake Michigan. "You know, when your mother wanted to adopt you, I never said a word against it."

I cross my hands over my chest, steeling myself as another round of shock hits me. So it's the truth. I was adopted.

But why is he telling me this now?

Is he throwing me off or simply trying to hurt me for whatever offense I'm still not sure I've committed?

"I didn't want some *vermin* having the Leon name," he continues. "Someone that had been abandoned in foster care like nothing. A Leon can never come from such a place. But your mother insisted. She couldn't have children of her own, and rather than permit me to get a child another way, she suggested adoption. So I took her to the most rundown center in Chicago I could find. I thought that once she saw how dirty and unfit the place was, she would change her mind." He shakes his head. "But then they brought you out. She took one look at you and fell in love with you. Your mother had died in childbirth, and your father didn't want you. My wife felt sorry for you. And I had to play along with all of that because I loved her. She was threatening to leave me, and this was the only way I could think of to make her stay. So I agreed to take you home. But I should have known better."

He turns to me grimly. "And before you think I'm heartless, know that I tried to see you as my own. I really did. But you didn't help matters. Some days, I would look at you and still see that impure blood of yours, and it would irritate me. I tried to raise you with as much class as possible, but you continuously befriended other vermin and shirked all your lessons on social castes. All my efforts were for nothing. Because you could never be what you're not."

He pivots his entire body now, his eyes hard and cold. "You've never been a Leon. This company has never been yours."

I bite my lips and smile at him, trying not to let the pain show. The words dash around in my head, frustration bludgeoning me.

But then there is a cruel kind of humor in this. All this time, I thought I was working hard to regain his trust and his affection when it was never there in the first place.

There was nothing I could ever do to make this man like me. Nothing.

All this was for nothing.

I can't say that I wasn't warned. James Coleman warned me, and so did my mother at times.

Forget about your father's approval, she would say. *You don't need him. Just be happy, alright? You just need to follow your heart and do what makes you happy.*

But instead, I did the exact opposite. I worked myself to

death for him, tossing aside morals and decency to feed his bottom line.

I sold my soul for a man who never cared about it.

Like a lit match, the dark anger flares up within me, and in that moment, I hate this man with every fiber of my being.

But just as quickly as it appears, the feeling disappears, leaving me hollow.

I stare at my father now and feel the anger melt off of me. With it goes the sense of responsibility that I held my entire life to uphold the LEON name. There was never anything I could have done.

But strangely, there's no feeling of loss to replace it, no more words to say. In fact, it's almost freeing.

I realize that for the longest time, what I've felt toward my father has not been love. It has been my duty.

Bonded by the Leon name. By our shared love for my mother. By the fact that he's my father.

Because I felt the duty to make the Leon name proud.

But stripped of all of that, what am I? What do I have? *Who* do I have?

Dara.

Her name whispers like a voice in my mind, like a balm to my wounded soul. It settles inside me, evoking a nearly crazed kind of joy that makes me want to burst out into peals of laughter.

For so long, I've fought it. I fought what she made me feel because I felt like by accepting that I loved her, I was betraying my company and the Leon name.

But I love her.

My entire life has been a simulation, but my love for her and Kenny is the only real thing that I have left. Spending time with the two of them has been the only thing I've looked forward to lately, the only thing that has kept me sane.

My duty is now to her and to my son.

All my reservations about being without Dara instantly rip and fall away like cobwebs from my mind. The chains are now unable to keep me tethered, and I feel lighter.

It's true that I don't deserve her.

Also true that she's too good for me.

But what if I become better? What if I become the kind of man who deserves her?

Our relationship began on a lie, but I can start setting things right by finally telling her the truth. And even if she rejects me, I'll find a way to win her back.

I'll give everything I have to keep her.

And so what if I'm too old for her? If she wants me, then I'll count myself the luckiest man in the world.

Fuck Samson Leon. Fuck everything he stands for.

Even if I have to give up everything, I will build it myself, from the ground up, if need be.

I will no longer remain tethered to this man who so clearly despises me.

And I will dedicate my life to making a family that is far happier than what I came from.

A chuckle leaves my mouth, and my father turns to me. He raises an eyebrow.

"Care to share what's so funny?" he asks.

I shake my head, then head to my desk. I only shut my laptop and pick it up before turning back to the door.

"Where are you going?" he asks with curiosity and annoyance in his voice. He's probably annoyed that he wasn't able to get the reaction he wanted out of me.

"You're not my father," I say. "So I don't think that's any of your business anymore."

His lips tighten, and then the ghost of another smile crosses his lips.

His next statement is the only thing that gets me to react and strikes a chill in my heart.

"If you're looking for Dara, then you should know she's likely already far gone."

~

"DARA!"

When I burst through the mansion doors, the first person that I happen on is Sophia.

"Where is she?" I grab her by the shoulders, and she squeaks at the intensity of my hold.

"Sir?"

"Where is Dara?"

"I don't know, sir."

"Master Leon."

I spin around, and Anna is behind me. She appears shocked by my vehemence, too, and takes a few steps back.

"Where is Dara? Is she in her room?"

"No. She went out to run an errand—"

"She left!"

A small boyish voice breaks through the atmosphere, and we both turn in unison. Kenny is standing at the top of the stairs, his face squeezed in frustration and his eyes splotchy like he's been crying.

"She left because you did something to her!" he says.

"Earlier, she was sitting in the garden meeting with Master Leon," Sophia says. "I didn't even know that she left."

God. My breath is scoring my chest, and I want to rage to the sky. I keep my eyes on my son, but he shakes his head and storms away. Even though his room is several steps inside, I hear a loud door slam.

I need to fix this.

I need to find her.

I whip out my phone, enabling the tracker I put on it so I could always find her. It's a safety precaution because making her a part of the LEON family ultimately endangered her as well. So, I need to be able to find her quickly if need be.

I'm already back in my car in under three minutes, and I whip out through the mansion gates like a crazed man. I complete the thirty-minute trip in about half that time, arriving at a small townhouse on the outskirts of Englewood.

I knock on the door, and it's answered by a large man in an apron.

"Can I help you?" he asks.

"My wife is here," I tell him. "I need to see her."

"Who's your wife?"

"Dara."

The man's eyebrows furrow. "That can't be right. Dara isn't married."

"I need to see her," I say firmly, and then attempt to walk past the man, but he blocks me.

I cock an eyebrow.

"You're not going anywhere until you explain to me exactly what's going on."

"I don't have time to explain shit to you," I snap. "I need to see my wife and make sure she's okay."

"She's not okay." Suddenly, he's flanked by another large, younger man who looks a lot like him. He crosses his hands over his chest, accusation glinting in his gaze. "She came here crying. Was that because of you? Did you do something?"

"She was crying?" Fuck. What the hell did that old bastard tell her?

"Let me see her."

"No." The man attempts to shove my back, but I'm too quick. I grab his wrist and twist it up. He bites out a curse but then grabs me by the shirt.

We glare at each other, both ready to throw down, when I hear, "Kane?"

I glance around wildly before focusing on a window open to the right of the wall.

Dara is sticking her head out, her eyebrows furrowed in confusion. Her eyes are red, and so is the tip of her nose. Her color is splotchy.

So she has been crying. A lot, by the looks of it.

I'm filled with a combination of guilt, relief, and anger at myself for making her like this. Myself and my father.

"Dara. Honey."

She shakes her head. "Don't call me that. Go away, Kane. I don't want to see you."

I try to enter the house, but he blocks me. And then two other large men flank him at his back.

I don't care. I'll go through them if need be.

"Go home, Kane," Dara says.

"Not until we talk."

She bites her lips. "Fine."

Her head pops back in, and the window shuts.

In just a few short minutes, though, she's squeezing herself through the two men, murmuring to them softly as she stands in front of them.

Despite everything, after seeing her, the tension in my chest eased that had been there for the past hour. It's the first time I can breathe.

I love her.

"Dara..."

"No." She holds up her hand. "You said you want to talk, but I only want to hear one thing from you. Is it true that your

293

Dad was going to give me an inheritance? Shares from his company?"

Shit. So he told her that. "Yes."

"And you knew about it," she continues. "So you were going to trick me by having me sign a document that willed my fortune to you? Without my knowledge?"

I want to lie, but I can't. I owe her the truth, at the very least. "Yes."

She swallows and then says. "Leave, Kane. I never want to see you again."

"Wait, Dara—"

"You know what's the saddest thing about it," she explodes. "If you had just asked me, I probably would have given it to you. You didn't need to lie. I would have given you the inheritance anyway."

She's not lying. I already know how she's been spending the money I gave her, not on lavish trips or shopping sprees. But on charities.

She has the most beautiful heart I've ever seen.

And judging by the look in her eyes. I just shattered it.

"I love you."

"Don't." Once more, she cuts me off with a hand, pain squeezing her features. "Don't even dare say that to me."

"It's the truth," I tell her. "I haven't lied to you during this whole conversation, and I'm not lying now. Yes, this entire thing started as a ruse, but I fell in love with you for real, Dara. Fuck why do you think I held on to that damn contract for so long? I didn't want to go through with it. I wasn't going to—"

"Stop," she says, her eyes filling with tears again, her voice cracking. The look on her face is heart-wrenching. "Please, I just can't take this anymore. Please, Kane, just leave. I can't breathe when you're here, so just go."

"I love you, Dara."

"This isn't about you anymore," she snaps. "I need space to think. I need to be away. If you truly love me, you would give me that."

The look in her eyes shows me she's not ready to hear anything I have to say. She won't believe it. The pain is too fresh, the betrayal too deep.

She may never believe anything I have to say ever again.

And perhaps the best thing I can do for her is to let her go.

And though it's like spitting out gravel and ripping out my heart, I finally tell her, "Alright. I'll give you space."

CHAPTER 33

Dara

I t's the most miserable week I can remember having in a long time.

And that's saying something because I seem to be a connoisseur of misery.

I end up crying the entire first night I spend at Lisa's. I try to do it quietly because I share the bed with Lisa. Her two brothers are also in the room next to us, and the walls are pretty thin, so I don't want anyone to hear me quietly sobbing into my pillows.

That would be more than embarrassing.

In addition to the embarrassment of them watching me argue with my fake husband on their front porch.

To their credit, they haven't mentioned anything about it. When Lisa's father brought us some dinner, he only said, "Sweetheart. Are you doing okay?"

And when I nodded and smiled weakly, he seemed to understand and gave me my space.

Her other two brothers, Brody and Andrew, have all come in at different intervals to ask Lisa mundane questions, which I know is just their excuse to check in on me.

I appreciate their concern, but I don't want them to worry.

When I cry at night, I muffle the sounds as the tears roll down my cheeks.

Then, in the morning, I wash my face as much as I can to hide the tear streaks.

Although, the red eyes and puffy face probably give me away.

I try to ignore the pitying looks they all give me at breakfast. At least Logan spent the night with a friend in the city, so I don't have to endure his pity, too.

Lisa at least tries to hide it, but the men keep scrutinizing me inconspicuously until her Dad coughs.

"Well," he says. "I think I can speak for everyone when I say it's nice having you here. And you can stay as long as you like, sweetheart. Brody will stay home with you today in case that man comes back."

I blush. "That's not necessary." I think I was pretty plain yesterday that I would no longer be manipulated by Kane, so I doubt he'll come back. He knows he can't deceive me anymore.

Or can he?

A traitorous part of me still wants to hear him out and still thinks there's an explanation that will justify what he did. Even though he admitted that everything his father had said was true. Our marriage was built on a lie.

You already knew it was built on a lie, I remind myself. *You just didn't know that you were one of the people being lied to.*

"You sure?" Brody asks, shoving a forkful of bacon into his mouth and chewing as he speaks. "Because I don't mind asking the chief for a day off."

I shake my head and smile. "No. I don't think Kane will come back here, but thank you, Brody, for the offer."

"Well, I'll be here in case he does." Her father says with a smile. "I work from home now."

"So will I," Lisa announces and when I shake my head, she rolls her eyes. "It's fine. I'm owed a few days off anyway, and even if I wasn't, I'm not leaving you alone. Not a chance."

"Lisa—"

"Don't bother babe. I already called off."

I shake my head but grin at her in gratitude. She reaches over and squeezes my hand in her lap.

But as nice as their kindness is, it's also a little bit stifling. I can't look into their eyes without feeling their pity and the painful reminder that I'm just a naive girl who got duped by a much richer and much smarter man.

And now, I don't know what to do next with my life.

Lisa tries to distract me that afternoon, by taking me out grocery shopping. I'm reluctant to leave the house in general, reluctant to accidentally run into Kane, but I agree to go because I can't exactly stay holed up forever, can I?

Throughout the trip, I go through the motions. I push the cart, pretending to pay attention to Lisa's usual chatter and feigning excitement over the discounts she finds. I barely hear her, even though I try to smile and respond to all the right cues.

Then, as we head back to the bus station, she finally ventures,

"So," she glances at me. "What are you going to do now?"

I stare at her. "What do you mean?"

"Well, according to what you told me you have this new inheritance coming from your..." She purses her lips. "Sort of ex-father-in-law?"

I grin. "Yeah. I guess that's one way to address him."

"Yeah. So you no longer need Kane's money."

I think about it, then nod. I haven't used Kane's card since I left. I don't want to spend his money anymore. I don't want to feel reliant.

But what am I going to do in the interim? I would certainly need to get a job.

That's not what Lisa is talking about, though.

"Are you going to accept it?" she asks. "The inheritance?"

I think about it. "I don't know if I have a choice." Samson didn't make it seem that way, but truthfully, I'm not sure I want his money either. I'm not sure I want to be involved with the Leons at all.

Their world seems far too complicated and secretive for me.

"I don't really want to think about that right now," I say.

Lisa nods. "That's fair. Well, let me know if you need anything. And like my Dad said, you're welcome to stay with us for as long as you would like."

"Thank you, Lisa," I say. "Seriously. You've been more than a friend to me on this."

"It's the least I can do, considering you cleared my student debt."

I blink at her, stunned. She smiles wryly.

"What? You didn't think I would realize it was you? What are the odds that a few weeks after my best friend marries a billionaire, a charitable organization decides to pay off all my student loans? And then does the same for Brody and Andrew, too?"

I blush, my face hot, and then duck my head. "I knew you wouldn't let me if I asked you directly."

"You're right. I wouldn't," she says. "But I can't say that I'm not grateful you did."

"I should have done more," I mumble, and she shakes her head.

"No, that would have pissed me off. I don't need your money or your husband's money. Alright? You're my best friend. And whether or not you get a giant inheritance or not, you'll always be my best friend. And I will always be here for you."

"I know," I say, feeling gratitude flitter across my chest. "I just…it didn't feel right for just me to have all that money and not do anything useful with it. And then Kane said I had to spend a minimum of fifty thousand a day, or he would do it himself. I didn't know what else to do. I guess, in a way, you did me a favor."

She snorts. "Right. You know a lot of women in your position would have gone on shopping sprees, right? Bought designer bags and whatever else."

"Yeah." I shudder a little. Designer stores have always intimidated me, and the ethics behind most of them bother me, so that was out of the question for me.

Lisa chuckled, and then we headed home.

The next day presents another challenge.

It's my first time back in class after what happened between Kane and Max.

Max acts normally during the lesson, although his eyes don't meet mine quite as often as they used to do. It's like he pointedly avoids looking at me.

After class, I tentatively approach him, and he gives me a ticked-off look out of the corner of his eyes.

"I don't want trouble," he says. "Is your boyfriend going to attack me out of nowhere?"

"He's my ex now," I say, chastised. "I'm so sorry about that. I didn't know he would fly off the handle like that. He's never done that before."

"Well, that's how it usually goes," he says, and then he sighs. "But I'm less pissed that he attacked me and more so worried about you. You went with him, knowing what he's capable of. If he's that violent, then—"

"We broke up," I cut him off. "He's my ex now. And he's never hit me before. He's usually not violent. I think he was just jealous."

Which didn't make sense at all if he didn't care about me from the beginning.

But I think it will probably do me well to stop trying to make sense of Kane's actions. The more I try to make sense of them, the more my head hurts.

Sympathy enters Max's gaze. "Look, I know how these things usually go. I've worked in a few domestic shelters. So if you need a place to stay or anything..."

I shake my head. "Thank you for the offer. But I think I'll be fine. I'm staying with a friend now."

"Okay," he grins. "But don't forget that I'm your friend too. Let me know if you need anything, okay?"

I nod, glad we finally got to make up. And then I go home.

For the next few days, I tried to keep busy, so I forget about Kane and everything that transpired between us.

But he doesn't make it easy. He texts me every day. He's so far kept up with his promise to give me space, but then I start getting texts like:

I'm sorry.

I know you don't want to hear this from me, but I never lied to you about one thing. I do love you.

I miss you.

You and Kenny are my life.

My heart cracks at that line, and my resolve wavers once

more. I can't do this. I can't listen to him text me these things and then just remain unwavering by it.

Not when I love him this much.

I need to block him and go somewhere far away, somewhere he can't reach me.

I roll over in bed. I miss Kenny so much, too, miss running my hand through his curly brown hair and miss his mischievous little smile. I wonder how he's doing in my absence if he's reverted to his old behavior. God, I so want to go back to the mansion if only just to check on him, but I see that for the excuse it is.

Because I want to see Kane too

Maybe I can go in the afternoon when he's at work?

No. I shake my head. I need to keep my distance for now

By the end of the week, I know I need to do something with myself. Staying at Lisa's house is starting to wear everyone thin. The house wasn't meant to house five people, much less six. And I don't know for how much longer Kane is going to stay away.

I'm still very weak when it comes to him.

So I come up with the crazy idea to leave the country for a few weeks.

I need to go somewhere unfamiliar but not entirely foreign to me at the same time.

I can't book the tickets using Kane's card, or he'll know exactly where I am.

So I call Anastasia and trust that she wouldn't tell Kane of my plan.

I just hope she can give me a week before her loyalty to Kane overpowers her friendship with me.

I TELL LISA AFTER DINNER, AS WE'RE ABOUT TO GET IN BED together. "I'm leaving tomorrow."

Her eyes widen and she pauses in the act of fluffing her pillow. "So soon?"

"Yes." I don't want to think too much about it because I'm going to end up talking myself out of it.

She glances at me. "Where will you go?"

"I can't tell you," I tell her. "But it's somewhere very far. I'll call you once I'm there."

Lisa's eyes are watery and she drops the pillow and hugs me. I hug her back.

"I'm going to miss you," she whispers, and I squeeze her even tighter.

The next day, Anastasia chartered a private jet for me and also had a car deliver me to the airport. Unlike the first time with Kane and Kenny, I don't enjoy this trip as much. It feels very lonely.

The whole trip is pretty much a blur. I faintly greet the driver, who comes to pick me up from the Charles de Gaule airport in France and drive me to Anastasia's mansion. Another man, the butler, I'm assuming, directs me through the grand house up to Anastasia's room.

"She'll be here soon," he tells me in heavily accented English.

"Thank you," I say and offer him a faint smile.

He nods and leaves me for a few seconds.

I glance around Anastasia's room. It looks pink and expensive. If I thought Kane's mansion looked ancient and elaborate, then Anastasia's room alone is about ten times that. There were Greek carvings by her window, two large art pieces flanking her bed, and at her bedside, a pink lamp looked to be carved out of alabaster.

And besides that, an odd black hat that appears out of place.

I frown as I approach the hat. It looks very familiar, and I wrack my brain to figure out where I've seen this before.

Suddenly, it hits me like a lightning bolt.

The door behind me opens with a heavy groan, and Anastasia's voice drifts in.

"Sorry I'm late, darling," she's saying. "My Dad wanted to meet with me about some dull business stuff, and then it went on and on..."

I turn around, and she pauses, cocking her head at me.

"Why are you looking at me like that?" she asks.

I shake my head, still reeling from the shock of what I just discovered. "I'm just wondering what my brother's hat is doing on your bedside table."

CHAPTER 34
Kane

I give Dara a week.

That's about all I can tolerate without seeing her. And in that week, I'm going stir crazy.

Kenny is still refusing to talk to me. Ever since he started school again, he's no longer holed up in his room, but even when he comes down for dinner, he's painfully quiet and only throws glares at me. All my attempts to form conversations with him fall flat.

I don't blame him. In his eyes, I drove away a woman he was coming to love as a mother.

I did drive her away. With my lies, my scheming. My refusal to accept what was right there in my face this entire time, the love for her that was starting to consume my soul.

It's crazy that before, I was so unwilling to admit that I loved her, but now it feels like love is even too mild a word for this all-consuming thing that is taking over my mind and body.

This painful void inside me that yawns wider and wider every moment I spend without her. She has consumed my dreams and my waking thoughts.

Right now, all I think about is how to get her back.

Even at work and with staff, I find myself rethinking my decisions and wondering how she'll feel about them. I have thoughts I never had before, like remembering the names of staff and being generally more considerate with my words and actions.

Several times, I ask myself, *What would she feel if she saw me do this?*

She's acting as my conscience.

Meanwhile, at the same time, I'm also trying to stop Leon from free-falling. Although we've isolated the cause of the leaks, the press is still running the story about stock manipulation. We've announced the new phones in an attempt to distract from it and it's only partially working.

Half the news articles talk about the revolutionary new phone, but the other half staunchly remains on the scandal.

There was not enough evidence found to make the allegations stick. Of course. My father isn't entirely insane, after all. He wouldn't want to fuck up his legacy entirely. He merely wanted to shake me up, and now that he's succeeded, he's clearly content to let his assistant take the fall for everything.

But the question is, what happens now?

I no longer owe my allegiance to Leon, and I plan on leaving the company sooner rather than later.

But at the same time, I don't want to let down all the people who have come to rely on me.

Despite whatever my father thinks, Leon will fall without me at this current moment. It needs a successor with the vision and willpower to lead them into the next phase.

I could give two fucks about my father or the other senior members of the board, but a lot of people have dedicated their lives to working for this company. They put their blood, sweat, and tears into innovation after innovation. They don't deserve to suffer for my father's games.

So, I plan to keep working until I find someone worthy enough to take over while I'm gone.

"It looks like we're on track to sell three million phones first week," Nathan says at the end of our meeting. It was a meeting between the marketing and development team, and while everyone else had filed out, Nathan remains lounging in the seat opposite my desk. "And there's been no word on *them* releasing their version."

"Good." My guess is Textra hasn't managed to finish manufacturing yet. They believed they still had a year to release their version of the phone.

But left to me, their version is never going to see the light of day.

"We're also collecting the evidence needed to sue them for it when the time comes," Nathan continues.

"Good," I say. "That's good."

I stare out the window, and once more, my mind drifts to Dara. *What is she doing now? Did she go to class today?*

Does she miss me as painfully as I do her?

"Are you okay?"

I turn back to Nathan, noting he's giving me an odd look. I raise an eyebrow.

"Yes. Why wouldn't I be?"

He shrugs. "Because you've been distracted throughout the whole meeting. And you're not the type of man that's easily distracted, especially when it comes to work."

He's right.

But Dara is here even now in a moment like this, always at the forefront of my mind.

I want to tell her about my day and see her eyes light up

when I tell her of my little wins. I want to hear her cooking analogies and cover her little giggles with my kiss.

I want to beg her for another chance.

But I can't. Because I told her I would give her space.

Stupid idea.

I still text her, though. I'm not good with romance, but I try to express myself in ways I haven't done before. Honest and vulnerable.

The last one is the hardest for me, but I do it for her. I bare my heart for her.

I want to show her everything, including the ugly sides of me. I have a feeling she wouldn't make me weak for crying over my mother's death. Or for the hurt I still feel towards my father.

She would understand.

So far, she hasn't replied to any of the texts, but she hasn't blocked me either. I'm holding out hope that there's a chance.

There has to be a chance. Because I don't stand any chance of letting her go.

"I'll be leaving Leon soon," I say rather than answer Nathan's question.

Nathan's eyebrows lift into his hairline. "Are you serious?"

"Yes. And I need someone to take over once I'm gone. Someone who knows what direction to push it in, who has a history with the employees."

Nathan immediately catches my drift and shakes his head frantically. "If you're asking me to take the job, the answer is no."

"You're the only one I can think of."

The head shaking continues. "I couldn't run this place like you, and it's laughable that you think I could. Plus, even if I tried, do you think I could put up with your Dad? I would strangle him and the rest of those old cronies within a week. No offense."

I smile as he continues.

"If you leave, then I'm leaving with you." He nods like it's final. "I'm serious. I'll go with you wherever it is you go."

"I don't even know what I'm doing. Or what I'll do after this." I haven't thought that far. I have a few options. I could join James Coleman or a few other companies who expressed interest. I could simply live out the rest of my life on my investments, which are in the billions.

Or I could start up a new company on my own.

"Well, when you figure it out, let me know," Nathan says. "Because I'm coming with you."

I smile in earnest now. "Thank you. It's nice knowing that I inspire such loyalty in a brilliant man like you."

Nathan frowns. "Are you sure you're okay? You're being unusually sentimental and...nice."

"I'm fine," I assure him. But I also can't continue like this.

I need to see Dara.

∾

A FEW HOURS LATER, I FIND MYSELF AT HER FRIEND'S doorstep again.

I knock, wondering vaguely if the behemoths are in. I don't necessarily care if they are or even if there's an entire army behind the door.

Nothing is going to keep me from her again.

The door opens, and a disgruntled-looking woman answers. I recognize her instantly. Lisa, Dara's best friend.

"What do you want?" she says in a sour tone.

I raise my eyebrow. I'm not used to being addressed like that, but I ignore it.

"I want to talk to Dara."

"She's not here."

"Where is she?"

"Why the fuck would I tell you?" she says. "And don't bother trying to track her phone. She left it behind."

Frustration lines my spine.

"Please." The word squeezes out of me, surprising both of us. "Please. I need to find her."

"Why? So you can hurt her again."

"I don't want to hurt her again, damn it. I love her." I shut my eyes as the honesty flows out of me. "I fucked up with her badly. I never expected to fall in love with her, but I did."

"Is that why you tried to steal from her? Why you tried to get her to sign away her inheritance?"

"I wasn't going to do it," I admit. "I had the document for weeks. I was trying to convince myself to go through with it but I couldn't. Because even then, I knew I loved her."

"I don't believe you."

She attempts to slam the door in my face, but I shove my foot through the opening, blocking it.

"Please," I say again.

She rolls her eyes. "Look, I really don't know where she went. And I don't think she's even in the country anymore. You lost her. That's it."

"You really don't know where she went?"

She shakes her head. "No. She wouldn't tell me because she knew you would come looking for her if she did. Now get lost."

I know I deserve her antagonism, so I nod and say, "Thank you."

She seems surprised by my acquiescence and then says grudgingly, "You're welcome. I guess."

And then I retract the foot from her door and turn around, hearing it slam behind me.

I run a hand over my face. I need to think of where she would go. I need to find her.

I take out my phone and scan through my bank apps.

She hasn't used any of her cards since the day we split up, I note.

Which means she's using money from another source.

I head back to my car, but my steps slow as I approach, spotting a figure dressed head-to-toe in black standing by it.

Even though it's been a few years, I recognize the man underneath the hoodie.

CARTER...

Same stance, wide-legged, with a defensive shoulder.

He's gotten a little taller, and more filled out, a far cry from the scrawny man who used to follow me around.

As I approach the car, I wait for all the rage that I had for him to muster up, but it doesn't. He's the least of my problems now.

"I don't have time for you," is all I say to him as I grab my car door, popping it open.

"We need to talk," he says and then grabs my arm. I immediately drive my elbow back, and he swiftly avoids the hit. But I'm not done. I spin around, propelling my knee up into his abdomen.

"Ooof!" The breath whooshes out of him as my knee makes contact.

Unsatisfied, I try for a punch, but he blocks it with his forearm.

I grab his shirt instead and yank him close before throwing him back into the car.

A part of me wants to beat the shit out of him, but I hesitate. I think about what Dara would think if I ended up killing her brother.

I push off him.

"I told you I don't have time for you, you bastard," I tell him.

"I know," he says, straightening his shirt. Accusation glints in his gaze. "You're too busy sleeping with my sister."

I cock my eyebrow. "She told you?"

"No," he says but doesn't clarify. I smirk.

"You've been spying on us," I smirk. "Wow. You really have more in common with the old man than I thought."

"If you're talking about your father, I'm going to kick your ass for that allegation."

"Tell me something," I watch his expression. "Are you really his son?"

A look of disgust fills his face. "Why the fuck would you ask me something like that?"

"Because I know something is going on between the two of you, something I'm not seeing." I shake my head. "But frankly, I don't have time to find out. So unless you know where your sister's run off to, I don't care what you have to say."

"I do know where she is."

I pause in the process of opening my car door again and shut my eyes.

Shit. Now I have to listen to him.

"But before I take you to her, I'm going to tell you the real story of what happened all those years ago," he says, eyes gleaming. "And trust me. It's way more fucked up than anything you could imagine."

CHAPTER 35

Dara

A few seconds of silence throbs between us as Anastasia
and I hold each other's gazes.

It almost feels like a stalemate, like we're in a Texas
standoff off, and we're both pointing guns at each other.

I cross my arms over my chest to let her know I mean
business. I'm no longer willing to let my ignorance slide.
Something very weird is going on here, and I need to figure
out what it is.

Anastasia finally relents with a sigh, rolling her neck.
"Jesus, this is going to be annoying. Honestly, I'm not even
sure where to start."

"You know my brother?" I ask, glancing at the incrimi-
nating hat again. I guess it would make sense, given the
longevity of her friendship with Kane, that she would know
Carter. But I never put the two together, honestly, since
neither of them ever mentioned him.

And Carter never mentioned her, either.

So that's why he was in France. I realize. *And at the
airport.*

It all makes sense now.

Anastasia smiles wryly at my question. "Does anyone ever truly know Carter?"

"Meaning?"

"Meaning that your brother is an extremely complicated man, and this is an extremely complicated story and I'm definitely not the right person to be telling it."

"You're the only one here," I say, throwing my hand out. "And you're the only one who can tell me the truth since both Kane and Carter are determined to hide it from me." I walk to her, take her hand in mine, and plead with every fiber of my being. "Please, Anastasia. I can't take being in the dark anymore."

"*Merde*," Anastasia mutters and then rolls her eyes. "Alright, fine. Take a seat. I'll tell you what I know. Mind you, it probably won't be the full story because Carter doesn't give anyone the full story, but it might help you fill in some gaps."

I sit eagerly in one of her loveseats and await her next words.

She slides into her bed and then leans her head back on her pillow, her face faintly worried.

"I met Carter at the Leon estate, back when I was sixteen and he was eighteen," she says. "I didn't think much of him. Just that he was Kane's friend who also worked for his Dad. And frankly, we didn't get along much the first time we met. He was a know-it-all, infuriating, and dismissive of everyone who wasn't as ambitious as he was. Called Kane and me rich spoiled brats. Kane didn't mind, but I did."

For some reason, there's something in her eyes that tells me there's more to the story, a stray emotion that feels deeper than hurt, but I restrain myself from investigating it. If I pry too much, she might stop talking, and her feelings for Carter aren't the point of the story.

"Anyway, I met him then and then didn't think much of it again. Until years later, when Carter showed up at my father's doorstep needing a place to stay."

"Why?"

"The story Carter told us is that he was driven out by Samson Leon," I say. "They had some sort of argument, and Carter had done something so bad that he had to leave the country; otherwise, Samson was going to find him and make him pay in blood."

I widen my eyes in shock now. Was that why my brother had gone into hiding? What did he do that was so bad?

I ask Anastasia the question, and she shakes her head. "Your guess is as good as mine, dear. I don't know what it was. But my Dad does."

"Your Dad?"

"Yes. There was no way he was just going to let Carter stay for no reason. After Carter showed up, he told my Dad he had something to tell him and only him. They had a private meeting that lasted for three hours. And whatever Carter showed him made my father protect him. He got him a place and a job in Paris to sustain himself. Even helped him change his entire identity." She adds. "He goes by Jean Pierre now."

I swallow and digest the information with some difficulty. "So you don't know what was said?"

Anastasia shakes her head. "No. And yes, he's been in Paris this entire time, but I don't know much about what he does here. I haven't told Kane about it because my father forced me to take an oath of secrecy. I couldn't tell Kane anything, or Dad would take half of my shopping budget." She shudders like it's the most horrible thing she can imagine.

"It's not like I was going to tell Kane anyway," she continues. "If he knew Carter was here, all hell would break loose. He would never forgive me, and he would probably kill Carter."

"Why?"

"It's another complicated story. But essentially, Kane thinks that Carter stole money from his father's company and fled."

"Did he?"

"I have no clue," she says. "Or at least I don't think that's the full story. My father wouldn't house a thief unless he had a really, *really* good reason for doing what he did."

I think about it.

What if stealing was the horrible thing that made Carter flee the country? But Samson also never mentioned anything about Carter stealing from him, either? He only spoke about my brother fondly. Kane, on the other hand, hates him for a seemingly good reason.

So who's right?

Are they both lying? Or were they both telling the truth but seeing the same situation in two completely different ways?

I now recall that Kane's cold treatment started when I mentioned I had seen Carter in France. *Did he think I was in on this too, on this scheme to steal from him?*

"Now, it's your turn," Anastasia says.

"My turn?"

"Yes. You still haven't told me why you ran away from Kane," she says and then holds up her hands. "I've been very patient so far."

I sigh, feeling weary. I don't want to get into it, but I guess I do owe her at least that for all her help.

I tell her the story briefly. "Well, essentially, Kane lied to me during our whole marriage. And nothing about it was real." I smile at her, feeling the tears once more pushing behind my eyes. "I mean, I knew in the beginning it wasn't real, but somewhere along the line, I guess I forgot."

"Oh, honey." Anastasia rises from her bed and walks to me, taking my hand in her. I swallow and blink multiple times to keep from crying.

"Look, I don't know what he did," she says. "I know Kane can be an idiot, especially when it has to do with his feelings. But I've never seen him as head over heels over someone as he was for you."

I shake my head. "It wasn't real, Anastasia."

"Are you kidding me?" She blinks incredulously. "He was ready to bite my head off when I disrespected you. He threatened to end our entire friendship over it, and trust me, he meant it." She shakes her head. "He's never done anything like that before with anyone he dated. Not even with me."

I shake my head again, denying her words, but then the door shifts.

I turn around and come face to face with Anastasia's father.

CHAPTER 36
Kane

There's a rustle of breeze in the silence following Carter's words. It punctuates how bizarre this is.

Carter stands before me with a grim look on his face. My former best friend, the man who stole my family's money and ran.

I swore I would kill him if I ever saw him again.

Except I can't kill him. Not because I've forgiven him for what he did but simply because he's Dara's brother, and I would never do anything to hurt her.

Part of the reason I searched so hard for Dara in the first place was to use her as bait to find Carter. I was going to show her off at galas around the world, everywhere the press could see. And once Carter saw that I had his sister in my grasp, he would come out of whatever hole he was hiding in to save her, and get her away from me. I was blinded by revenge.

Of course, that plan fell flat once I actually met Dara and discovered that Carter didn't give two shits about her. He hadn't even bothered contacting her when he was gone. I want to kill him for that alone.

"Are you ready to tell me what it is, or are you just going to stare at my face the entire time?" I snarl. I might have agreed to hear him out, but that doesn't mean I have to be happy about it.

A snort echoes in the air. "You haven't changed a little."

"Whether I've changed or not is not your fucking business," I say. "Tell me where your sister is, or get lost."

"I'll tell you." He crosses his arms over his chest. "But to get there, we need to start from the beginning. All the way back to our parents."

"Our parents?"

"Yeah. They knew each other, did you know?" His eyes darken, reminding me so much of his sister's when she's upset. "Turns out our parents go way back."

I don't respond. I knew my father and Carter's father had been old college friends. He told me as much when Carter came to stay with us for the first time. I was curious about their relationship. My father didn't have a lot of people he called friends, especially those not in the same social class as he was. David Dalton was special, an anomaly, a poor man who had somehow surmounted that 'grievous fault' in my father's eyes.

I assume something eventually happened to break that friendship, but Samson remained obsessed with the Daltons ever since.

I gesture for Carter to get in the car. It looks like this story is going to take a while, so we might as well drive as we talk.

Carter nods and obeys.

"They went into business together," Carter says as I pull out of the parking lot. "Your Dad and my Dad. They were both students at UChicago, and they were roommates, I think. Your Dad liked my Dad because he was so brilliant, the best in his class. And despite Samson Leon's snobbery, my father found something good in him."

I say nothing but vaguely wonder if Dara's father was anything like her. She sees the good in everyone.

"Your grandfather's company was going bankrupt at the time, but Samson still clung to his British aristocratic lineage."

That part rang true. My Dad certainly had an obsession with British aristocracy, which was why he sent me to England for school. He also claimed a distant Russian family on his mother's side, so some of his high school studies were completed in an exchange program in Moscow.

As a matter of fact, my childhood was spent in a conglomerate of European countries, where my father hoped I would learn class and good breeding.

"That's where my Dad comes in." A wistful, prideful smile crosses his lips. "David was super smart, and since high school, he had been working on a brand new design for a revolutionary new camera. A camera that could adapt automatically to different skin tones and lighting, using artificial intelligence to predict the best edits for a picture. Sound familiar?"

"Cut the crap and tell me what you're trying to say."

"That's the camera that revived Leon Inc.," he says, leaning forward and turning to me. In the rearview mirror, I watch the anger pulse in his eyes. "The camera that made your company now worth a billion dollars. That camera was created by my father."

He's lying.

My instinct is to deny everything he's saying as a lie. But I restrain myself, scrutinizing his expression instead.

If he's lying to me, then he's lying to himself, too,

because he appears and sounds utterly convinced by the words he's saying.

"Samson told my Dad that he would find investors for the project," Carter continued. "They were friends, but of course, since your Dad is a raging snob, in addition to being a massive asshole, he always thought he was better than his friend. He wanted to own the patents, and the majority split the profits. He thought he had every right to it since he was doing David a favor. But my Dad was smarter than that. He refused to take the deal, and then came the first wrench in their friendship. The second was the thing that twisted the knife in Samson Leon's heart." He relaxes back in his seat. "Beverly."

"My mother?"

"Yes. At the time, she was Samson's beautiful high society girlfriend, the darling of the Beaufort family. They'd been friends for years, and it was assumed they would marry each other. But she never loved him. Instead, she fell in love with his best friend. The poor nobody genius inventor."

"What?"

"Your Mom was one of the first investors that Samson got for the camera. That's how she met my Dad. Your mother fell in love with my Dad, and your Dad couldn't take it. Looking at it from his angle, David is refusing to sell his patent to him and now stealing his girl. That was the last straw."

Carter points to me, his eyes glittering. "But do you think Samson came out and said how he felt? Do you think your Dad is the type that communicates his feelings like a normal human being?" Carter's laugh is humorless. "Of course not. So, instead, what Samson did was frame my Dad for a crime he didn't commit. He had my Dad sent to jail rather than admit that he was jealous of your mother's feelings for my Dad, feelings my Dad did not reciprocate. And he stole

David's design and scrubbed every evidence that he created it."

I shake my head. Everything he said sounds too crazy to be true. My father might be a cruel bastard sometimes, but this seems too far.

Then again, reality often has a very weird way of being stranger than fiction. After all, I've fallen in love with my fake wife, who is my former best friend's sister.

"If your father truly owns the patent, why didn't he sue Samson when he got out?" I ask.

"Because my Dad was framed for murder," he said. "Dad didn't think he was ever getting out. So he sold the patent to your mother, Beverly, in return for lawyer fees and money to take care of his family while he was in jail. He also told her that he suspected Samson had framed him for the murder of a homeless man. He told her to stay away from Samson. But of course, she didn't. Their families were intertwined and even if she believed that Samson framed him, which she didn't, there was no way to get out of the wedding. Her family and Samson's family had planned it since they were kids. So the next thing my father heard was that Beverly had married your father."

"No," I say, shaking my head firmly. I can tentatively believe whatever horrible thing he says about Samson.

He can convince me that my father is a vindictive psychopath.

But my mother… "She would never have married him if he really did those things."

Carter raises an eyebrow. "Do I need to remind you how these upper-class families go? Your mother's family was very powerful and influential, and they wanted this marriage whether she wanted it or not. Plus, as I mentioned, she didn't entirely believe David at the time. Samson has a very clever way of pretending to be what he's not. He pretended for long enough with her. And by the time she discovered who he really was, it was too late. She'd been married to him for years at that point and suddenly realized that she made a mistake. So, she set about trying to make things right."

My eyes widen. "What do you mean?"

"She began looking for evidence of Samson's guilt, without his knowledge, of course. She tried reaching out to my father in jail, but he didn't reply to any of her messages. He didn't want anything to do with her or the Leons. Luckily, she still had the patent that was now worth billions of dollars and her shares in the company."

"So why not give the patent back to David?"

"She couldn't. Even if David agreed to meet with her, it was too dangerous. Your father had contacts in the police force, and some of them oversaw the prison. If Samson even had a whiff of what she was doing, there's a possibility he would have staged a nasty accident for David. He would have killed my Dad before he allowed the truth to be revealed. And Beverly knew it."

I clench my hand on the steering wheel, teeth grinding. Something is slowly splintering in my mind. Carter's words are like a pick-axe, carefully taking apart everything I thought I knew, destroying the perfectly crafted family I thought I had.

My father, the great Samson Leon, was a thief who framed a man for murder.

My mother, so warm and loving, kept his secret for all these years.

It's a bitter pill to swallow, and everything inside me is crying out for me to deny the claims.

But Carter speaks with absolute confidence, and I have no choice but to listen to his story.

"Your mother had a plan, though," Carter continues. "Samson had the chief of police in his back pockets, but Beverly wasn't without power. She was a Beaufort, after all. She just needed to act without her husband or her parents finding out. And she did. She talked a judge friend of hers into granting David parole. Thankfully, new evidence came up, and the case was appealed in court. He also earned some credit due to his good behavior in prison, so he was let out early." The grim look reappears on his face. "Your father never knew for sure if your mother had anything to do with the pardon. But he made her pay for it regardless."

"What do you mean?"

He sighs. "I was conceived while my Dad was still in jail. My mother at the time was an old friend who visited him. They slowly fell in love over the years. I was sixteen when my Dad got out of jail. Of course, by that point, most of his life was gone. He couldn't start over, so he resigned himself to a simple life as an electrician instead. But Samson was furious that he'd been let out. He suspected Beverly might have had something to do with it. Of course, he didn't know Beverly suspected him of framing David. He simply thought she did it because she was still in love with David after all these years. So Samson came to find me and offered me a job. He promised me that he would take care of my family if I worked for him. It all seemed too good to be true. And it was. Because what he really wanted was a tool to keep his wife in line."

Suddenly, a memory flashes through my mind. The first day Carter arrived, my parents had a huge fight, one of their biggest to date. My mother was adamant that Samson 'take him back.' I assumed at the time that it was because she didn't like Carter, but everything from that day on proved me wrong. After that, she was warm and affectionate toward him and treated him as well as me.

So I just chucked up the incident as another of my mother's emotional outbursts that often didn't make any sense.

Or at least, I thought they didn't make sense. Now I'm realizing I just wasn't thinking hard enough.

"My Dad was against me working for the Leons, but he wouldn't explain to me why. Maybe he wanted to keep me safe, or maybe he didn't think I would believe him. At the time, I couldn't afford to go to college, and Dara was just born. My Mom died giving birth to her. I wanted better for her than what I had. So, I agreed to work for Samson. My father and I had a big fight about it. He forbade me, but I didn't care. We didn't have the greatest relationship to start with, and I barely knew him since he had spent most of my life behind bars. So I let him know he couldn't tell me what to do. He even told me he would disown me if I worked for Samson. But I knew we needed the money. So I did it anyway."

I rub my hands over my head, suddenly so tired of this story. What a fucking mess. "Say I believe you. Is this you trying to tell me that you stole the money because you felt it was your right to? Because of what my father did to yours?"

"I never stole anything," he snaps. "Everything I took, your mother gave me. How did you think I accessed it in the first place?"

I frown. "I assumed you memorized my passwords."

He rolls his eyes. "Really? As paranoid as you are, you thought it was that easy to memorize your password, much less get access to your laptop?"

I shrug. Carter is pretty smart when he wants to be, and I assumed he had found a way to hack it.

"Your mother gave me that money. It might come as a

surprise to you, but your mother owns the largest shares of Leon."

I nearly gape at him as another bolt of shock hits me. He nods.

"She's the controlling member, not your father. His shares aren't enough. And when she died, she left her shares to you, me, and Dara." He cocks her head. "As you can imagine, your father was not very happy about the split. That's why he almost crashed Leon Inc. the first time, by leaking the Smart TV designs all those years ago. And then he blamed me for it."

"That's not what was said at her will reading." There, the shares had been split between me and Samson, with the latter taking the lion's share.

"The will they read to you was a fake," he says. "I have the real will. As well as a recording of Beverly confessing to all your father's crimes and everyone involved." He hesitates a second before he admits, "I also have a key to where she keeps the real patent."

"Where?"

"It's in her brooch," he says. "That's why I took it. She was scared that your father would eventually catch on to what she was doing and would steal it from you before you had a chance to learn the truth."

My hands tighten on the wheel as I drive.

"How am I to believe anything you are telling me right now?" I ask. "You show up out of the blue and make my father out to be this monster."

"I can show you the videos your mother left behind if you don't believe me. But if you didn't already believe your father was a monster before I showed up, then you're more naive than I thought," he says. "But that's why your mother could never tell you these things. You were too wrapped up in

Samson, too willing to do just about anything to please him. She knew if she told you, you wouldn't believe her. Your father had already convinced most of the shareholders that she was half mad anyway. She thought he would do the same with you."

I want to deny everything he just said as the indignation and anger rises within. But then it sinks just as fast, shame taking its place.

I wouldn't have believed her.

But she tried to tell me in her own way, and I didn't listen to her then.

Ignore your father and just be happy.

Don't let him control you or your thoughts.

Your father is not who you think he is.

Don't become him.

Now, suddenly, I remember all the times she encouraged me to distance myself from Samson. But I never listened.

"That's why she told me all this instead," he says. "I was the only one who would believe her."

"Fuck." I swear as the breath rasps in my chest. "So why not come forward with this earlier? Why wait till now?"

He's silent for a few seconds and then says. "That story can wait until we get to where we're going."

"Which is?"

"France."

I stare at him for a few seconds and then press a button on my dashboard to call number one on my contact list.

Pope answers on the third ring. "Yes, sir?"

"Is Kenny still in class?"

"Yes. I'm sitting here observing him, and he's behaving remarkably well." Pope is supposed to observe Kenny during his first few weeks of school to ensure that he's doing as promised and to make sure there are no more misunderstandings with his friends.

"Okay." I bite my lip, debating on what to do next. I could pull Kenny out of class to fly to France with me, but I don't want to mess with his schedule so early in the school term.

And he's been looking forward to being in school, so much so that he even agreed to have Pope sit in his classes. He wanted to see his friends and be able to go over to their house after. I don't want to take that from him.

Also, if this turns out to be a part of some sick scheme Carter cooked up, I don't want Kenny involved. I won't endanger my son.

"I want a full security detail on Kenny," I say. "Immediately. Call Ruford's men. I'm flying to France, but I'll be back tonight or tomorrow morning at the latest."

"Okay, sir," Pope says, and even though I can hear the question in his voice, he doesn't ask me anything.

After I hang up, I feel Carter's gaze on the side of my face.

"What?" I ask.

"Nothing," he says. "It's just weird that you have a son now."

"My son is none of your business," is all I say. I'm not ready to forgive Carter or pretend like we're friends again. I'm not even sure if the story he just told me is true.

All I know is that I want to see Dara. If she's in Paris, then that's where I need to be.

CHAPTER 37
Dara

I blink at Anastasia's Dad, startled by his sudden entrance.

"Hello, Mr. Coleman," I greet formally, unsure how to address him. "Thank you so much for letting me stay at your home."

"No, Mr. Coleman." He strides to me, tucking his hand into his loose linen pants. "Just call me James. I'm not that stuffy troglodyte that you call a father-in-law."

"Oh…um..okay." I'm not sure how to react to that either. I look to Anastasia for direction, and she rolls her eyes at her father.

"Dad, we were having a private conversation."

"Then maybe you should have closed the door, so I didn't catch morsels of that 'private' conversation," he retorts smoothly as he sits on the other loveseat facing me. "Of course, now that I did, I have no choice but to come in and clarify a few things."

Anastasia sighs, but her father ignores her leaning back on the seat and pinning me with his gaze.

"You want to know what your brother showed me that ensured that I let him stay here," he asks.

My heart stutters. I nod.

He raises an eyebrow. "I suppose now is as good a time as any. We've held onto this secret too long anyway." He shrugs. "It was a video of Kane's mother."

"Beverly?" Anastasia inquires.

"Yes," he says. "In it, she told me of every atrocity Samson Leon had committed. There's a pretty long list of things, too, including framing your father for murder."

"My Dad?" I frown. "Wait, what?"

James nods. "You didn't know your father went to jail?"

"I did," I admit, swallowing past the sudden shock that seized my throat. "But I didn't think it was for murder. I thought it was maybe petty theft. Or not paying taxes or something." My father never spoke about it, and I didn't want to make him feel bad by asking.

James shakes his head, and my stomach sinks further. A terrible feeling tears through me.

My Dad was accused of murder.

"Don't worry," James waves his hand suddenly, drawing me out of my thoughts. He shakes his head. "He didn't do it."

He didn't.

"Kane's father framed him for the crime."

Another bolt of shock has me jerking up. "Wha-how? Why? Samson told me he and my Dad were friends?"

James smiles humorlessly. "I'm sure he did. But Samson doesn't use that word the way the rest of us do. He has the unique ability to simultaneously admire and loathe someone at the same time. That was how it was between him and your father. It's the way it is between him and me, too." He shrugs like he couldn't care less. "Although he would probably tell you we're friends, he had no problem trying to sabotage my business when he thought I was poaching his son and also when he felt my friendship with Beverly was too close. I have no doubt that he'll stab me in the back again, given half the chance."

"You were friends with Kane's mother?" Anastasia asks next, while I'm still reeling from the words. None of this is what I thought it was.

It's far more convoluted than anything I can imagine.

"Yes," he says. "We ran in the same social ties. Our families knew each other, and we were probably cousins from a few generations back. And though Samson tried very hard to get everyone else to believe Beverly was going crazy after her multiple miscarriages, I never bought it. I always knew that he did something to her, but I could never prove it." Frustration lines his forehead. "Beverly, of course, played along to lull Samson into a false sense of security. So she could move around and do what she needed to do to bring him down."

"What do you mean?" I ask.

"Beverly was troubled, but she wasn't an idiot. She knew that Samson was capable of murder, and despite his proclaimed 'love' for her, the minute she didn't fall in line, he could kill her without a second thought. So she played the game, pretending to be docile. Easily controlled. The whole time she's working. She helped your father get out of jail, pulling a lot of strings behind Samson's back to make it happen. And that was only the beginning of an extremely sophisticated plan to take down Samson."

"Her own husband?" I frown.

"Yes. The marriage wasn't her choice. But that's a story for another day." He taps the table. "You see, Beverly technically owned the majority shares of Samson's company, but she acted more as a silent shareholder. She never so much as showed her face, so Samson never suspected that she wanted to do more than be a wife and mother. He didn't think she had the balls or the intelligence to defy him, even though he destroyed the man she loved. David Dalton."

"My Dad," I whisper, eyes wide. "Kane's mother was in love with my father?"

"Yes. He didn't return her feelings, at least not to the same level she did, but he loved her in his own way. That was why Samson framed your father for murder. Because he was jealous of Beverly's feelings for David."

"That's…" I shake my head and blow out a breath. "Insane."

"Oh, trust me. It gets even crazier. Beverly, despite her love for David, initially believed he was guilty of killing that man, at least unintentionally. Samson did a very good job of placing DNA evidence at the scene and even produced a falsified CCTV footage of someone who looked like David performing the crime. But eventually, as their marriage soured, Beverly got suspicious. She started snooping around and found correspondence that showed what he did. She tried to make it right, but your father refused to talk to her. He felt betrayed and had too much pride to forgive her."

"Sounds like my Dad," I murmur faintly and James offers me an apologetic smile.

"I think David was scared as well of what Samson would do when he found out that his wife was reaching out to him, so he told Beverly to stay away. But she didn't give up. She did, however, slow down when Samson hired your brother as his assistant. I think he started to suspect her then, and she knew that if she made a single wrong move, he would kill your brother or have him framed, too. So she had to be very careful with the plan to take him down. And careful she was."

"What plan?"

"She collected evidence against her husband. Recorded phone calls. Kept copies of contracts. Everything. She was so clever at it, but one day, she got caught by Carter. Then, she had to tell him what was going on. And he decided to help her. But then Samson started catching on. Beverly knew his life was in danger, so she sent Carter away to me. She knew I was the only one who would believe him. And then, she died in a surprising trip down the stairs."

His tone leaves no room for misinterpretation. Anastasia and I share a look.

Anastasia's eyes are as shocked as mine. "You think Samson killed his own wife?"

"I think that man is capable of anything to get what he wants," he says. "Your brother came to me with the video evidence and showed everything they'd done. Told me that I was the only one he could trust. I believed him and sheltered him. Together, we carried out the rest of Beverly's plan. When your brother left the Leon's, it was framed as a theft so that Samson would never suspect that Carter knew what Beverly did. But Samson hunted him down still."

We're both silent for beats. My heart is racing.

"I don't understand," I say. "If Carter had all that evidence against Samson, then why didn't he just come out with it? Or, at the very least, tell Kane?"

"Kane wouldn't have believed Carter over his own father," he says. "And while Kane loved his mother, he believed she was insane too. Samson had convinced him of that fact. Additionally, Samson had to be taken down in one fell swoop, like a hydra. You couldn't do it with just evidence. You needed to ensure you showed the evidence to the right people because, at the time, Samson had a lot of powerful friends. One wrong move would jeopardize his father and Dara," he says. "Your brother also knew he couldn't jeopardize you. He wanted to protect you."

"Protect me?" My head is whirling. It's too much. It's all

too much. "Why didn't he tell me? Why did he just leave? And..." I sigh. "Why didn't Samson come for me then?"

"He tried. But by that time, Carter tipped off your Dad, and the two of you moved."

I remember it now. Dad and I didn't move just once, but several times. For a few years, we even lived out of Chicago.

And a few other things start adding up...like Dad's paranoia, his insistence I never use any social media apps or even have so much as sign up for a credit card. It was like he was trying to avoid leaving any digital footprint.

His eyes flash. "You're a far more important piece in this than you realize. After all, you have some ownership of the patent. Perhaps he thought by getting you on his side, he could get you to sign over your shares and legitimize his claim. Then, if he could frustrate Kane enough to leave the company and kill Carter, then all of Beverly's shares would be his, too. There would be no one left to contest it."

"Fucker," Anastasia swears. "That's why he's been so mean to Kane lately and why he tried to sink his own company."

"He only did enough to drive Kane crazy," James points out. "He used Kane to drive the company up to where it is now, and he wanted Kane to leave everything behind. And like an evil genius, his plan would be complete."

And like that, on cue, my phone dings.

It's a new message.

I glance down. It's a new phone, and the only contacts on there are Lisa's. But the message is from the same number that sent me the picture. Samson's email.

After everything I just found out about him, my heart pounds as I read it.

Dear, I've been trying to reach you on your phone, but it's not going through. I only hope you see this message in time. I have a plan to keep your fortune safe from my son. He might be able to claim some of it through marriage, but I have some documents you can sign to prevent this. Meet me tomorrow at my estate at 4:00 pm.

Samson Leon.

I stare back at James, my heart pounding. Documents to keep the fortune safe or to sign over my shares to him?

I don't know what to believe. It's all so overwhelming.

"This is insane," Anastasia says, voicing out my panic.

"Yes," James says and rises. "I'll give you time to ruminate. I've called your brother and let him know you're here. He'll explain the rest to you when he gets back. But you should get some sleep."

But I can't sleep. Even after a cup of soothing tea that Anastasia brews for me, sleep is the farthest thing from my mind.

I'm too horrified by everything I just heard.

My Dad was framed for a crime he didn't commit. And then my brother was working for the man who framed him.

Was that the cause of the rift between my Dad and brother?

Why did Carter not warn me about this when he came back? To keep me safe because I was married to Kane? Maybe he thought I would ask Kane questions, and it would eventually get back to Samson, thereby destroying their plan.

Ah, thinking is making my head hurt.

I close my eyes and attempt once more to sleep, but they fly open when the door creaks.

My heart pounds, and I sit up, staring into the darkness at a large shape entering the bedroom.

But as the familiar scent hits me, that fear turns to a different turmoil

It's Kane.

CHAPTER 38

Kane

My heart tightens in my chest, squeezing painfully as Dara sits up in bed. Her hair falls in waves down her back, and her eyes are red as if she's been crying.

And she's so damn precious that *I* feel like crying.

She's here. She's really here.

She squints in the darkness. "Kane?"

"Yes," I answer, voice hoarse. "Sorry, I didn't mean to wake you, I just wanted to see you for a second."

After an eight-hour flight and a drive that felt like an eternity, I couldn't stop myself from coming up to see her. I just needed one look to assure myself that she was within my grasp again.

And then one look turned into another and another.

I have no idea how long I've been standing here drinking her in.

It's only been a week without her, but I miss her so fucking much.

Anastasia doesn't look surprised to see me or Carter at her doorstep today. She just rolled her eyes at him and said,

"Really? You couldn't keep a secret from him for two seconds?"

"It's nice to see you too." He smiles and brushes a kiss on her forehead as he enters. I eye both of them before settling back on Anastasia. She avoids my eyes guiltily.

So she knew where he was this entire time. She knew he was here.

She finally ventures a peek up at me and nods like she knows what I am thinking. "Yeah, I know. I'm sorry I couldn't tell you. My Dad made me promise not to tell anyone."

"This is where you've been hiding?" I ask Carter, suddenly recalling that Dara mentioned she saw him at the Charles De Gaulle Airport when we first arrived in France.

It doesn't take a genius to figure out the rest. No wonder not even my Dad's best PI's couldn't find him. James Coleman has enough money to make anyone disappear.

"Are you mad at me?" Anastasia asks in a small voice.

I shake my head.

I do feel a little betrayed, but given everything Carter told me on the way here, I get it. As humiliating as it is to admit, I did have a massive blindspot when it came to my father.

I believed my father when he told me that Carter stole our money and ran off. I believed him when he told me my mother was troubled, although her frequent outbursts didn't help matters.

If Anastasia told me Carter was here, I likely would have told my father without question. That is if his spies hadn't figured it out first.

"I understand," I told her, and to prove it, I flicked her forehead like I used to when we were kids.

She smiles in relief.

"Is she here?" I ask, my heart racing. There are a lot of

things I have to digest today, and a lot of new information is being thrown at me. Right now, I don't care about any of that. At the forefront of my mind is Dara.

She is still my priority, the only thing that matters.

Anastasia nods. "It's pretty late, though. And she's had a rough day, especially after the conversation we just had with my Dad."

"James?"

"Yes. He told us what a deranged individual your Dad is. No offense."

"Wait, he told her? Everything?" Carter asks.

"He told her enough," she says, eyeing him. "Though, I would have preferred you told me at least some of it."

"I told you as much as I dared," he says. "I couldn't risk anything getting back to Samson for him to learn everything we had planned."

"I wouldn't have told him."

"Yes, but you wouldn't have been able to hide your loathing for him, and he would have figured out that you knew something."

"Well, I hate him anyway. And Dara knows now...And she's probably in shock."

"I need to see her," I say to Anastasia. "If only for a minute."

Anastasia smiles a little softly. "You really are in love with her, aren't you?"

I nod. "She's everything to me."

Her smile widens. "I told her as much, but she wouldn't believe me. I think you're going to have to do a lot of convincing."

I will convince her. I have to because there is no way I am living without her.

As I leave them at the entrance, I hear her say to Carter,

"Who would have thought the great Kane Leon would fall so madly in love? And with your sister, of all people?"

"Don't remind me," Carter responds in a dry tone.

"Hey, it's isn't so bad. I'm like *his* sister, and look at us."

Their conversation falls to the background as I jog up the stairs, counting the breaths till I reach her.

And now we're here, staring at each other.

Dara doesn't look as mad as she was the last time we spoke, but that could only be because she's half asleep. I walk closer to her and brush my hands over her hair. She doesn't flinch or move away from my touch, and I secretly count that as a win.

"He told me…" She shakes her head. "Anastasia told me that your Dad framed my Dad for murder."

I nod. "Yes. I just found that out myself. Carter told me."

"Carter's here?"

I nod again, but I lean forward.

"My Dad said you hated Carter," she mentions.

"I did," I admit.

"So you didn't come looking for me because he told you to?"

"No," I admit, hating the fresh betrayal that appears in her gaze. I've lied to her so many times from the very beginning of our relationship. I can only hope she forgives me for it. "I came looking for you because I wanted revenge on Carter. He stole…well, at least I thought he stole money from my company, and he disappeared right after. I thought I could use you to lure him out of hiding, and that's why I went to find you in the first place. And then, when I found you, Dad mentioned that he wanted to give you part ownership of Leon Inc."

"And that's why you offered to marry me?"

Telling the truth is like shards of glass scraping over my vocal cords. But I do it anyway. "Yes."

Pain blooms in her eyes, and she swallows. I put my hand on her cheek, wanting to take it away from her, wishing it was mine instead.

"He also said that your mother knew about what your Dad did."

"You heard the whole story."

She nods. "Yes. But I have to admit, I'm still trying to wrap my head around it. The whole thing sounds like a bad soap opera."

"I'm trying to wrap my head around it, too," I admit. "But right at this moment, I don't care about any of that."

"You don't?"

"No," I say, caressing her cheek. "All I care about is you." I allow her to see the desperation in my face. "I love you, Dara. I need you. I can't lose you."

Her expression shifts, and she moves away from me.

"Because your mother left me shares of the company." Her voice is bitter.

"I don't care about those shares," I tell her. "I was going to leave Leon anyway, and my plan hasn't changed. I can sign over my shares to you and your brother if you want."

Her head snaps to me, and her eyes widen again. "You would do that?"

"I would. I don't give a damn about Leon or any of that anymore. My greed and my commitment to that company almost cost me the two best things that ever happened to me. My son. And you."

Her expression softens, but she fights to hide it, looking everywhere but at me. She doesn't quite believe me yet, and I understand.

But I'm not going to give up.

I'm going to get her back, even if I have to bare my soul to do it.

"I'm adopted. Did Samson tell you?"

Her mouth drops open slightly. She shakes her head.

"I recently found out myself. But I wasn't surprised. My whole life, I felt like I constantly had to prove something to my father in order to earn his love. I felt inferior and like I was disappointing him by simply existing. It made me work harder to prove myself, and I've done a lot of despicable things on that path. Including what I planned to do to you."

The hurt flashes in her eyes again, but when I reach out and touch her cheek again, she doesn't flinch back. I savor the softness, the pure connection that I missed. "I'm not trying to find an excuse for what I was going to do to you. I was an idiot who thought it was okay to take advantage of people for my own selfish needs. But I don't think that anymore. And I'm so fucking sorry that I did in the first place. There are a lot of things that will probably come out in the next few days, things we don't know about our parents. Know that I'm so fucking sorry about what that man did to your father. You probably deserve better than me, and it's going to be hard for you to trust me or even love me again. But I'll wait until you do. I'll spend every single second of my life proving myself to you again. Every time you tell me to leave, I'll be just beyond your door, kneeling, waiting for you to give me crumbs of your love again. And I'll kneel forever if it comes to it."

"Kane," she whispers after my speech, emotion taking over her expression. She shakes her head, and her hands slowly come up to touch my face.

My heart soars.

I can't help it anymore.

I kiss her.

The kiss starts slow and sultry, but our hunger quickly turns it desperate. I want to inhale her. Her taste. Her beauty. Her softness. I want it all.

I want her so damn much.

She drags my body on top of hers, but I flip us over so she's sitting astride me.

I want her to control this.

"Use me," I tell her. "Take what you want. I'll be whatever you need."

Her eyes are dark with desire, and she bites her lips. Her hands shake as she clutches my shirt, tearing it up so she can run her hand over my head.

I moan, my head falling back. I missed her touch, gentle and hesitant but right on the verge of wild.

Kisses trail down my neck, and it feels like tiny bombs setting off in my body. Dara moves against my legs wantonly, but it's nothing compared to when she leans in to whisper in my ear, "Take me. Hard and fast."

Fuck me.

There's nothing else I can do but to oblige. I fuse our lips once more, swallowing her moans as my fingers find her pussy wet for me. Her legs shake as I pluck her clit, before thrusting a finger in her entrance, getting her ready for me. She mewls, moving into my touch, her eyes shutting and her face flush with ecstasy.

She's mine.

I roll over so she's under me again, and I kiss down her body until I get to her pussy. I push down her shorts and lick her slit, tasting her essence. She bites off a little scream, but I want to hear it, so I do more. I want her to go as crazy for me as I feel for her.

It doesn't take long to get her there, gasping and shaking and begging.

"Please," she grasps my shoulders, her entire body trembling. "Please."

I can't hold back anymore.

I shift up, tearing my trousers open and pulling out my cock. The edge of madness flits through my brain, so I press my lips into her neck, sucking hard. Dara likes her skin between my teeth, judging from the way she grasps me and moans.

And when I finally enter her, I stare into her eyes and give her the words I hope she'll remember forever.

"I love you, Dara Dalton. And I'll love you for the rest of my life."

CHAPTER 39

Dara

When my eyes flutter open the next day, Kane is gone. I'm tempted to think that last night was a dream, but the marks on my body say otherwise. He was animalistic in his lust yesterday like he wanted to devour me, and as rough as it was, it was exactly what I needed.

And then after, he made slow, gentle love to me again, whispering those words in my ears. *I love you.* He'd said it again and again, even as he stroked deep inside me, staring into my eyes each time.

I love you, Dara Dalton. And I'll love you for the rest of my life.

I shiver at the memory, lust weaving through me once more as I roll onto my back.

I'm still not sure if I believe him, honestly. I want to, but it's hard to trust my instincts when it comes to Kane. My feelings for him cloud my judgment and I don't know if I believe him truly or if I simply want to believe him because it would make things easier.

I don't know if the warmth and affection I saw in his eyes were real or if all this is another game to him.

I run my hand over my face, wiping the sleep from my eyes.

What I do know is that I love him. I'm so irrevocably in love with Kane that it's not even funny. Even a week apart wasn't enough to dull my feelings.

Something tells me that we could spend years apart without seeing each other, and I would still be in love with him.

The question is what I'm going to do about it because, despite my love for Kane, I refuse to let myself be lied to and deceived anymore.

I roll over in my bed and turn to the other side, taking a second to admire the cream accents and antique decor. I also spot the indent still on the mattress. Kane lay behind me, between me and the door. His arms had curled protectively around me when I slept.

His spot is still warm.

There's also a cup of coffee on the nightstand, steam spiraling from the top of it. When I reach over and grab the coffee, a note is stuck at the bottom. *I'm downstairs. K.*

He wrote in his straight, efficient handwriting. Although there's nothing remotely romantic about the note, it still makes my heart skip a beat.

I take a sip of the coffee, my eyes falling closed in bliss. A hint of sugar and a dash of cream. It's the perfect cup.

He knows me so well.

I get out of bed, stretching and yawning as I do. Then I head to the bathroom, wash my face, brush my teeth, and head out.

I follow the sound of voices as I descend the stairs, and it leads me right into the living room.

I pause at the entrance as the occupants of the room turn to look at me. Carter, Anastasia, Kane, and James are all there, and by the looks on their faces, they'd all been involved in a pretty intense conversation before I walked in.

Kane moves first, walking to me and taking my hand. He brings it up to his lips, pressing a kiss on the back of it. "Good morning," he murmurs.

"You left," I tell him and I'm not sure why it sounds like an accusation. He smirks.

"I didn't want to wake you," he says and then reaches down, brushing his lips over mine.

"Really? In front of me?" I hear my brother's voice out sourly, and we both turn to regard him. I try to go to Carter next, but Kane has me tucked firmly against his side.

Carter rolls his eyes at Kane and then walks to me anyway. He pulls me out of Kane's arms and hugs me. "How are you holding up?"

"As well as can be expected," I say and glance up at him. He tucks my hair behind my ears tenderly. I think he used to do that when I was younger.

But I'm not a little girl anymore, so I say, "James told me everything. Is that what you couldn't tell me? That was why you disappeared?"

He nods. "I had to cut off all contact with you after Samson started monitoring my movements. His men got close. I couldn't have him targeting you guys, too."

I understand that, but I still ask, "You couldn't even reach out when Dad was sick?"

His eyes grew sorrowful. "I didn't know. I had to go off the grid for a while because Samson's people found me. I was kidnapped, and although I escaped, I had to lay low. And by the time I made it back to Paris and got your letters…" He shakes his head and lays a hand over his chest as his heart aches. "He was already gone by that point. I'm so sorry. So so sorry for everything."

He draws me closer, and I hug him back, swallowing down the tears. A part of me isn't ready to accept his apology. The part of me that saw my father suffer in so much pain.

Nevertheless, I can't deny that it probably hurt Carter even more to stay away from us, knowing what he knew.

"For what it's worth," James says. "I tried to send your father money, but he wouldn't accept it. He probably thought this was a sick trick from Samson since he knew me as Samson's friend."

"My Dad hated charity," I say. This was why it broke him when I eventually had to drop out of school to take care of him.

He never wanted me to do that, especially since his disease had no cure anyway.

But a part of me can't help but wonder what would have happened if my father had less pride. If he'd accepted help from Beverly or James, would our lives have been easier? Would I not have had to drop out of college? Would I have been able to afford a more fitting end for him?

But then, I also wouldn't have met Kane.

And as painful as it is to admit, I knew if my father had another chance, he would probably do everything the same.

He'd prefer to end things on his terms all the way.

I table all that for a different day, focusing on what's at hand. "So what happens now?"

"We planned a sting already," Carter says. "I was in Chicago when Anastasia told me you left. I was meeting with the newly elected chief of police." He turns back to James. "It took a while to get him on board. I also needed to make sure that he wasn't bought off by Samson."

"And?" James inquires.

"He's clean," Carter says. "And we have to move as quickly as possible. Today, we fly back to Chicago and get to his house. We need one more crucial piece of evidence before your father goes down, and the police chief is trying to secretly secure a search warrant to get it first."

Kane nods, and his expression is empty. We might as well be talking about a stranger.

"Are you okay with this?" I ask Kane.

He shoots me a look.

"After what he did to your Dad? You're really going to ask me that?"

"Yes, but…" I don't hold Kane responsible for what his father did. From what Anastasia told me last night, Kane's childhood wasn't exactly the easiest either.

"I'm more than okay with it," Kane says. "Samson Leon has ruined too many lives. He almost ruined yours, and he was the reason you had to suffer all those years with your Dad. He deserves to rot in hell for the rest of his life."

I stare into his eyes and see the truth within. Then I offer him the words that I don't think anyone has said to him yet. "I'm sorry about what happened to your mother."

His expression tightens. He swallows and then nods. I know he's still processing the details surrounding his mother's death, and it will take him time.

And I want to be there for him if he needs me.

"I still don't think a search warrant is the way to go," James says. "One of Samson's friends on the police force could tip him off if the search warrant is approved. By that time, he may have destroyed the evidence already."

"What is this evidence?" I ask.

"A burn book," Carter says. "Or a folder more so. It has the names of everyone Samson has ever made illicit deals with, including the former chief of police. Samson kept evidence in case he ever got in trouble that he could use to blackmail his way out of it. We need that, or he's going to be out of prison the second after we put him in."

"I know where it is," Kane says, his eyes flashing darkly. When we turn to him, he smiles grimly. "I used to be very snoopy as a teenager. I found it a while ago, but I never really understood what it meant until now. He keeps it in his study."

"It would be easier if someone could sneak it out," Carter muses.

"I can get it," Kane says, and James shakes his head.

"It can't be you. He might suspect you after your last argument," he says. "This is the most delicate part of this entire plan. One wrong move could alert Samson, and he goes into hiding. And that's it. That's the end."

"I can do it," I suggest, and all eyes fall on me. "Samson trusts me."

"No," Carter and Kane say in unison.

They both eye each other, like they don't like agreeing with each other, and then turn back to me.

"It's too dangerous again," they parrot again, and this time they glare at each other.

Anastasia giggles, and I roll my eyes.

"I'm the only one here who he won't suspect," I say. "He wants to meet me anyway. He said as much in his message. All I have to do is get in his study and swipe the book, correct? Should be easy."

"Nothing with my father is easy," Kane says. "You're not doing this."

"Good thing it's not your decision alone," I say. "That man destroyed my father and nearly did the same to my brother. Carter didn't even get to say goodbye to Dad because of it. I'm not letting Samson get away with it. I'm doing this."

I see the battle take place in Kane's eyes. He doesn't want

to fight with me. He's trying to get on my good side and do what makes me happy.

At the same time, he doesn't want to put me in danger.

"He's dangerous," he says.

"So am I," I say.

Kane cracks a smile, and I feel like a child wearing boxing gloves. "You're definitely dangerous to my heart."

"Ew," Anastasia says.

"That was pretty bad," Carter concurs. "Has he always been this much of a sap?"

"Young love does that to you," James grins.

"But what about Kenny?" The thought finally hits me with a significant amount of panic. "Did you just leave him behind?"

"Relax. Kenny is safe. Before I left, I had a full security detail on him, plus Pope. No one is getting close to him."

"Okay," Carter claps his hands together. "We don't have much time. Let's get to work."

∽

KANE HELPS ME CRAFT A REPLY TO SAMSON, AGREEING TO meet with him at his home.

Then we leave France quicker than we arrived. We go over the plan on the flight back. Carter goes over it again, and then Kane reiterates it once we're in the car.

It's to the point I can probably recite every word if I need to.

"I get it," I tell Kane when he tries to tell me the plan for the fifth time. "You don't have to go over it again."

"But I need you to understand that you can't say anything that makes him suspicious," Kane says. "Let him lead the conversation. Play along. Then we stage a distraction. I'll have Samson's secretary call him pretending that the police are at Samson's estate, asking questions. This will cause him to leave the room. The burn book is a black folder on the third column of his bookcase and the key is in his right drawer. If you can't find it in time, just get out. And if you give us the safe word, we'll come get you out. You remember the safe word?"

"Beaver."

"It will be funny to see how you work that one into the conversation," Carter mutters from the other seat in the van. Along with him, there were about three policemen in front who picked us up from the airport. They're in civilian clothes so they don't give themselves away.

Carter had the entire thing planned to a T.

Everything will be fine.

Still, I'm a little nervous when they drop me off at the bus station. Kane gives me a final long kiss before I leave and whispers, "Come back to me. Alright?"

I nod.

I miss his chatter and overprotection on the taxi ride to Samson's estate. All I have is my thoughts to keep me company and they become increasingly more panicked.

Everything will be fine. Just stick to the plan.

I know Kane, Carter, and the police are following me at a discreet distance, and they'll be parked close by, but it's still nerve-wracking to go in by myself.

Just act normal.

Samson Leon's mansion is bigger than Kane's and has so much white marble that it reminds me of a mausoleum. As we drive through the gates, and up the driveway, a woman in a suit waits at the entrance.

"Master Leon has been waiting for you," she says, her eyes darting to the side.

I nod and swallow. Here goes nothing.

She leads me inside, through a long dark hallway, until we get to a door. She knocks three times and then leaves before the door opens to reveal Samson wearing a red robe and loose pants.

He smiles when he sees me.

"Hello dear," he says. "Come in."

"Hi, Mr. Leon," I say, walking in and trying not to jump when I hear the door close behind me. My eyes scan the room, especially the book cabinet. *The third column. Key in the right drawer.*

Samson moves around to block my vision, sitting at the head of the table. His eyes are shrewd and gaze-cutting.

"You said you wanted to see me about the will?" I ask.

"Yes. But first, you're going to take off that recording device you're wearing."

Lead falls in my stomach.

My heart ratchets in my chest.

"What?" I stutter. "I'm not —"

"Don't insult me with a lie, dear. I know that you were in France with him."

"Yes, but I—"

"While you were there, I heard a strange rumor that the chief of police wanted to issue a search warrant," he says, and just like that, my entire heart clenches in my chest. "You're going to explain to me why. Right after you take off that listening device. Take it off right now, or my grandson is going to take a nasty tumble off a high place."

I widen my eyes. "Kenny."

Samson gives a cruel smile. "I picked him up from school a few minutes ago. Of course, it was a hassle to get him away with all the eyes on him, but thankfully, Kenny played along when I told him that I was taking him to meet you. Luckily, he's very good at escaping from his guardians. But I couldn't have them tipping Kane off, so I had to pay off the school security, and my men had to knock out the driver and the bodyguards."

My heart cracks in two. My panic is now through the roof. I should probably be scared for myself, but all I can think about is Kenny.

Without hesitation, I rip off the tiny mic on my shirt button, throwing it to the floor. Then I step on it and crush it.

Samson grins. "Good. Now we can speak so much more candidly."

CHAPTER 40

Kane

A roar tears out of me the second the sound disconnects. I tear out of the van, and I'm on my way out of the forest where they have us perched inside.

A hand grabs my arm, but I throw it off, storming through the forest.

"Kane." It's Carter's voice but I'm not listening.

"Fuck you," I tell him. I can't believe they fucking convinced me to let her do this. I can't believe that I didn't keep her safe.

And now she's in danger. I'm getting her out of there.

"Kane, you're going to jeopardize the entire thing."

"You think I give a fuck about that," I glare at him and the FBI agent who stepped out of the van with him. "I knew this was a bad idea, knew it from the beginning. I don't give a fuck about Leon or getting revenge. But if anything happens to Dara, I will be your enemy number one. Understood?"

"You think I predicted this," Carter snaps. "You think I would just send my sister in there without any kind of backup?"

I finally pause but the breath is still rushing out of me like a bull. Kenny is in danger and so is Dara.

The two most important people in my life.

I need to save them.

"We have eyes on her," Carter says, coming closer and gesturing with his chin to a tree in the distance. I squint at it and finally see a hint of…something.

"A sniper," Carter murmurs to me. "Courtesy of James. The cops don't know we have one, but if Samson makes one wrong move toward her, I'm going to put a bullet in his skull and be done with it."

Perhaps my first thought should have been horror that Carter could so coldly murder my father.

But the bigger part of me is worried that the sniper might miss and hit Dara instead.

"And what exactly do you think it's going to do to Dara to see a man killed right in front of her."

Carter's jaw clenches. "As far as I'm concerned, that man killed our father. Dara should be happy to see him dead."

I shake my head. He doesn't know his sister at all. "You're an asshole. I almost wished you had just murdered Samson Leon in the first place, and left Dara and me out of this little vendetta."

"Is that what you think this is?" Carter's tone is harsh. "A little vendetta?"

"Yes." I look him straight in the eyes when I say it. "My son and my wife are in danger because of you. And I'm going to get them out. So figure out whatever you're going to do with that information but, if you try to stop me, you'll regret it."

And with that, I turn around and walk off.

Luckily, I placed a tracker on Kenny before I left. I put it in a week ago after he started acting out, placing it in the watch Dara gave him. He never takes off that watch.

I pull up the location on my phone as I walk and frown at the screen.

It says Kenny is in Samson's mansion too.

Of course. Samson probably plans to use him as a bargaining chip for a hostage negotiation.

Which means he plans to kill Dara.

My heart jumps into my throat. I can't let that happen. She and Kenny are my world. If anything happens to either of them…

As I approach the house, I walk briskly, following the directions on the map. I don't know what I'll meet once I'm there. I don't care if I die on this mission.

As long as Kenny and Dara walk out of here, I'm happy.

I stick to the shadows to avoid being seen, but there isn't anyone here. Samson probably had the house cleared out of most servants, so no one would know what he's doing here today.

The same way he probably had the house cleared out when he killed my mother.

Kenny is in a bedroom on the third floor, the one that used to be mine. As I creep close enough to peek through the keyhole, I spot my son.

Relief rushes through me.

He's alive, sitting on the bed and glaring at the two men by the door with their backs turned to me.

His hands are crossed stubbornly in front of him.

"You said Dara was going to meet me here," he says. "It's been thirty minutes. Where is she?"

The men glance at each other but they don't reply, turning away from him.

I can tell from Kenny's eye movement that he's trying to

figure a way out of it. My son may not know exactly what's going on, but he knows it's strange. His grandfather has never shown this amount of interest in him before.

I analyze the men, their positions, and the guns at their hips.

Silencer on.

Perfect.

A plan is formulated in my head, and I play it over and over again, ensuring the scenario is perfect so my son doesn't get injured.

Then, once I'm sure I have all my bases covered, I act.

I knock on the door, three times like Samson orders all his servants to do.

One of the men approaches the door, palming his gun, but before he can pull it open completely, I push the door into him, then drive my fist into his face.

As he howls and bumbles back, I grab the gun in his holster and take out his partner with a shot to the chest.

The man falls back, and I notice Kenny jerks before I turn and point the gun to the other one's head.

His eyes are wide with surprise. *How did you do that?* I can see the question in his gaze.

The truth is I've trained extensively for scenarios like this. As the son of one of the wealthiest men in the country, I'm aware of what I present. I've always assumed I would be kidnapped at some point, so I trained in several martial arts in preparation, so when the time came, I would be able to escape.

Or save the ones I love.

"Turn away and close your eyes, Kenny," I say. I hate that he had to see me shoot someone, but I'll try to protect him now.

"My eyes are closed," Kenny says, sounding remarkably

calm about the entire thing. The other assailant's eyes widen as I shift the gun and shoot him in the legs.

"Don't make a sound," I tell him as he falls to the ground, biting off curses. "Or I'll kill you."

At that point, I hear the sound of feet and glance over, pointing my gun at the door.

But it's two cops from the van who arrive.

One of them glances at the men on the floor, and his eyes widen with surprise.

The other gives me a look of reproach.

I shrug, not feeling even the tinge of guilt. They would have killed my son without a second thought if Samson ordered them to.

As the cops take over, I run to Kenny, snatching him close. He holds me tight, his hands squeezing me.

"I knew you would come," he whispers.

I nod, feeling relief choke me. "Are you okay? Are you hurt?"

He shakes his head. "I knew you would come for me."

"Of course. I'll find you anywhere. I'll always come for you," I say and he hugs me even tighter. "I'm sorry that I had to shoot someone in front of you."

"Is he dead?"

Hopefully.

"Probably not," I say instead. Then I step back. "Stay here with the cops, alright. I have to go get Dara."

Kenny nods, eyes wide. "I love you, Dad."

Even through the horror of the situation, I find it in me to smile. "I love you too."

I ruffle his hair one last time before I rush out to find Dara.

All I have to do is get her out of there. The sniper can take care of Samson but I don't want Dara to have to see it.

At the door, I take a few steps back and then drive my leg through the door, breaking the lock.

The door swings open, but fear has me freezing.

Samson and Dara are sitting, staring at each other. Dara's whole body is tensed up and soon I see why.

Samson's right arm is at an odd angle underneath the desk, aimed at Dara.

He's holding a gun.

Fuck.

Samson grins. "It seems that you know everything, and it's the end after all. But at least, I have the pleasure of taking this one down with me."

God.

He's going to kill her.

It's like a bolt of lightning hits me, and I'm running before my mind makes sense of my actions. I grab Dara and yank her to the floor, throwing my body over hers as a gun explodes.

Pain tears through my side, and Dara screams. I expect another shot, but instead, a crash sounds.

The next thing I see is Samson lying beside us, his eyes vacant. A red dot in the middle of his head.

"Oh my God," Dara wheezes underneath me and I roll off her, grabbing her face.

"Are you okay?" My eyes scan her body, looking for any bleeding. "Are you hit?"

"No," she shakes her head frantically, then she freezes when she sees my side. She reaches out pale-faced. "He got you."

"It's fine." The wound stings when she touches it, but I don't show it, face smiling. "It's a flesh wound. I'm just so fucking glad you're okay."

"That was..." She shakes her head and swallows. Her face

is still pale, eyes haunted. "You saved my life. You took a bullet for me."

"Because you are my life."

"He could have killed you." Tears fill her eyes. Her shoulders are shaking, likely from delayed shock and emotion. "He shot you."

"I would have died happy knowing that you were safe."

"Kane, I..." She seems lost for words, shaking her head and crying. "I don't know what to say."

I smile. "Just tell me you love me."

"I love you." The words burst out of her. "I love you so much. If anything happened to you, I would—"

"Shh. I'm fine," I grin, kissing the tears of her cheeks and her lips. "And for what it's worth, I love you very much too."

Epilogue

DARA

I stand in the spacious, elaborate dressing room, admiring the wedding gown that shimmers to the floor. It has a sweetheart bodice and a voluminous multilayered beaded skirt that looks like it's dotted with diamonds.

The most beautiful gown I've ever seen is now draped on my body.

I almost felt too scared to touch it the first time I saw it, in an upscale atelier in Paris. Anastasia dragged me there for wedding shopping the day after Kane proposed to me under a starlit sky.

It had been a romantic proposal, on my birthday, with everyone I loved in attendance. Kane was down on one knee, his eyes glowing like two stars themselves.

"I didn't do things right the first time," he confessed. "I did everything wrong. But I want to do it perfectly this time. I want you to know what I feel for you. Love is too mild a word for it. I'm obsessed with you, devoted to you. And I want to be obsessed and devoted to you forever. Will you marry me?"

The speech had been so moving, I wasn't the only one

teary-eyed. And the rest of the well-wishers had cheered as I nodded and he swept me to him in a kiss.

Kane loves me.

I can no longer doubt his love after he risked his life for me. When he stormed into that room, relief and horror spiraled through me. Relief that he was here, but horror that he was now in danger. His father had a gun. I thought we might both die there.

But Kane protected me. And I will never forget that.

Even after that incident, he continuously showed his love for me. He insisted on giving me his shares of Leon even though I told him I didn't want it. He buys me thoughtful gifts every day, just because.

He bought me this beautiful wedding dress too.

While dress shopping, I actually picked a different dress. This one was two hundred thousand dollars, and it felt wasteful to spend that much money on a dress I'd only wear for a day. So, I went with something more sensible.

But Anastasia already saw my reaction to this dress and ratted me out to Kane.

A few days later, the dress was waiting for me at the fitting.

"Oh my God." I hear from behind me and spin around. Anastasia is standing by the door in a beautiful pink bridesmaid gown that shows off her luscious curves. "You look like…Elizabeth Taylor."

"You do look good." Lisa appears behind her in a similar dress. "So good I could cry. Even though I think I look stupid."

"You can't look stupid," Anastasia says. "These bridesmaid dresses are custom-made Givenchy. Mulberry silk. They cost about fifty-thousand a piece."

"Great. I look expensively stupid."

Anastasia rolls her eyes at her, and I grin at the two of them.

As two of my bridesmaids, the women have gotten pretty close. And though they bicker, I see a friendship forming, especially since Anastasia insists on introducing Lisa to every eligible bachelor she knows.

There's another knock on the door, and Lisa's Dad appears, along with Kenny.

The latter's eyes widen. "Wow, Mom. You look like a million bucks."

My heart skips a beat like it does whenever Kenny calls me Mom. It's something he started doing recently, and I've been loving it.

"Thank you," I say, trying not to get emotional.

"You do look amazing," Lisa's Dad, Ernest, says. "I wish your father was here to see you."

"Somehow, I feel like he is," I say. I feel his proud presence with me, now more than ever.

Ernest smiles. "Then I hope he allows me the courtesy of walking you down the aisle."

"Can we do it, like soon?" Kenny asks, tugging at his collar. "This suit is itchy."

I reach out and kiss his cheek. "Sure thing, Ken Ken."

The wedding is held at the Chateaux De Versailles, a ridiculously luxurious venue that Anastasia insisted on. The wide halls are lined with golden ornamental pieces, a gilded fountain behind me, and rows of glittering crystal chandeliers in the center.

"It's the best in Paris," Anastasia says. And the way it looks, she's probably right.

There are about a hundred-odd people in the hall, most of them guests we flew in. I instantly spot Lisa's brothers, who wave at me, and Max, who sends me a wink, sitting next to Brianna.

I don't miss the way the two look at each other and know that something has probably started there. I'll quiz her about it later.

Pope is sitting in a fitted suit at the front of the hall, and he grins proudly. Next to him are two boys who look exactly like him. One of them has a stain on his shirt that looks suspiciously like a wedding cake.

Anna is seated on the other side of them, and she shoots me a watery smile before wiping her eyes with her napkin. Oscar and Harold give me a thumbs up.

After smiling and waving at them, I face forward.

My bridesmaids line the path. Sophia, Lacey, Faith, May, and Gemma. All the friends I made at Kane's estate in their beautiful dresses.

Then, my attention is snagged by Kane.

He looks amazing in a black suit. His eyes are intense on mine as I get closer.

I'm still so in awe of him.

I can't believe this magnificent man standing there is all mine.

And I'm his.

Kane

I step out of my Mustang, ignoring the looks I get as I walk to the busy bakery. There is a line out front, and some of those people have probably been waiting hours. They shoot me dirty looks, and I smile as I cut to the front.

It's nice having VIP access to the best new pastry shop in the city.

I nod at the hostess as I walk in.

The scent of warm bread wraps around me, along with cinnamon and nutmeg. The seats of the French-style bakery are packed, but that's not what I'm here for.

Instead, I head behind the counter and down the hall to the office.

Where my very pregnant wife stands behind her desk.

She looks up when I walk in.

"Hey," she grins. "I didn't know you were coming in for lunch."

"I didn't know myself," I stride to her and draw her close. She smells like vanilla and home. A scent that is uniquely her.

"What are you doing here in the middle of the day then?"

I take every excuse to get off of work and see you.

"Because I thought you would like an audit of how your company is doing, Mrs. Leon."

"Oh, this again." She rolls her eyes. Even though she told me she was not interested in the company, I transferred all my shares to her.

It's the least I could do, considering everything Samson did. The company should have been hers, and her brother's anyway.

I still stayed on in my CEO role, though, mostly at Dara and Carter's request. I couldn't abandon Leon Inc., especially at a crucial time like that. We dealt with the scandal from the stock manipulation, plus the scandal regarding my father's death. And then, all his crimes began coming out one by one, leading to Dara's Dad being fully exonerated.

Several members of the board, including Marvin Hayes, had to be ousted for their role in Samson's crimes. Leon suffered in stocks, but the X3 sales saved us.

The phone has been selling hot ever since its launch, and Textra didn't even bother releasing their dupe.

And in the following weeks, our stocks have been slowly climbing up, our profits soaring.

I love to tell Dara about how well her company is doing every day.

"Come on," Dara says, amusement dripping from her voice. "Tell me why you're really here."

I sigh, caught.

"Your brother was pissing me off," I tell her, nuzzling her neck. "So I needed my personal brand of sunshine to make it better."

She giggles. "What did he do now?"

With Carter now on the board, things are both easier and harder. We see eye to eye on most things, but when we disagree, we're both bullheaded.

Carter wants us to release version two of the X3 next year, but I think we should take at least two years between releases. I see the merit of his opinion, and he likely sees the merit of mine, but we're both stuck in our ways.

At this point, I probably should compromise, but sheer stubbornness prevents me from doing so.

"I might need you to come in and vote," I admit, and I kiss her in that spot that makes her shiver.

"So you came to argue your case."

"Mmhmm." I drop even more kisses along the trail of her neck.

"Then why aren't you saying anything," she whispers, her voice suddenly husky.

"Because this is me arguing my case." I nip her skin, and she lets out a little gasp that fires me up.

Before I can do more, the door bursts open, and a sour voice says, "I should have known you would come tattling to her."

I turn and smirk at Carter, standing in the doorway. "I beat you to it."

"You think so?" He crosses his arms and sticks his nose in the air. "It won't matter. My sister is obviously smart enough to tell that I'm right."

I feel the laughter bubbling up in Dara's body. "The two of you have a strange friendship."

"We're not friends," we say simultaneously, and they look at each other and frown.

"Right." She rolls her eyes. "Both of you sit."

"Why?" I ask.

"Because I know neither of you has eaten anything today, and before I make my decision, I need to make sure you have. Now sit."

We sit.

She shakes her head, muttering something to herself as she walks out.

"She's getting bossy with pregnancy," Carter comments.

I nod in agreement.

Ultimately, when Dara gets back, we both argue our case over a plate of bagel sandwiches. And even though I eventually lose and she sides with Carter, I'm smiling the entire way through.

Because I've won in the way that matters.

I have Dara and my son.

I have everything I need.

The End

~

Did you enjoy this read? Then check out Trapped with the Grumpy Single Dad: An Enemies to Lovers Small Town Romance by Anna Pierson on Amazon

Sneak Peek of Trapped with the Grumpy Single Dad

I was supposed to hire my best friend's sister as a favor, not sleep with her.

When my best friend calls in a favor, I offer his little sister a job.

Imagining the awkward girl I teased in school,

I never expected the striking beauty who walked into my office.

Her haunted hazel eyes make me want to shield her from the world.

But she doesn't trust easily, and I won't risk my heart again.

Chemistry and passion consume us, and one night I let my guard down.

She came alive in my arms, and I knew I needed her in my life.

Except in the harsh light of morning when reality kicks in.

I could lose everything. My daughter, my business, and my best friend.

But it might be worth it if Carissa says she'll be mine.

Did you enjoy this read? Then check out My Grumpy Single Daddy: An Off-Limits Age Gap Romance by Anna Pierson on Amazon

Printed in Great Britain
by Amazon